THE TALMAGE POWELL CRIME MEGAPACK®

THE TALMAGE POWELL CRIME MEGAPACK®

TALMAGE POWELL

WILDSIDE PRESS

Published by Wildside Press LLC.
wildsidepress.com | bcmystery.com

CONTENTS

INTRODUCTION

Talmage Powell (1920-2000) was one of the all-time great mystery writers of the pulps (and later the digest mystery magazines). He claimed to have written more than 500 short stories (and I have no reason to doubt him—I am working on a bibliography of his work, and so far I can document 373 magazine stories…and who knows how many are out there under pseudonyms or buried in obscure magazines!) His pen names included Robert Hart Davis, Robert Henry, Milton T. Lamb, Milton T. Land, Jack McCready, Anne Talmage, and Dave Sands. Some (like Robert Hart Davis) were "house names" shared by many different authors. (Bill Pronzini also wrote as "Robert Hart Davis," for example.) His work appeared in *Dime Mystery*, *Black Mask*, *Ellery Queen's Mystery Magazine*, *Alfred Hitchcock's Magazine*, *Manhunt*, and many, many more

He wrote his first novel, *The Smasher*, in 1959. He went on to pen 11 more novels under his own name, 4 as "Ellery Queen," and 2 novelizations of the TV series *Mission: Impossible*. Clearly, though short stories were his first love.

Enjoy!

—John Betancourt
Publisher, Wildside Press

CRIME GETS A HEAD

Originally published in **Ten Detective Aces,** *September 1943,*
under the pseudonym "Milton T. Lamb".

CHAPTER 1

Percival Smith, my boss, was reading a book written by some guy named Freud when the phone rang. He didn't look up from the book. He said, with a nod, "Answer it, Willie."

I was glad to, glad of the chance to do something. Percival Smith has long periods of silence when's he not very good company. I'd been twiddling my thumbs and trying to doze for the last hour.

I got out of my chair, walked to his desk, and picked the phone up. I said, "Yeah?" A torchy voice asked, "The Smith Agency?"

"None other," I said, thinking that the female who owned the voice must be plenty easy on the eyes.

"Is Mr. Smith in?"

The boss kept reading. I nudged him with my elbow and pointed to the phone. He frowned at me, shook his head, and looked back at his book.

I said, "I'm sorry, but he's not here. Can I help you? This is Aberstein. I'm his assistant."

"I'm Alicia Droyster," the voice said. "I…"

I covered the mouthpiece with my hand. "The Droyster dame, boss!"

He sat up at that, closed his book with a pop. He reached out a hand which the little blonde dish at Central Barber Shop manicures twice every week.

The Droyster dame was saying something about a calling card and a Great Dane dog, when I broke in. "Just a minute. The boss has just blew in."

I handed him the phone, stepped back to watch him. He began asking Alicia Droyster a lot of questions. His eyes sort of got warm-looking and I could see his hand get tight on the phone. Well, I been with him long enough to know the signs. I wondered what in hell it would be this time.

Smith can get into more messes in five minutes than you or me could in ten years. He began to smile and it made my stomach nearly do a flip over.

I wished he would tell the Droyster dame good-by and hang up. But I knew from the way he was grinning that he wouldn't do that. Smith is a private shamus because he wants to be. And that kind of guy always hunts trouble.

I moved around the desk and sat down. I was already betting myself three to one that Smith would find what he was hunting—if Alicia Droyster hired him.

Two days ago, Mark Droyster, Alicia's loving hubby, had gone home late in the afternoon, gone in his bedroom, and rigged up a contraption with coat hangers and a sawed-off shotgun. I thought it was a very messy way for a guy to kill himself. When they found Droyster there hadn't been anything left of his head.

The bulls had marked it up as suicide without thinking about it much, and Droyster had been put six feet under late yesterday. It had been a very private funeral. Alicia Droyster, a sawbones named Lawrence Jordan, the preacher and pallbearers were all the people the Droyster dame would let come into the cemetery.

As usual, the boys on the news sheets made a big splash with it. This Mark Droyster had been as tough as a bulldog. He'd started as a kid selling papers, muscled his way up in a rough and ready style until he was a big shot. But when he cashed in his chips, the newshounds hinted that he was busted. It was odds around town that losing his dough had put him in such a funk that he killed himself.

But I didn't see it that way. Like the boss says, I may be sort of dumb, but I couldn't get it in my head that Droyster was the kind of guy to bump himself off. It didn't jibe with the way he had come up. You don't beat your way to the top like he did only to kick off. If you lose your dough, you go after it again.

The whole thing smelled to me like a red herring, and now to have Alicia Droyster calling Smith…

The boss put the phone down, leaned back in his chair. "Perhaps I don't give you enough credit, Willie."

"Yeah?"

"Droyster—the remarks you made about his death might be nearer right than I thought."

The boss was usually blessing me out. He didn't say things to make me feel good and I wanted to make the most of it. "Well, boss, now that you realize just how smart I can be sometimes…"

He laughed. "Oh, Willie, climb down. Alicia Droyster might simply be running a case of nerves—or greed." He frowned, and it didn't fit his face much. He looked back at me.

"Droyster was really broke, Willie, as flat as a tramp. Even the house he bought for his wife is mortgaged to the hilt. She said nothing to the police about his suicide, yet now she tells me she thinks it was murder. It doesn't add up nicely."

I didn't get what he was driving at. I said, "Uh huh."

He began sort of talking to himself. "All Droyster had left was insurance. And they do not pay off for suicide."

I sat up straight. "Yeah! I get it! Nerves—or greed. If it was really suicide, the insurance isn't worth the ink it took to print it. But if it was murder..."

He laughed softly, "I must give you a raise, Willie."

"Honest?"

He looked at me a minute, then waved his hands, shook his head. He pushed his chair back from his desk. "Come along, Einstein, we'll see the widow." He crossed the thick carpet of his office to get his hat.

I heard him muttering, "A raise—honest?" Then he laughed a little, but, cripes, I didn't mean nothing.

The big house that Droyster had bought for his wife gave me the creeps. It was a huge chunk of stone in the middle of a lot big enough for a park.

The boss paid the hackie who had brought us down and the cab pulled away. I tagged along as the boss opened an iron gate and started up the walk.

He didn't talk any when we reached the door. He punched the bell and in a few seconds a big-bellied guy in a butler's get-up opened the door.

"Mr. Smith to see Mrs. Droyster," the boss said. "She's expecting me."

The butler led us in. The inside of the house knocked my eyes out. There were pictures on the walls, rich drapes, and the furniture smelled of the good old mazuma. I went to my ankles in a rug that covered the whole floor. I thought it was no wonder Droyster had gone busted.

The butler tugged a couple of doors open. "You may wait in the library," he said, giving me a look that made me wonder if my hair—what there is of it—was combed.

I followed the boss and the butler waddled off to find the Droyster dame.

The boss began looking over the books that the walls seemed to be made of. I looked and spotted a big chair. But I didn't get to sit down. Somebody said. "Hello, Mr. Smith. I'm glad you came right down."

I turned and got set back on my heels. This was my first close-up of her and it was plenty all right. She had more than enough to go with the voice: a figure that could model bathing suits, a face that would drive a guy to drink, and long hair that was as black as the spots on the ten of spades.

She looked at me, then at the boss. Then she frowned. But everybody does that when they first see me and Smith together. And maybe we are sort of odd. He's the guy they invented all fancy words like elegant to coin. He's got his own tailor and his shoes cost twenty-five bucks. To top it off, he's got a sort of air about him that makes you think of Park Avenue.

And me—well, I'm just Willie Aberstein. It don't do much good to send my clothes to the cleaners. I guess I'm too short and too broad; a kid once screamed when he ran around a dark corner, smacked into me, and got a gander at my face. But I can't help that. I was never a daisy and having every pug in the east punch the face hasn't helped it any.

The boss said, "Mr. Aberstein, my assistant."

I nodded. "Pleased to meet you."

She came on in the room, waved us to a chair. I beat Smith to the big chair. She walked back and forth a little. Then she said, "You know why I called you here, Mr. Smith. I'm almost positive poor Mark was murdered." She tried to make her chin quiver, but it didn't go off. I marked her down a notch in my book.

"The calling card I mentioned," she went on after a minute. She reached into the pocket of her green dress and pulled out a white card. "I found this under the bed in my husband's room this morning." She held out the card to Smith.

Me and the boss both got up and I got a squint at the card over his shoulder. It was a very loud-talking card. It said:

A. H. Newell, Investments.

Right then and there I patted myself on the back. If Al Newell was mixed up in this, the whole business of Droyster killing himself by blowing off his kink was the bunk. I'd guessed right when I read the papers.

Al Newell owned part of a dog track that Droyster had promoted. I had wondered why the coppers had let the thing slide without so much as a how-do-you-do to Droyster's corpse. Maybe I knew why now.

Newell sort of had his way in City Hall. He was a slick-haired young guy who could tell people what to do. He had the dames, the dough, and the wrong kind of boys working for him.

The boss slipped the card into his pocket. "The card doesn't mean much, Mrs. Droyster. Simply that Al Newell was in the room where your husband met his end." He offered Alicia Droyster a cigarette, but she didn't take it. The boss lighted a smoke for himself.

"Perhaps Newell was in the room yesterday or even today. When did you find the card, anyway?"

"Just a few hours ago."

"And who has been in the room? You know, someone might have deliberately planted the card under the bed."

She shook her head in a very serious way. "No one has been in there. Not even the housekeeper. I haven't allowed the room to be touched." She tried the chin quiver again. "You—you know how those things are."

"Of course, Mrs. Droyster," the boss said in a nice way. But I could see he thought it was a lot of pap. He knocked his ashes into a metal tray. He was tired of sparring. He said:

"You think Al Newell killed your husband and dropped the card from his pocket when he bent over your husband's body?"

She didn't have to force her chin to quiver then. "I didn't say that! Don't get me wrong, Mr. Smith. Al Newell—I'm only telling you the facts."

The boss nodded. "And what about the Great Dane dog you mentioned over the phone?"

She was beginning to twist her fingers. "That was Jackie. He disappeared."

The boss almost laughed. "I don't follow you."

"It does sound silly, I suppose. But it makes me feel afraid somehow. You see, my husband loved the dog almost as well as he—as he did me. Night before last, I heard the dog yelping out in back. Then he barked in pain and that's the last I know of him. He was out at the little house we use for storage. I made a quick search out there but didn't find the dog. He has simply vanished."

I didn't think the bait was very good. What was she trying to get us to do? Pin a murder rap on somebody so she could cash Droyster's insurance?

The boss said, "I'm afraid I can do nothing. If there was something else you could tell me…"

"There is!" She seemed out of wind, like she had gone nine rounds. "There is! A man named Joe Dance phoned me. He promised to give me definite facts about my husband's death, which no one else knows. I'm to meet him tonight at nine o'clock at the Greenleaf Bar on Canal Street."

"That's better," the boss said. "You want Willie and me to interview Mr. Dance?"

She nodded in a hurry.

"Very well," Smith said, "we will take the case. It will cost you one thousand—cash."

That one was almost below the belt and it jolted her. Then she smiled. "That's about all I have left, Mr. Smith"—I could almost see her thoughts—thousands of dollars of insurance money—"but I'm sure it will be worth it."

CHAPTER 2

The guy who named it the Greenleaf Bar must have been punch-drunk. Or just plain drunk. It should have been called the Smokehouse. The place was jammed when me and the boss got there, and it was some brawl.

Me and the boss wrestled our way in. The tobacco smoke made my eyes burn.

Some of the big punks saw the boss and it was a scream to see them make room for him. But they knew Percival Smith. They knew he looked as soft as a wet sponge when he's more like a chunk of stone. He has shot more than one guy and he can handle his dukes. Me, I'm ready, but I'd want five to two before I'd take the boss on in what he calls fisticuffs.

A Greek and a slick-looking kid were working out behind the bar.

I thought for a minute the Greek was going to hug Smith. "Smeeth! You lika some gooda Scotch?"

The boss nodded. I said, "Give me some bourbon, Nick."

The Greek brought our drinks. The boss pulled out a five spot, waved it back and forth in front of Nick's eyes.

After the Greek digested the sight of the five, the boss said, "What are they saying about the dog track, Nick?"

The Greek looked all around, then back at Smith. "She'sa keep running. She'sa belong to Newell now."

"So?"

The Greek hunched his shoulders. He began swiping the bar with a towel. "There wasa no contract."

"A thieves' agreement between Newell and Droyster personally, eh?" The boss downed a little of the Scotch and made a face.

"One more thing, Nick," he said. "Where is Pete Lorentz? Pete's been booking my bets for over a year now. He's cost me a grand or so. Three days ago I placed a bet with him on White Lady. He was supposed to bring my winnings to my office, but I haven't laid eyes on him."

I remembered that. The boss had sure been in a stew because he thought Lorentz had run out. The odds on White Lady had been right and the boss had made a killing. He'd called all over town for Pete before he decided the bookie had taken a powder.

The Greek hunched his shoulders again.

The boss said, "Well, where's Pete?"

Nick grunted. "You keepa the five dollar, Smeeth. Pete—he'sa none my business."

The boss was never one to dicker. He peeled five more off his roll. Nick licked his lips.

"I tella you then, Smeeth. Pete leave town. He have the fight with Mark Droyster the day Droyster killa himself. Pete—he mop floor over witha Droyster."

"And where did Pete go?"

"She'sa big mystery. No one see Pete since he hava the fight."

"Okay, Nick," the boss said. The Greek grabbed the dough. Smith said, "That drunk down the line needs a drink."

"You no tella what I say?"

"Have I ever, Nick?"

"No, you gooda fran, Smeeth." Nick moved away.

The boss and me parked in a booth to wait on Joe Dance. I kept looking at the clock behind the bar every now and then. Nine o'clock came, but Joe Dance didn't show up. I had another bourbon.

At ten, the boss said, "Dance isn't coming, Willie. Let's be toddling."

We went outside and the boss told me to hail a cab. I flagged one to the curb and we got in.

Smith gave the hackie Al Newell's address, which isn't far from Alicia Droyster's.

"You think we ought to go there, boss?"

"It's a lead." He didn't say nothing more for awhile. Then he said, "You know, Willie, it's all rather queer."

"What is?"

"Joe Dance and Pete Lorentz are great pals—and they both work for Newell."

I said, "Uh huh."

Smith said, "Look at it this way. Droyster and Newell own a dog track together. Droyster is dead—suicide they say—and Lorentz has vanished. To top that, Dance breaks an appointment with us."

"Maybe we should hunt Dance, boss."

He laughed. "We shall, Willie. We shall call on a great number of people."

* * * *

When we got uptown, the cab turned a corner beside the Jackson building. That's where Smith's office is. The boss was looking out the cab as we went around the corner. He sucked in his breath like he had been punched in the stomach.

"Hold it!" he said. "We'll get out here."

The hackie pulled over and the boss tossed a piece of folding money at him.

I nearly had to sprint to keep up with him. "What in blazes, boss?"

He didn't say nothing. He just pointed up. I said, "Cripes!" There was a light in the boss' office. And we sure as hell hadn't left it burning.

The elevators had quit for the night, but Smith likes to be close to the ground. So we only had four flights to go up.

The boss must have thought it was time for a little road work, the way he took those stairs. We came to the fourth floor and I was winded. My tongue was hanging out, but Smith hadn't even started to sweat.

He whispered, "Keep those big feet quiet, Willie." Then he motioned to me and started toward his office like we were creeping up on a punch-drunk guy in a ring.

The light was still on. I began to get a tight, cold feeling in the pit of my stomach. I filled my paw with the old equalizer. Smith got out his key.

I had the room pretty well covered and he got the key in the lock without making a sound.

He twisted the key and banged the door open hard. I was all set to start throwing lead.

Then the air went out of me with a fizz. I put the gun back in my pocket and me and Smith looked at each other. Then we looked at the guy standing in the middle of the office.

He was a big bruiser, taller than me and just as broad. He had on a shiny old suit and a hat that looked like he found it at a dogfight. He could be a nasty egg sometimes. He was a plainclothes dick. They called him Bedrock Hannrihan, mainly, I guess, because he always dug to bedrock on a case and he didn't give a damn how he did the digging.

"Hello, Smith," he said, "this is more luck than I bargained for."

Me and Smith looked around the office. Hannrihan had been having fun. He had pulled the desk to one side, the big radio the boss loves away from the wall. He had even pulled the couch out in the middle of the room.

But the boss kept his temper. He didn't sound mad. "What do you want, Hannrihan?"

"Does it matter?"

"It does."

I said, "Have you got a warrant?"

I thought for a minute Hannrihan was going to bite me. "Listen, ape," he said, "I don't like you. You're a smart aleck. You talk too smart. Just because you could beat a few guys' heads off a few years ago and have a couple of Broadway dolls around, you think you are a gent."

I took a step toward him. The boss said, "Easy, Willie." He looked at Hannrihan. "Perhaps Willie is right. This sort of thing usually calls for a warrant."

"Now, now, Smith. You're not going to be that way are you?"

The boss looked at the mess Hannrihan had made. "Were you going to try the bookcase next? What the hell are you looking for anyway?"

Hannrihan smiled. "A corpse. Somebody squealed on you, Smith, said I'd find Joe Dance's body here."

My chin nearly hit my toes. "Joe Dance!"

Smith sort of stiffened. "Whoever called you, Hannrihan, must have recently escaped from the insane asylum. Have you checked there?"

Hannrihan said, "I'm not kidding, Smith. Now shall I get a warrant?"

"Why get a warrant now?" I said. "You've just about covered the place. The boss won't mind you finishing." I was giving him plenty of the Bronx cheer in my tone. "Why don't you look in that closet over there, you grinning ape? Maybe we killed Dance, for no reason at all, and stuffed his body in that closet."

Hannrihan's face was about to gush blood. "I'll do that, Mr. Aberstein," he said soft-like. "I'll look there."

He crossed the office and I couldn't help it; I laughed until my head roared. The big dummy yanked the closet door open. The laugh choked up in my throat. I staggered back like I'd been punched with a hard left jab.

There was a coat hanging in the closet, but I didn't even see that. I couldn't see anything but Joe Dance's eyes. There were three of them, and the one in the middle of his forehead had spilled red down over his face. He'd never tell us anything about Droyster.

I couldn't move. I had to hang to the edge of the desk. Hannrihan started to turn around. But I couldn't do a thing about it. It took the boss to do that.

He swarmed all over the big cop. Hannrihan yelped, swung, but the boss hit him in the back of the neck with a rabbit punch.

Hannrihan went stiff, bounced up on his toes. His eyes rolled back. The boss hit him again and the floor caught the big dick.

I'd seen Smith do that before. His old man had wanted Smith to be a doctor; the boss knew every nerve center in a guy's body. That's what he had done to Hannrihan. I knew the big dick would be out ten or fifteen minutes until the nerves started working again.

The boss bent and looked at Dance. "Probably a thirty-eight slug, Willie," he said. "It's parked in the middle of Joe's brain—if he has one."

He closed the closet door. He took a look at me and laughed. "Feel sick?"

I nodded.

He stepped over Hannrihan. "Well, come along, Willie. We'll snap you out of it. We've a very busy night ahead of us."

"You're telling me!" I wobbled out the door.

* * * *

On the way to Newell's place, which is some dump, the boss relaxed in the cab like he was coming home from a picture show. Me, I opened the window and poked my head out. I kept seeing Joe Dance and the cold air helped.

"All we've got so far," the boss muttered, "is Mark Droyster dead, a dog track now owned in its entirety by Al Newell, a widow who wants insurance, a bookie named Lorentz who had a fight with Droyster and made tracks, and the corpse of Joe Dance in the office of the Smith Agency."

"Yeah, and a big bull who saw the corpse."

The boss fired a smoke. I said, "Honest, boss, I was just making with sarcasm when I told Hannrihan to look in the closet. Cripes, I never dreamed that Joe Dance…"

"I haven't blamed you, have I?"

"No, but still it makes me feel punk, me causing that ape to look in the closet."

"Oh, forget it, Willie. He would have looked sooner or later anyway."

"Well, that sort of makes me feel better." Then I remembered those three eyes of Dance's and had to get my head out of the window where the wind could hit it quick. It's fine, the things cold air will do for you. It sort of knocked the grogginess out of my head.

The boss laughed. "Feel better?"

"I don't know. I guess so. Wonder what we'll find at Newell's?"

"Your guess is as good as mine."

Well, I guessed all the way down. I was sure we'd find plenty. But I was wrong. We didn't find nothing. Newell's apartment was as quiet as a graveyard. The boss kept buzzing the buzzer.

After awhile I said, "Nobody's going to answer, boss."

He looked at me kind of funny like. "That's quite obvious," he snapped. He tried the knob. The door was locked. "I wonder if the fire escape—"

He broke off when a door down the hall opened. We looked, and I could have hung around there awhile. The blonde standing in the doorway was some babe.

"I heard you ringing," she said. "If you're looking for Mr. Newell, you won't find him."

The boss gave her a million dollar smile. "Yes?" he said.

She smiled back. Then she frowned a little. "Mr. Newell is in jail."

"Jail!" I said, and the boss gave me a dirty look.

The blonde nodded. "I can't understand it. He hardly knew my name and he looked like such a nice fellow, yet he burst into my apartment this afternoon. He was so drunk he could hardly walk. He seemed to think I was some woman named Susan. I got him in the bedroom, locked him in, and called the police." She giggled.

"What time was that?" the boss asked.

"About four o'clock. I—"

"Thanks very much, Susan."

"But I'm not Susan, I tell you. I…" But me and the boss were already on our way.

* * * *

Down in the street again, the boss took a quick gander about. There was no bulls around, so we started walking.

I was sort of dizzy. I thought we'd come here and have a little fun choking the truth out of Newell about Joe Dance. But now…

The boss said, "It would be a nice alibi, being in jail."

"Cripes, it would!"

"But I'm not so sure, Willie."

"Well, I don't know nothing, it seems like." We walked on a little. There wasn't many people out and we kept our eyes peeled for coppers.

Then an idea popped into my mind. "Listen, boss," I said, "I got an angle. That sawbones, the one who went to the funeral with the Droyster dame. And, say: What about Alicia Droyster herself?"

"You mean Doctor Lawrence Jordan?"

"That's right."

"That's too weak, Willie. Lack of motive. And I think Mrs. Droyster is out. It would be too risky for her to call us if she…"

"I'm not so sure, boss. People do the damndest things. Maybe she's hoping we'll pin it on somebody else. Maybe…"

"Stop it, Willie. I didn't hire you to play Sherlock."

"Aw, gee, boss. I was just trying to help."

He slapped me on the shoulder.

"When I need you, I'll whistle. Now come along, Willie, it suddenly occurs to me that I am a great lover of dogs."

"You what…?" But he didn't answer.

We walked a block, then turned into an alley that ran to the next street. It was a fairly wide alley and pretty dark.

We passed a platform that was used for loading I guessed. It was all messed up with old crates and boxes and big sheets of paper.

I knew we were headed for Droyster's. It wasn't far this way, taking short cuts. The boss didn't want to use cabs much. Cops have a nasty habit of talking to cabbies.

Thinking about cops was bad. Hannrihan was chasing all over town by this time. I laid myself four to one that me and the boss was being talked about plenty on the police short wave.

I had to wipe my face with a handkerchief. What those cops would do if they caught us…

I never had the chance to put the handkerchief back in my pocket. A car had turned in the alley at our backs. Its headlights made a lot of light in that alley.

I turned around. The car was coming like a cannonball.

"The end of the street, boss. We're close. Let's go!"

He gave me a hard shove. "You fool! We'd never outrun them. Dive for that doorway over there!"

I scrambled across the alley. The car wasn't a prowl car because there was no siren.

Whoever was in the car had a gun. He started using it. It sounded like a bowling alley with all the alleys full of guys making strikes. A bullet yanked at my coat sleeve.

I hit concrete nearly head first, rolled into the doorway. I got Bessie out of my pocket. Bessie talked back to the birds in the car. But I'm better with my fists than a gun and all Bessie's bullets missed.

A bullet hit the steel door behind me. I heard the boss get his Spanish going. Somebody in the car yelped. The door behind me took another slug. Bessie roared again and I had the fun of busting a window out of the car.

Then the car was gone and I got up. I had got a glimpse of the guy driving the car. I couldn't be sure, but there isn't two guys like that in this world. He was the guy me and the boss wanted to see—Al Newell.

Percival Smith had been behind a steel garbage can. He got up, blew smoke out of his gun. He met me in the middle of the alley.

I had lost my handkerchief. I had to wipe sweat on my coat sleeve. "Some fun, boss. Me getting over there was a good idea. It made a split target of us."

"Which surprised and rattled them," Smith said, "and which enabled us to converge our fire on them from both flanks."

"Yeah, yeah," I said, quick-like. "It was okay." Once he got started talking like that, he was hard to stop.

My ticker was just getting back down in my chest where it belonged. We took a few steps and the old heart started doing tricks again. But you couldn't blame it. Not with that harness bull's whistle going like it was. He was around the corner somewhere and he must have been blowing himself blue in the face.

The sound of the whistle got louder. I moaned, "They heard the shooting, boss."

"Yes, and this alley will be swarming with cops in two minutes."

He grabbed my arm, turned me around, and we started running back up the alley.

The cop kept blowing his whistle.

"That loading platform we passed," the boss said. "We'll shake them there."

Another whistle began blasting at the other end of the alley.

"Oh, oh," I said, "a cop at each end!"

We got to the platform. It was about waist high. We climbed up.

Those whistles were sure making a noise. Any second now the bulls would be coming in the alley—one from each end.

I didn't feel so hot. I remembered everything I had ever heard about the electric chair. It was like being in the ring with the other guy and the referee both punching you.

I unlimbered Bessie. The boss made a nasty sound in his throat. He grabbed my wrist, squeezed, and I nearly yelled.

"Aberstein, some day I'm going to fire you! Put that damn gun up!"

I did what he said, but I couldn't see any way out of this jam but to maybe kill a cop.

Percival Smith shook my shoulder. "Get a move on, Willie!" He didn't sound like any elegant guy now. He sounded tough.

He talked fast, in a whisper. "There's no chance of fighting our way out of this. There's nothing we can do but hide. Quick, get under this paper."

He lifted a big sheet of the old wrapping paper that had been around some of the crates or boxes.

I got it then. I dropped down, scooted up under the paper. I lay against the wall. The boss got in beside me. The paper covered us. I hoped he had fixed it to look like somebody had just thrown the paper there.

The alley got quiet. That meant the coppers were sneaking along in the dark.

It took a long time for the cops to meet down in front of the platform.

It was ink black and hot under the paper. Somebody stepped up on the platform. He turned on a flashlight and light passed across the paper. I set my teeth to keep them from chattering.

"Maybe they were all in the car," one of the cops said.

The other one didn't answer. I heard him turn a crate over. He walked toward the paper that covered us. I reached slowly for the old equalizer. Smith felt my movement. He got his fingers around my wrist.

Somebody else out in the alley said, "What's up, Kelley?" The alley sounded full of cops.

The bull on the platform said, "We're not sure. There was a lot of shooting here in the alley a few minutes ago, but we don't find anything now. Must have all been in the car that came tearing out the alley."

Smith and me lay like two store dummies, right where Kelley could have reached out and touched us. Then after awhile Kelley got off the platform. Lady Luck was riding with us for a few seconds.

The boss wouldn't let me move for a long time after they left. Just when I thought it was move or go crazy, the boss said, "All right, Willie. Take a look."

I pushed the paper back, raised my head. I sounded like I was choking on something. "They're gone, boss."

We pushed the paper back and got up. Smith dusted himself off with his hands, wiped his hands on a handkerchief. He straightened his tie and we were ready to push off.

We took it easy getting out of the alley. We came to the street, and Smith hailed a cab.

He said, "Willie, this lark is becoming a bit too grim."

"You're telling me!"

"It will be most gratifying to meet the gentleman who is causing us this discomfiture."

He wasn't kidding. It would be nice to get our hands on the gent who had put the corpse in the closet and us behind the old black ball.

The cab turned a corner. Droyster's house wasn't far away.

CHAPTER 3

We didn't use the front entrance this time. We sneaked across the lawn. It was a little after eleven, but there was a light on in the front corner room. We went toward the light.

We had to be careful getting close to the window. There was some dry shrubbery growing under the window and you could make a lot of noise walking in it.

We got to where we could see into the room. There was a good-looking doll in the room—Alicia Droyster.

She had on a fancy evening gown cut low in back. There was a guy with her I didn't recognize. He was young, slim, and had a small mustache.

They must have just come in from someplace. Alicia Droyster was mixing drinks. She handed the guy a glass that made my mouth water.

They touched glasses, downed the drinks. Then this guy put his arms around her and they started getting mushy. My knees got weak just watching. I could have looked at that for awhile, but Smith had seen enough. He pulled me away by the arm.

Out on the lawn, he said under his breath, "How very interesting!"

"You mean them two?"

"Yes, that was Alicia Droyster and Doctor Lawrence Jordan."

"Jordan! Boss, I told you—"

"Not so loud!"

"That sawbones, boss, I'll give you eight to three—"

"For heaven's sake, Willie, stop the deducting."

I didn't say nothing more. But it would sure be a laugh, I thought, if I was right.

We didn't have no trouble at all getting into the little storage house. The boss has a fine ring of keys.

He swung the door open. He shielded his pencil flash with his hand so nobody in the big house up front could see it.

There was some old furniture and books in the front room, piled all around.

The boss eased the door shut behind us.

"What are we looking for, boss?"

"I don't know."

"You what—? You mean we get shot at by Newell, hide from the cops..."

He grabbed my arm. "Newell? Did you say Newell?"

"Sure, boss, he was driving that car! I—I was so excited I didn't think to tell you before."

"Newell," the boss muttered like he had found a present of some kind, "Newell was driving the car, eh?"

Then he said, "Well, come along, Willie. We'll still seek our treasure."

"For pity's sake, boss, what kind of treasure?"

"I told you I don't know. Now shut up." He played the light around the room.

"Well, can't you just sort of give me an idea?"

"We're hunting whatever Jackie, the Great Dane dog, found here. Remember, Willie? The dog came here and barked. Then he vanished. If we find his corpse, or the thing he was after, we have found our treasure."

I thought of Bedrock Hannrihan hunting all over town. "I hope we find it."

We didn't find nothing downstairs but a lot of junk. We went upstairs. There were only three rooms here. The first was empty except for dust all over the floor. We walked to the door of the second room.

The boss threw his light into the room. This room held plenty—too much. I took one look and got sick.

He was in the middle of the floor, what was left of him, lying on his back. His feet and body looked okay. But his whole head was gone. I shut my eyes.

When I opened them again, I was sort of sagging against the door, like a fighter hangs onto the ropes. Percival Smith was looking over the headless gent like he might look over a dozen roses.

I got my stomach well swallowed and took a look myself. He had been a big man. His clothes were dusty and wrinkled. There was no blood around on the floor.

Smith said, "Know him?"

"Maybe—if I could see his face."

The boss laughed. I tried a grin.

"This lovely specimen, Willie," Percival Smith said, "is our old friend—Mark Droyster!"

That knocked the sickness out of me. "Droy—you're telling me that's Mark Droyster? It couldn't be! Droyster was buried yesterday!"

"Not actually." The boss held out his hand, shined the light on it. On his palm was a ring and a small blue book. "Droyster's ring, Willie. I just took it off the corpse."

"And the book?"

"A bank book. It was on the floor, under the small of his back. I got it while you were taking a count. It's a very interesting book."

I said, "Uh huh?"

"It shows a withdrawal of fifty-seven thousand dollars made three days ago by Droyster."

I whistled. "This sure gums up things, boss. Anybody most would kill for that much money."

"Yes, it is a complication. Unknown to the world, Droyster possessed a fortune three days ago."

"But why is his corpse here, boss?"

"You can play Sherlock on that if you want to, Willie."

I said, "Uh huh." I pointed at the corpse. "And that's why the dog came here."

"That's right. He came and barked. The murderer, for his own purposes, had taken Droyster's corpse from the casket. The casket, due to the condition of the body, was never opened. The dog came here, found Droyster, and the murderer did something to the dog to silence him. Mrs. Droyster came and looked, but not very well. However, she did scare the killer off. He'll have to return and dispose of this body."

"Well," I said, "I don't understand every bit of your lingo. And I'm in one fine muddle. But if the killer has to come back, why can't we lay for him here?"

"In the first place he might fool us and not return. And in the second, we've got to find the murderer before Hannrihan finds us."

Even the mention of it made my mouth get dry. "Let's not talk about Hannrihan, boss."

We started back down the stairs. The boss turned off his light.

I whispered, "Where do we go from here?"

"Where would you like to go? Take your pick. You have Alicia Droyster, Doctor Lawrence Jordan, an absent bookie named Pete Lorentz, and our friend, Al Newell, to choose from."

"Let's see the sawbones!"

"Later. First we'll see Newell." He started to open the front door. "And, Willie, you can begin to earn your pay. I'm whistling for you now. We might have to beat the truth from Newell."

"Lead me to it!"

He pulled the front door open.

I said, "I'll wring Newell's neck, boss. I'll break him in two. I'll…"

"Do nothing of the kind!" a voice said. Somebody else had a pencil flash. They threw it on us, standing so the light couldn't be seen from the big house.

Percival Smith said, "Hello, Newell."

"Hello, Smith, I've got a gun. So be careful. Now get back inside. I don't want snoopers from the house."

Newell moved from the yard to the porch. I could see his face above the flash.

Just like he was asking Newell in for a drink, Smith opened the door with his passkey.

"Go on in," Newell said. He took a step toward us.

There wasn't nothing to do but backpedal. Newell herded us to a back room. He didn't get close to us. He wasn't taking chances.

"Smith," he said, "I had a devil of a time trailing you down here. In fact, I've been having a devil of a time all night—and just because of you."

"That," Percival Smith said, "is mutual. That was a very smart trick, Newell, putting the remains of Joe Dance in my office and calling the bulls."

"What the hell are you talking about, Smith? You're nuts!"

"Am I? Joe Dance worked for you. He was about to tell me a few things about Droyster's death. You inherited a very rich dog track from Droyster and you were afraid Dance would spoil it by talking."

Newell brought his gun up a little. I wished I could get some moisture in my mouth. Newell said, "So you know about the track?"

"Of course, what do you think I do with my time, knit? How much does the track payoff, Newell? Ten grand a month? Enough to commit murder for?"

"All right," Newell said in a sort of ice-like voice, "I'll show you my hand—since I've got the gun. The track does payoff plenty. Mark Droyster never knew, because I kept the books and he was tied up in a dozen other different places. But I didn't kill him or Joe Dance."

"And you trailed us all the way down here to tell me that?" Smith said.

Newell laughed. "Don't be funny. I came here to do what I tried to do earlier tonight."

The boss just said, "Yes?" but my knees were banging together. I looked at Newell's gun. It must be awful lonesome, I thought, with six feet of dirt over your face. But I couldn't get close to Newell, not close enough to do nothing.

The boss said, "Earlier tonight you tried to kill us, Newell. Now you say you are going to finish it. Yet you claim you are a very innocent boy. I think you are a very funny boy. You tried to make me and the police think you were drunk this afternoon, when Dance's corpse was planted in my office. You—"

"I was drunk, if you must know. I was in jail until just a few minutes before I found you and Gargantua in the alley." He leveled the gun at Smith's head. "I think you know too much, Smith. Maybe I should knock you off."

"You tried hard enough once already," I said.

Newell laughed. "Tried? There in the alley? That's a joke. If I'd tried, you wouldn't be kicking now." He threw the light toward the boss. "No, Smith, I don't want to kill you. In the alley tonight I merely tried to wing you, lay you up for a few days with a bullet in the leg. Or maybe scare you off the Droyster case. But I didn't really expect that. You're too dumb to keep your nose clean."

Smith said, "Perhaps you need another drink, Newell—to sober you up. What are you driving at, anyway?"

"I've decided to change my tactics, Smith. Instead of putting you and that baboon in the hospital, I'm going to buy you off this case."

The boss rubbed his hands together. "How interesting!"

"Two grand, Smith, to forget Droyster's suicide?"

"Gracious!" Percival Smith said. "Willie, we must choose more generous company. We'll settle for four thousand, Newell."

"You're a fool, Smith!"

"Four thousand?"

Well, I'd never thought the boss would do that. I'd sooner look at Newell's gun than have Smith do this kind of business. "Cripes, boss, don't do it! We—"

Newell said, "I must be crazy, but I'll give you three grand."

"It's a deal," the boss said.

That must have made Newell happy. He laughed. "I've heard different about you, Smith, but I guess you like dough as well as the next one."

"Money is money, no matter what type hand handles it."

This was slaying me and I'm not kidding. Me and Smith maybe don't do everything real gentle, but having him do this was like finding out there is no Santa Claus. "Boss…"

Newell threw the light more on me. "The gorilla doesn't like your way of working, Smith."

"He will," the boss said, "when I whistle."

I got it then. Newell put the back end of the pencil flash in his mouth. He still kept his light on us, but having the flash in his mouth freed his left hand. He used the hand to drag out a pocketbook that was just about busting with dough. He put the pocketbook between his knees. He got three one grand bills from it with his left hand. I was set.

Newell moved closer to hand the three grand to the boss.

He let the gun point away from me a little. That was bad. I was on my toes, just like in the good old ring days. The boss reached out for the three grand. He whistled real soft between his teeth.

I let go. It was a wallop that would have floored the champ ten or twelve years ago. Newell saw it coming, tried to swing the gun. The gun got all tangled up in the boss' fingers. My knuckles smashed Newell's cheek and the flash popped out of his mouth. He staggered, but he hung to the gun.

The boss twisted. I stepped in and hit Newell again. It was fine. The punk nearly left the floor. He sailed clear across the small room. I heard him hit the floor.

The boss picked up the flash, threw it on Al Newell.

Newell made a couple of tries and got his pins under him. The boss kept the gun on Newell. I picked up the slim punk's dough, put it back in the pocketbook, and handed it to him.

His eyes were nasty looking in the light from the flash. "I'll remember this, Smith!"

"Tish, tish, such talk—when I've got the gun." He cocked his head, looked at Newell a minute. "It will be a shame, Newell, a downright shame."

"What do you mean?"

"That face of yours, it's so handsome."

Newell lost some of his fire. "Listen now, Smith…"

"Willie will make mincemeat of you, Newell—unless you tell us the whole story of the guy in the closet."

"Now look here, Smith! You'd better watch your step. It wouldn't be healthy if you set that gorilla on me!"

"Indeed it wouldn't—for you. Come now, tell me. You killed Droyster to get the dog track, didn't you? Dance found out and you killed him to cover it."

"No, Smith, you're all wrong." He was sort of having trouble with his voice. It kept shaking like a hula dancer. "I swear you're wrong! I didn't even know Dance was dead until my lawyer came to headquarters tonight to get me out of jail."

The boss didn't say nothing for awhile. Then he said, "Okay, Al, if that's the way you want it. How many of your boys are outside?"

"None, Smith, I came alone."

"Very well. We can't stay here all night. If you want to be stubborn, we'll have to have a little tea party someplace. Would you like some tea, Willie?"

"Sure thing, boss."

"No, Smith, don't do it." He was nearly crying.

"Take him in tow, Willie," the boss said. "And if he gets away, I'll have your hide."

I grabbed Newell by the shoulder. He was scared silly. He let me turn him around. I got his left arm in a hammer hold. I got my gun in my other hand and planted it in the middle of Newell's back. He was in a bad way.

The boss turned off the light. "Let's go."

We went out the front again. I almost had to hold Newell up while the boss locked the door. We were out on the porch of the little house. The moon was playing around behind clouds.

"Listen, Smith," Newell begged, "I've seen a couple of guys you have worked over and I don't want it. I'll tell you all about Droyster, if you'll make this elephant turn me loose. You're right, it wasn't suicide. It was the most fantastic—"

And that's as far as he got. Somebody in a patch of bushes not ten feet away had a gun. He used it. It sounded like an earthquake, the gun going off. Newell slammed into me when the slug hit him. Then the somebody made a quick take off out of the bushes. Before me or the boss could get our roscoes going, the somebody was already around the corner of Droyster's big house and gone.

Smith snapped, "We've got to get out of here." Lights went on in the big house. "Hurt bad, Newell?"

"In the side."

"Let's get the guy, boss," I said.

"We'd never catch him now. Better let Newell go, Willie, he should get to a doctor."

A door slammed up at the big house. Somebody yelled. More lights went on.

I turned Newell loose. He wobbled off, nearly on his last legs.

"You and me, boss?" I said. We were already legging it across the lawn.

"We're going on a little errand. Too bad we couldn't have hung onto Newell. But if we had tried, he might have died on us."

"What kind of errand, boss?"

"We're going to dig a grave, Willie."

CHAPTER 4

Me and the boss shinnied over the iron fence that was supposed to keep people out of the graveyard. I didn't much want to move when we got inside the fence. There wasn't nothing but tombstones and graves all around. The way the moon was shining didn't make them look any better.

"Do we just have to do this, boss?"

"Of course. What's wrong?"

"Nothing—I guess. I sort of would like to get out of here, though."

He laughed and gave me a push with his hand. I wished I could laugh. I wonder what it is like to have a regular job so you can sleep at night instead of messing around in graveyards with a killer loose someplace and the cops just praying for a chance to get you in the little room at headquarters.

I followed the boss. He looked at tombstones every little bit. Finally he pointed to a big chunk of some kind of fancy stone, marble, I guess.

"This is it, Willie. Start digging."

We had gone by Smith's apartment on the way down here. The boss had found a short-handled spade way back in a closet. He had once used the spade for flower beds, but we wasn't planting petunias now.

He handed me the spade. I took off my coat, wiped the sweat off my face, and went to work.

I was about three feet down when I heard the voice. "What are you doing there?"

Then a light smacked me. I turned around gentle-like. I couldn't see the guy holding the light.

He said, "Are you the same one that was here last night?"

I shook my head. Where in hell was Smith? I took a step toward the light.

"Hold it!" the guy said. "I'm the caretaker here and I've got a gun on you. One more move and I'll give it to you."

He wasn't kidding.

He went on after a minute, "What's so interesting in that grave, anyway?"

What the devil could I say? I didn't know what he was talking about even if my throat and tongue hadn't been so numb.

"Didn't you hear me?" he growled. "Last night somebody came here and now you. Why?"

I shook my head again. Damn that Smith!

Then I saw the shadow behind the caretaker. Smith hit him hard with his automatic. The sound of the gun on the caretaker's skull sort of made me sick. He dropped his light and fell on the loose dirt I had dug.

"Cripes, boss, I was wondering…"

"Where I was? Merely taking care of you, Willie. That headstone over there made a nice hiding place." He looked down at the caretaker. "Someone here last night, eh? How interesting!" Then he told me, "Keep working, Willie. This is no holiday."

I went back at it. It was hot work. The closer I got to the coffin, the hotter it seemed to get.

I got the lid off the pine box with a screwdriver the boss had brought along. I handed the lid up to him. He was getting all in a huff.

"Hurry, Willie! Get busy—open the casket!"

That took longer. My hands had too much sweat on them to do what Smith wanted them to do.

This had been one more night, I thought. Nothing could floor me now. But when I opened that casket, I damn near passed out.

The moonlight that came into the grave made things plain enough to see. I wish it hadn't. There was a Great Dane dog stuffed in the casket. Blood was all over the inside, on the shiny white cloth. Somebody had cut the dog's throat wide open…

Smith got down in the grave so fast I thought he had fallen. He pushed me back, which was fine, and started messing around in the casket with his hands. I shut my eyes on that.

In a minute he stood up. He was holding a white pillow that had been dyed in spots with blood. He crammed the pillow under his coat and it made stiff, cracking noises.

Percival Smith laughed, reached in his vest pocket, and got out a calling card, his own card.

"It began with a card, Willie. It might as well end that way." It looked goofy to me, but he put the card on the dead dog's head, right in sight.

We climbed out of the hole. "Do we fill the grave back, boss?"

"No, but we'll have to tie the caretaker and hide him somewhere. I don't want him to find that card."

The caretaker was still out. We tied him up with our neckties and gagged him with Smith's handkerchief.

We got out of the graveyard fast, went back over the fence. We walked a block or two, and Smith flagged a cab that passed. "The Jackson Building," he told the driver.

When we got back to the office, Smith turned on the light just like he was going to read awhile. He put the bloody pillow he had got from the casket on the desk. I looked in the closet to make sure Hannrihan had got Joe Dance's body out of there. He had.

Smith smoked a cigarette, walked around the office. He lighted another smoke from the old butt.

When he got through with that one, he looked at his wrist watch. "It's been five minutes since we came back, Willie. You can turn off the light now."

He pushed a couple of chairs together over in the corner. I turned off the light.

"Sit over here, Willie," Smith said.

I went over and parked beside him in one of the chairs.

"Well," I said, "this is all okay, I guess. But what's the idea?"

"I'm hungry," he said.

"Cripes, boss, who the hell are we waiting for?"

"Whoever finds my calling card."

"And who'll that be?"

"Perhaps the police," he said.

"Oh, Lord!"

"Or perhaps the mild gentleman who left Joe Dance in the closet."

"That's better."

Smith didn't talk anymore. He leaned back in his chair. I knew we were in for a long wait.

After what seemed like a hundred years, I started to tell the boss it was no soap. I wanted to get out of here. This hanging around didn't make me feel any too good.

But Smith caught my arm before I could say anything. And I heard it too—somebody putting a passkey in the lock.

The door swung back, covering us. The guy waited a minute, then came in. He was good-sized. I made a guess—Pete Lorentz, the bookie who had taken a powder.

He saw the bloody pillow in the light from outside. His breath made a funny sound. He jumped at the desk, got his hands on the pillow.

Smith turned the light on.

The guy wheeled around. Smith covered him with his automatic. I'd been all wet. This guy wasn't Pete Lorentz.

Smith made a little bow. "You almost got away with it," he said, "and it was a scheme worthy of a genius." He grinned at the guy. He said, "Mark Droyster—the man who wouldn't stay dead!"

Droyster didn't look so good. He hadn't had any sleep, and he needed a shave badly.

He didn't say nothing. He just looked at Smith and the Spanish in Smith's hand.

"Come on, Willie," the boss said, "we're taking him in."

But I didn't move. Somebody else had come in the office. He gave the orders, "No, Smith, you're not taking him in. Drop your gun. You, Aberstein, line up beside him."

The boss let the gun go. It bumped on the floor. Me and the boss turned around. Al Newell was bent over a little from the slug he had taken. There were two guys with Newell. Ike Clark, a little hophead, and Harry Haines, a skinny, tall gent who had shot his own brother a couple of years before.

Newell pushed the door shut. "You can scram in a moment, Droyster. If I let Smith take you in, people will know you are alive and I lose my dog track. So I'll help you, even though you did plug me earlier tonight."

My head was spinning. I finally got my jaw back up where it ought to be. "I thought that was Droyster's stiff in the storage house. I—"

"So did a lot of people, monkey," Newell said. "It was a fine plot, the nicest business deal Droyster ever cooked up. And I'm going to help him push it through. I'll take you to Hannrihan, Smith. Think he'll ever believe you when you claim Droyster is still alive? You'll tell him that the corpse in the storage house is not Droyster but Pete Lorentz.' But will he believe it? Can you prove it? We'll claim the corpse really is Droyster. So the only mystery the cops will have is why wasn't Droyster's corpse in the grave?"

It looked plenty bad. If Droyster got away from here, no telling where he'd be this time tomorrow.

Newell nodded to Ike Clark and Harry Haines. "Let's get a move on."

The two torpedoes pulled their rods. The boss fired a smoke. "Are you quite sure, Newell, that you and Droyster haven't overlooked anything?" The way he said it and the way he looked at Newell sort of did things to the slim punk.

"What do you mean?" Newell said. He held out a hand to slow Clark and Haines down.

"Shall we go back to the beginning?" the boss said. "Back to what drove Droyster to this?"

Newell and Droyster looked at each other. Droyster said, "Talk fast, and it had better be good. If I've slipped, I want to know it, but if you're stalling…"

"In the first place," Smith said, "you were slipping all around. Your house was mortgaged, your business enterprises—thanks to men like Newell handling the books—were shot to hell. Your whole life was exploding in your face, money evaporating, your wife giving you the air for Doctor Lawrence Jordan. You were losing, had lost, everything. You had been a big shot, now you were sinking to the level of a tramp. No man who has had your money and power, Droyster, would give it up without a fight. It hurt to see yourself as an old, broken bum, with people laughing and shaking their heads behind your back.

"But you had fifty-seven grand that no one knew about." The boss laughed, puffed his fag. "This is the first case on record where a man killed other people for his own money. That's exactly what you did. You were finished. There was only one way out—get away, start over. For a start you needed money. And the only way to keep your fifty-seven grand was to die here and be another man someplace else. That fifty thousand dollars wouldn't have lasted long, what with all your debts, if you'd tried to leave in a legal manner."

The boss sat down like he had all the sweet time he needed. The others watched him like buzzards. Me, I was soaking my shirt with sweat.

"When Pete Lorentz gave you the beating," the boss said, "you got your big idea. It was a hard pill to swallow, having a two-by-four bookie beat hell out of you. It showed just how far you had slipped. You were so enraged you wanted to kill—and thinking about it started the plan in your mind.

"You killed Pete with a shotgun, Droyster. With your clothes and ring on him, and his head gone, everyone thought it was you. Neither of you had ever been fingerprinted. You knew Lawrence Jordan would swear the corpse was you, even if he did have a few doubts. He was that anxious to get your wife."

The boss put out his cigarette, fired another one. "So you were a dead man—with a nice stake of fifty-seven grand, no strings attached. But Newell happened to go into the room, drop a calling card, and your wife, wanting insurance, called me in. Perhaps Newell suspected the truth about you, Droyster.

"He dropped a few words around Joe Dance, and Joe thought to make himself a pile of dough by spilling it. But you had been hiding close around. You killed Dance and brought him up here, then called the police.

"Were you in that storage house most of the time, Droyster? Is there a phone extension there?"

"In the attic," Droyster said, "I heard Dance phone my wife and I heard her phone you."

The boss nodded. "That's why the Great Dane went out to the storage house, because you were there. He barked with joy and you slashed his throat to silence him. That was the same day you killed Pete Lorentz.

"That night you sneaked back into your house. You knew you simply couldn't have Pete up and vanish. If his draft board should put him in 1-A and the F.B.I. went looking for him, it might have upset your scheme. You had to get Pete's body out of the coffin, mutilate it more, and plant it someplace where it could be found, with papers to show his true identity, several days later.

"You took the dog's body back into the house when you went after Pete. You took Pete out of the casket, put the dog in, knowing the casket would not be opened because of the horrible condition of the body. You knew it might take a day or so to dispose of Pete's body, which was very ticklish business; so for safe-keeping you put your fifty-seven grand in the casket—in that blood-stained, satin pillow.

"You went to the graveyard last night, but the caretaker scared you off. You couldn't get rid of Pete's body sooner, and tonight I was on the case. You had to watch other things than the cemetery."

"You talk well, Smith," Droyster said, "but where's the slip? Give out—and hurry!"

Smith smiled at Droyster. "Let me finish. Newell gave you a bit of help all along. First he tried to gun us off the case, later to buy us off. He really wanted that dog track. You were hiding outside, Droyster, when we came out of the storage house. You heard Newell almost break down; so you took a shot at him.

"Naturally, I was wondering all along, since I found the corpse in the storage house, what the devil was in the casket. So Willie and I went to the cemetery. We found your money, left my card where you'd think I accidentally dropped it. You were pretty close on our heels. You found the card as I hoped.

"I left the light on long enough so that you'd not think I suspected you of shadowing me. You watched from across the street until the light went off. You waited until you thought we had gone, then you came to find your money."

I saw just a little bit of sweat on the boss' face. That made my knees bang. If Smith was sweating...

"Poppycock!" Droyster said. "He's stalling. Take him on, Newell."

Newell nodded. He started to say something, but the door crashed open.

Bless his heart! Bedrock Hannrihan looked like the answer to my prayers. "Smith—" he howled. Then he flopped on the floor as Ike Clark got his roscoe going. I hit Newell and Newell hit the floor.

It was some party. Hannrihan's gun went like a cannon. Droyster was cursing a blue streak. Somebody hit a chair. Ike Clark screamed.

Somebody slung a slug my way. It caught me in the leg, knocked me down. I looked up to see Harry Haines. The boss and me don't like people that shoot at us. The boss shot Haines in the neck.

The bullet in my leg kept me on the floor. I rolled around. I was scared sick with all the lead flying loose. I rolled into Newell. He was drawing a bead on the boss and I hit him, I broke his nose with that one and blood went everywhere.

Then it stopped and my ears rang. Ike Clark was doubled up in front of the desk. Haines was on his back, blood coming out of his neck, Newell was over at the wall holding his nose and moaning.

Droyster hadn't been touched. He dropped his gun, looked at the boss, and said, "You win, Smith."

Hannrihan took a look at Droyster. "Cripes! I'm going nuts!"

The boss said, "Yes, quite true." Then he helped me to my feet. "It's only a flesh wound, Willie." Then the boss turned to Hannrihan. He wised the big dick up to all that had happened.

"I talked myself blue in the face," the boss finished, "and had just run out when you got here. I knew as long as the light stayed on there was a chance it would attract you or one of your boys."

Hannrihan kept the live ones covered. "The light attracted me, all right. I passed and saw it. I've been combing the town for you all night, Smith."

The boss tossed the bloody pillow to Hannrihan. "Watch the rent in the cloth," Smith said. "There's fifty-seven grand in that pillow!"

Hannrihan whistled.

"You may use my phone to get the meat wagon and reinforcements," Smith told him. "Willie and I are leaving now."

The boss helped me downstairs. Hannrihan's car was at the curb. We got a cab. "Central hospital," Smith told the driver. He turned to me. "We'll get that leg dressed, Willie. Then we eat."

I leaned back. The morning air tasted sort of good. The sun came up. I hadn't ever noticed before how good it looked, all red and everything.

I looked at the boss. He was looking at me. I don't know why, but the first thing I knew we were grinning at each other and shaking hands to beat hell.

YOUR CRIME IS MY CRIME

Originally published in **New Detective Magazine,** *May 1946.*

The city of Baltimore lay sweltering in the sluggish heat of the autumn night. A searing, fitful breeze off the bay lay its hot tongue on the dinginess of Pratt Street, bringing tired, stringy-haired women to doorways, causing babies to whimper in their grotesque sleep. On Redwood Street, a few offices in concrete and steel buildings blazed with light as brokers figured clients' margins, or tried to guess how many points above 103 Acme Steel would be four weeks from today. Lower East Baltimore Street teemed with sweat-boiled, jostling bodies. A newsboy hawked his wares, rearranging newspapers and magazines laid along the grimy curb and held prisoner from the faint breeze by paperweights.

A burlesque barker added his voice to the din and the air-conditioned penny arcades were jammed, offering refuge from the heat for the price of a pinball game and hot dog smeared with sweet relish. Shooting galleries reminded passing veterans of things they wanted to forget, and bartenders worked like machines, pouring streams of cool liquid over damp bars, while the laughter of men was joined by the tinkling laughter of women and juke boxes and sweating four-piece orchestras pounded a never-ending rhythm. Street cars clanged and horns blared as taxis snaked toward curbs for fares and into the stream of traffic again.

In John Hopkins, a quartet of specialists studied a case of leukemia and wagged their heads over it, knowing it to be incurable. In surgery a famed obstetrician finished a Caesarian and the new life was rushed to an incubator.

It was people. It was sound and silence, life and death. It was kinship, for no matter what a man was doing that hot night in Baltimore, there was another doing or thinking a similar act—even to murder.

Save for the man in the small apartment on Mount Royal Avenue. He was quite alone in his decision, his act—for there was, after all, only one John Brennan.

He stood looking at the slim steady girl with the brunette hair and the rotund, bald man who sat on the couch beside her. They looked back at him and the silence was heavy, broken only by the angry hum of traffic on the street below and the laboring whir of an exhaust fan somewhere in the building.

The rotund, bald, red-nosed man stood up his bulldog jaw quivering on the black cigar clamped between his teeth. "But you can't mean this, John! Now that you're back, you're staying right here—in Baltimore. We need you. Jean," he glanced at the girl who looked at John Brennan so steadily, "and me. The force needs you. And the city, John. We've been waiting for you to come back—me and Jean and the force and the city. We've waited a long time. When V-J day came—"

Brennan turned from the window. He'd been a big, strapping, lean-bellied man once. Now he wasn't. He felt only the ghost of himself.

He broke in, "V-J day was just another day in a hospital for me, MacLaren—and for a lot of other guys." His voice was almost savage, bringing the heavy silence back again. Then he added, "Sorry." He waited a moment and said, "Thanks for coming by, Inspector MacLaren. Tell the boys on the force—"

The ash on MacLaren's cigar glowed. "I'll tell them you're coming back, John." He moved over beside the younger man, the man who looked and felt old. He took Brennan's elbows in his hands and gripped until the tall, gaunt man winced. "You remember Donnavan, don't you, John? Donnavan is dead."

Brennan closed his eyes. "Sure," he said, "I remember Donnavan. A pug-nosed, red-a headed kid in school—the flivver we used to chase around together in."

"That was Donnavan," Inspector MacLaren said. "And you remember him as a red-headed rookie, too, John. The way he kept his shield shined and gun oiled. He worshipped you Brennan—and he was right."

"No," Brennan husked. "Donnavan was wrong."

"But you remember, don't you?" MacLaren released Brennan's elbows and sat down again, slowly, stiffly. "Now he's dead, Donnavan is. He never had a chance to tell us what crook killed him. He only had time to say one thing, Brennan. He said, 'I was trying to do it up like Brennan—but I guess I just ain't man enough.'"

MacLaren stopped and that brought the heavy silence again. Once more the bald man got up, paced back and forth. He wheeled on Brennan abruptly. "Then let's forget Donnavan—let's just think of all the decent people and the rats who are going to hurt some of them in the years ahead."

"Let the decent people look out for themselves," Brennan said. "Dammit, I've told you I'm tired. I'm sick of fighting for decent people! I'm through—washed up. Who the hell are the decent people to depend on me to look after them?"

"Just people," the girl on the couch told him softly.

Brennan almost snarled at her, "Not you too, Jean!" Then, "Sorry—look, MacLaren, I've never known anything but fighting. As soon as I was old enough and had sense enough to pass a civil service exam, I been fighting. First on the force—then to make the world safe for decent people. All right! I've made it safe! Now I'm tired. Who are you and Joe Doaks to tell me, 'Here, Brennan! Here's a gun, Brennan. Keep on fighting, Brennan. Make us safe.' What gives anybody the right to put the finger on me—me?—and say, 'Finish your job! Keep us safe!'"

"Nothing," MacLaren agreed, "gives anybody that right—except you, John. But as long as this world stands the right guys are going to have to keep swatting back the ears of the wrong guys. To hold them back. Safety and freedom are like gold—you got to keep 'em polished."

Brennan sat down heavily and reached for a cigarette. His hands were trembling. "Then a let Joe polish a while!"

"But a lot of Joes can't," MacLaren said quietly. "They try, but a lot of them are like Donnavan. He polished his life right out of his body, Brennan, fighting the wrong Joes here while you were trimming them over there. That job over there is done now, but Donnavan is still dead. We've drawn a blank on Donnavan's kill—but you could get the guys who killed Donnavan. And the wrong Joes who are going to hurt a lot of other people, every day, every year. You can do it because you're Brennan. I guess that's the answer to your question, John. The way you got born. The way your brain thinks and your body moves. Some men are born with music in their fingers. For every one of those a hundred are born who try but fail. Just like a hundred Donnavans are killed trying to stop the wrong Joes while only one Brennan is born." Cigar smoke gushed from MacLaren's heavy mouth. "So it ain't a job you can pick up or turn down, Brennan. It's something you got born to do!"

"Like hell," Brennan said harshly. "If I got born for it, then I'm dead and come to life again. I tell you I'm through, MacLaren! I'm going to Chicago and sell insurance, and be one of the right Joes the Brennans are keeping safe!"

The silence hung a long while this time. MacLaren and Brennan looked at each other; then Brennan looked away, and MacLaren said heavily, "Well, here's hoping you have a good time living with yourself."

Brennan bared his teeth to snarl back, but the other picked up his hat, went out the door, and a few moments later Brennan heard the hum of the elevator.

He felt the slim, soft hand glide into his. He turned on the couch and looked into hazel eyes. He could read nothing there. "You'll like it okay, Jean? Being the wife of an insurance salesman?"

She laid her head on his shoulder so that her lips touched his neck lightly just above his shirt collar. "I've waited too long to want anything except to be John Brennan's wife," she said, and if there was a hint of a hollowness in her voice. Brennan made himself not notice it.

"Swell," he breathed, "we'll set 'em on fire." But the heartiness in his voice was almost like laughter in a tomb. Sweat beaded his brow, his upper lip, though the apartment was cool. The words of MacLaren were running around in his brain—*Donnavan dead—the right Joes...* Damn MacLaren anyway! Why did the old fool have to come here tonight, Brennan's homecoming night?

"Baby," he told Jean, the suddenness of his voice startling her. "We're forgetting. This is a special night, a hell of a special night. Which club do we hit first?"

Coming out on the street was like walking into an oven. They strolled down Mount Royal, passing the patch of grass and benches the city fathers called a park. Young couples—and a few older ones, too—occupied the benches, lost in worlds of their own. *Right Joes*, Brennan thought. *Like gold*, he thought, *polish safety and freedom—born for it.*

He turned his face away, gripped Jean's hand. His wife's hand, he reminded himself. They'd stood in City Hall and been married only a few hours ago. After all the months of waiting, the months of lying in the hospital when all the other Joes were going home—or nearly all of them. Some had been there in the white-walled ward with Brennan; some were occupying enemy territory; some weren't ever coming. *Don't forget the Joes who stayed, America*, he'd thought.

And now, walking down Mount Royal he was hurrying his new wife to a little place he knew on Charles. Somehow her hand felt cold in his.

A man could walk past the Tic-Toc Club and never know it was there. A plain crystal door opening from the sidewalk gave entrance to a flight of heavily carpeted stairs. At the head of the stairway was an El and, turning there, Brennan and his dark-haired wife were in the Tic-Toc. To their left was the check room with a pert blonde. To their right were doors leading to the lounges. Ahead was the chrome and blue leather bar and beyond that the club with its small tables, soft-footed waiters, and dance floor large enough for a dozen couples of midgets perhaps.

Brennan checked his hat. The place was filled, but not jammed, not roiling with people like a beehive. Brennan and Jean filed through the bar and a waiter showed them to a table.

Brennan smiled at his wife and said, "Dance?"

"I'd love it."

But after a moment of milling on the small floor, she clutched him hard. She was trembling a little and there might have been a stifled sob in her voice. "John, I—we're trying too hard, darling. We're rusty on our dancing. An old married couple!" she finally managed the laugh. "Let's have a drink."

"Let's have a lot of them," Brennan agreed. Back at their table, he was seating Jean when he felt the presence at his elbow. Brennan turned and for a moment he didn't recognize the face. It had been an old face the last time he'd seen it; now it was ancient, heavy, hanging, topped with milk white hair. Brennan said, "Giovani!"

"Hello, John," Giovani smiled. "Glad to see you back. Order up—it's on the house."

Brennan moved around to his chair. He introduced Jean; then asked, "On the house?"

Giovani's slow smile came again, ghostly in the valleys of his face. "The Tic-Toc belongs to me now," he said. "Hard work, and all that. They're real things." He hesitated a moment. "I want to give you the best tonight, John. I'm never forgetting what you did for my son, Tony. I was a poor bartender here then with a sick wife and a bewildered boy who had nobody to look after him, keep him straight. Nobody but a guy named Brennan."

A guy named Brennan. Tony. Another life, now dead; even the embers of it held no glowing coals. "I didn't give Tony a break to be remembered," he said. "He was a good kid, deep down. Just like you say he was—bewildered."

"Sure," Giovani said, "Tony was a good kid—but it took you, Brennan, to show him the strength in your arm, then slap him on the back and help him find a job. I don't know what the Giovanis in this world would do sometimes without the Brennans."

"You'd get along," Brennan said, fingering the stem of his cocktail glass. "And how is Tony?"

Grey tinged Giovani's face. "You ain't heard? No, I guess not. Tony is dead, Brennan. No—wait—sit still. Don't tell me you're sorry. I know you are; we're sorry, all of us. But he died in Italy, Brennan, back on Anzio. I guess it was somehow right for Tony to die there in Italy—if he had to die. No—sit still. This should be a glad night for you, John." Giovani wheeled, strode quickly to the bandstand. He signaled the drummer and the lad on the skins rattled the glasses on the tables with a crashing roll. Giovani held up his hands, smiled his wan smile that could never be quite right with his kid one of the Americans who wouldn't be coming back.

Giovani said in the silence that rippled over the place, "Friends, all of you are my regular patrons. Giovani, he try to maka da place lika de beeg happy family," he grinned over his Italian accent, dropped it again and went on, "Many of you will remember a certain man by sight. All of you have heard of him—if you're residents of Baltimore. You remember that he gave every man a break, fingered criminals with a touch of magic and had his name in headlines more than once. He is as indispensible to society's health as a dose of good old-fashioned castor oil. A cop. An ex-soldier. Our newspapers have informed us from time to time that he has won the Purple Heart, the Silver Star. You—"

Somebody in the crowd said, "Brennan? John Brennan?"

"Right." Giovani laughed. "He's just introduced me to his wife, and since the Tic-Toc crowd is one-a beeg happy family, I think we owe the newlyweds a toast."

Reluctantly Brennan rose to his feet. He felt Jean's eyes like stars upon him. Light flared up, and he was surprised at the faces he saw and remembered. Nicholson over there, a bigwig in politics. A straight guy who'd innocently been in a terrific jam once with a blackmailing dame. Nicholson waved, beaming. And at the corner table near the dance floor—Andy Mondello was scowling darkly. From the way he dressed now and the looks of the blonde with him, Mondello had been running things pretty much his way recently. A bad lad, that one.

Then somebody who was drinking that toast, some Joe at a table on the fringes of the crowd said, "Welcome home, Brennan! You're one Johnny that ain't putting up his gun!"

The words rumbled and rolled in his mind like gunfire in a dark cavern. He felt himself putting his knuckles on the small table, heard words tearing out of his mouth.

"And who the hell says I ain't? You're telling me how to run my life?"

"But Brennan—" Giovani began. "He didn't mean—"

"I know what I'm saying," Brennan said harshly, realizing that for a moment he hadn't, but unable to backtrack. He glanced about at their frozen faces. His teeth went on edge. Condemning him. Calling him rat. Rat was he? How many of them could face the things he'd faced all his life? Watching him like Romans glaring at a faltering gladiator. Expecting things of him, things they couldn't do themselves. His throat constricted.

He choked off, stood trembling. Life still existed on earth, but he wouldn't have known it from this room. No one moved. No one breathed even, it seemed. They simply sat and stared, not knowing how to take him and he cringed a little and felt the heavy beads of sweat gathering and dropping off his nose. Then he grabbed Jean's hand, hurried toward the check room, wanting to run, or turn and curse.

Then he heard the first sound behind him. It was one person clapping his hands, softly applauding John Brennan—Andy Mondello. Andy was standing on his feet, laughing, applauding. Then Giovani finally got the orchestra going and Brennan clutched Jean's hand and ran down the stairs.

He ran harder toward that front door than he'd ever run in his life. And Jean clutched his fingers and sobbed a little.

By eleven o'clock he was beginning to have trouble navigating, and by midnight, when he and Jean blew into the Century Club, the double bourbons he was inhaling had begun to numb him and make him feel a little sick. But it wasn't a whiskey sickness, and he wished miserably that it were.

They'd kept running into people. Marcellene Grayson, for example. She'd come over to their table in Twenty-One. Rich, blonde, svelte, she had everything a woman could want. A serious-faced nice looking guy had been with her. Her husband. And she looked as though she deserved a guy like that now. Once she hadn't. She'd been an excitement-crazy kid, going straight to hell, chasing around with a young punk because she thought it was fun. Maybe she'd even tampered with dope a little, Brennan never knew for sure.

He knew only that when the punk had killed a man and their paths had crossed, he'd shown Marcellene Grayson exactly what she was headed for. The punk had drawn life and Brennan had scared hell out of the rich Miss Grayson, given her a tongue-lashing, and made her believe he was ogre enough to send her to the penitentiary if she didn't act like a lady.

So tonight when she'd seen John Brennan, moisture had come in Marcellene Grayson's eyes, and her husband had shaken Brennan's hand; it was at that point that Brennan had got the hell out of Twenty-One.

Now, watching a juggler in a tan and green silk outfit do his act in the Century Club, Brennan wondered how much longer it would take him to get drunk.

Beside him Jean was silent. Then she was saying something about being back in a moment. He nodded hazily and was aware that Jean had left the table.

A pang went through him. He wasn't being fair to Jean. A swell damn homecoming! Everything was wrong. So very wrong. He shouldn't have planned any kind of short vacation in Baltimore. He should have kept right on moving, to Chicago and a nice, quiet, safe insurance job, where he could look at a cop and say "Sucker! Keep on being a civil servant—but if you every try to climb off the grinding treadmill of sordid life and sudden death and be a normal human, watch them kick you in the teeth!"

The floor show continued in a clatter of orchestral sound and a blurred line of girls in abbreviated costumes. Someone sat down at his table, and Brennan thought it was Jean. But when he looked up, he saw a man. A very small man, with a pointed face that was shriveled and wizened, with pointed ears and a darting, pointed tongue.

The man's mouth was jerking spasmodically at the corner. He said, "Brennan! Thank—"

"You're Mouser Cline," Brennan remembered.

The little man's eyes lost some of their wildness. He seemed less out of breath. "Yeah, that's me, Brennan. You're a great guy for remembering."

Brennan was stonily silent.

"I been chasing all over town," Mouser said, his eyes darting to the door. "Huntin' you, Brennan. It's all around that you're back. In the paper and everything." He reached out one claw-like, quivering hand, clutched at Brennan's sleeve. "You've got to help me, Brennan. You'll give a guy a break and not tell him to peddle his papers." Mouser wheezed, daubed his narrow, pointed forehead with a handkerchief. "I'm still running my book, Brennan, like always. Straight and square and giving the suckers a break. I—It's about the only thing a guy like me can do—but I do it clean."

"And somebody's after your scalp?" Brennan asked coldly.

"That's right," Mouser sobbed. "Andy Mondello has been putting the finger on the bookies, making them run things his way. His way means a crooked way, a lot more money, and Mondello gets his share. But I don't play that way, Brennan. Since that time you took your own time to talk to a judge for me, I tried to play the game like Brennan would. It ain't cost me yet—but I don't want Mondello to bury me in the bay, Brennan."

"I ain't a cop," Brennan said stonily, "You'll get along without me, Mouser. I'm through."

He slammed up from the table, twisted his way out of the club. Faces turned to stare at him, and Mouser Cline's voice was rising, bringing a waiter and a pair of bouncers on the double: "I can't help needing you, Brennan. You're murdering me—"

* * * *

Brennan sat in the dark apartment for a long time, stone sober, his head in his hands. He wondered where Jean had gone when she'd left their table in the Century Club. But it didn't matter. Waiters had seen him leave, the hatcheck girl. They'd tell Jean he'd gone, and she would come on here, to the apartment.

He lighted a cigarette and it tasted flat. He turned on the radio, clicked it off again before it had warmed. Then he heard a key in the door. The click of her heels, the sound of her breathing. "It's just me, baby," he said.

She flicked on the light.

"They told me you'd left the Century Club," Jean said. "So I came on here. I didn't know that I'd find you here."

"I wanted to pack," he said. "We're leaving for Chicago as soon as we can get a train."

She opened her bag, drew out an envelope, handed it to him.

"What's this?"

"Tickets to Chicago," she said. She was quiet a moment and tears welled up in her eyes. "That's where I've been, John. I—I guess I knew we'd be leaving for Chicago tonight."

He stood with the tickets in his hand, looking at her. He saw the unbidden tears in her eyes. He saw a stranger. He saw that a part of her, somewhere tonight, had died. She hadn't been a stranger when she'd met his train.

He saw she wasn't going to say anything more. She had bought tickets, two of them. She was going with him, that part of her that hadn't died. Without complaining. Without arguing, without a word of regret on her lips. Going because she felt she had been born for this, to be John Brennan's wife.

All night he'd been thinking only of himself. Maybe it wasn't so hot to be in her shoes, either, being born for something and not flinching from it, not running.

He turned and stared out the window. A few lights met his gaze. But his mind was seeing something more; the dingy part of Pratt Street, the milling crowds on East Baltimore, the newsboy and bur-le-cue barker and penny arcade crowd. Johns Hopkins and life and death.

Giovani and his kid Tony. Tony had died, sure, but every man had to die, and Tony might have died in the electric chair, or lived bitterly in and out of grey prison walls. And for all her wealth Marcellene Grayson could have died in the gutter, along with a poverty-stricken, uneducated pack of ratty little guys like Mouser Cline.

He saw a red-headed rookie named Donnavan, polishing a nutty kind of gold with his life's blood, and rows of white crosses over men who'd been fighting side by side with Donnavan even though oceans and thousands of miles had separated them.

He saw Inspector MacLaren out in the night, heard the aged man's words: *It's the way you got born, Brennan, the way your brain works and your body moves.* And Mouser had said, *You're murdering me...*

He could take no credit for having these things Mouser didn't have, either. He'd just got born that way. It wasn't as if he'd created something with his own hands to have and to hold exclusively.

Donnavan had tried to give, but hadn't had it, only his life. And Brennan knew in that moment that a man who had those things, those workings of his brain and movements of his body, had no right to withhold them. No more than he did the air mankind breathed.

And if he withheld those things—what was it MacLaren had said? *Here's hoping you'll have a good time living with yourself...*

He would have a rotten time, Brennan knew now. Wondering how many Marcellene Graysons were sliding in the gutter; how many Giovanis were knowing their boys were going to the electric chair; how many Mouser Clines he had condemned to death and how many Mondellos were riding roughshod through life... And knowing, living with himself in the long years ahead, that the Donnavans had bled for nothing.

Sure, he couldn't do much in one lifetime, and he himself would die one of these days. But there'd be others born his way, lots of them, if he helped to make it possible now.

He turned slowly from the window. His gaze met Jean's. "These tickets—now that it's here—I'd make a lousy insurance salesman, hon."

"I know you would," she said. Then her arms were about him, clutching him very tightly. She was laughing, and tears were streaming down her cheeks. "I'm alive again—"

He said, "You know, it's funny. But I feel the same way myself."

KILLER BE GOOD

Originally published in **New Detective Magazine,** *December 1952.*

CHAPTER 1

I was murdered at exactly eleven o'clock on a Monday evening. I am able to recall the time exactly because the tall clock in the foyer was striking the hour as I shoved the papers to the back of the desk and started up the long, dark stairway to the upper hall.

There were many things on my mind that night. I wondered where Vicky was, for one thing. She'd said at dinner that she was playing bridge at Thelma Grigsby's tonight. Was it okay with me? Sure, I said. I had some work to do anyway. She'd pouted prettily, her hair like spun gold about her face in the soft candle light in the dining room—Vicky always liked dinner by candlelight.

"If only you could be a husband and an important man at the same time, Doug," she'd said. "All this work and no play—"

"Gives mama spending money," I said.

After dinner I went in the study. For a moment I stood looking at the desk. I didn't want to sit down to it and face the mass of papers on it. I was tired, and I had that pain across my abdomen again. Maybe I was developing an ulcer. Was it worth it, the work and strain required to keep a few steps ahead of the rest?

Then I pushed the smothered feeling aside, ripped the cellophane off a fresh package of cigarettes, and sat at the cluttered desk.

I heard Vicky pass through the hallway and without quite realizing it I listened until I heard the car start in the driveway outside. The motor raced until it sounded as if it would throw a rod. Vicky had never been able to get a motor started smoothly.

I heard the motor whisper away to an idle and the liquid, golden sound of her voice came through the open study window that overlooked the driveway.

"Mr. Shoffner, we'll cut some glads for the house tomorrow morning."

I heard the old, tired voice of Wendel Shoffner answer, "Yes, mum." He was our gardener and general handy man. He'd been with us a month now, a tired, sagging man with watery blue eyes and baggy pants.

The car engine raced again as Vicky left the driveway. Shoffner's slow footsteps crunched by the window as he went to his room over the garage. I was still too taken with lassitude to get to work. Could we afford a glad garden and a man to keep it and the grounds up? Of course we couldn't. You don't live that way on the pay of an investigator attached to the office of the district attorney. But there are ways. You don't have to act in an illegal manner, either. You just have to stretch a point here and there. Politics, some people call it.

I told myself that I had to get rid of this feeling of depression, the nagging sense that I was caged and on a treadmill. I had to shake loose the insinuation in my mind that it was all for nothing. Life was still sweet, very much so.

I wanted to live a very long time that night.

Lew Whitfield phoned me about nine o'clock. He had been elected D.A. a year ago on a reform platform. He was a short, deliberate man, given to flesh and losing his hair. He smoked black cigars and lived with his slender, greying wife and six children in a rambling barn of a house. "Only place big enough to hold the brood," he would explain. There were croquet and badminton courts in his yard. His lawn was like the hide of a mangy dog, scuffed bare of its pitiful, dried-up grass by the pounding of many childish feet. He romped with his kids until his balding head gleamed with sweat and his breath grew short, and they tumbled all over him when he went into the house to sit down. Through it all he moved as placidly as a good-natured elephant.

"Going over the Sigmon brief, Doug?" he asked that night on the phone. A radio was blaring and a kid was screaming laughter in his house.

"Just starting on it," I said. The Sigmon case wasn't particularly fresh or interesting. It happened a dozen times a day in different parts of the country. Loren Sigmon, a scrawny, underfed, cheap punk. His girl friend, after an argument, had tipped us that he was the boy we were looking for to clean up a filling station robbery. Maybe they made up and she, in that sudden reversal of emotion that takes hold of such women, told him that he'd better scram before the coppers came. Or perhaps she was still angry and threw it in his teeth that he was going to jail, when he showed at her place. He wouldn't tell us about that. He wouldn't talk about anything. But we had him. I'd gone to her place not quite in time to keep him from shooting her to death.

Lew tried to tell me something about the Sigmon case over the radio and the noise of his children.

Then he said, "It isn't important. Put it aside and bring Vicky on over. We'll have coffee after canasta."

"Sorry. Vicky's out to win us a set of ashtrays or something at Thelma Grigsby's tonight."

We hung up, and I rocked back in the desk chair, smoking and thinking. You live along for years, and then somehow you start doing that. Thinking. Questioning. What have I done with the thirty three years of my life?

College, an investigator's job with an insurance outfit. The war. And you remember the eruption of emotion that swept the country, the release from boredom, from the everyday treadmill that seems to have captured you. You return and meet Vicky and marry her. Then you set to work to build a future.

Yet one night, without warning, without reason, you find yourself unable to work, sitting and thinking...

I threw the pencil I'd been toying with on the desk. Dammit, I knew what was wrong with me. I was lonely. I wanted the sound of Vicky's voice. I wished she were here to go with me to Lew Whitfield's house. I wanted the noise of his kids, and Vicky's eyes lighting as she looked at a dress Lew's wife had made.

"Marge, however do you do it!" Yes, I could hear every inflection of her voice in my imagination.

Or perhaps she'd put her head next to the oldest Whitfield child, Sharon, over Sharon's high school homework.

And then later we'd leave the Whitfields and drive across town, the soft Florida night a caress in our faces. We might stop someplace and dance a few minutes. Then home—and the warm darkness.

I was still very much in love with Vicky. That night I hoped we would have many, many years together.

* * * *

At ten o'clock the phone rang a second time. I was deep in some notes Lew had made on a joint at the edge of town which was taking, we thought, illegal bets. Minor, but important. You go after those things and splash them big to keep the public convinced of your worth as a public servant. You like to keep the voters saying, "No organized crime in our community." In our case it was true, as true as in any place in the nation. This was saying a lot, considering that we were in a Florida resort town on the Gulf coast while right across the state from us on the Atlantic side lay a city which had attracted the Kefauver committee itself.

On the second skirl, I picked up the phone. "Doug? Is Vicky busy at the moment?"

I caught my breath. My hand went a little chill on the phone. The voice was that of Thelma Grigsby. Her bridge parties never broke up as early as ten o'clock.

"She isn't here," I said. I hesitated. "Didn't she stop by your place?"

"Why, no. Was she planning to?"

"No," I said, surprised at how fast the word jumped out of me. "I just thought she might. I'll tell her you phoned when she gets in."

"Doug—is anything wrong?"

"Of course not. Why do you ask?"

"Oh, just a silly feeling the tone of your voice gave me." She laughed. "Old worry bird, that's me. We'll be looking at you, Doug."

"Sure," I said.

I replaced the phone and sat there looking at it for a moment. It had never occurred to me to mistrust Vicky. She came and went pretty much as she pleased. But tonight my tired mind began asking questions. Was there something behind her absences during the past few weeks? Was this, tonight, a simple matter of her having changed her mind about attending the bridge party? If so, why hadn't she returned home? There were several places in Santa Maria, movies, the homes of friends, where she might have gone alone, of course. But she hated to go anywhere for a good time alone.

I found it hard to break the chain of thought, once it had started. She had taken an interest in water skiing recently, which occupied most of her afternoons. She was rehearsing a play with a little theater group, and that took several of her evenings. Had she really been at those places? Was there another man?

The question cut through my consciousness with a pain as acute as physical torture. I couldn't sit still any longer. I had to get up and walk about the study. The very silence of the house, the oppressive heat of the night ate away at me.

It happened. Hell, it happened so many times every day that a man was a complete fool to think it could never happen to him.

I'd never fooled myself into thinking that nine men out of ten who looked at Vicky wouldn't like to take her from me. I'd never blamed them, and I'd never been of a jealous disposition. She had that natural animal magnetism that was felt the moment she entered a room. Blonde, golden, a tall, striking woman. She knew how to dress to advantage, but that attraction would have been felt had she donned a mother hubbard.

Yet I had never once believed that any other man would ever succeed in stirring Vicky's feelings to the point that would lose her to me. She was too damn forthright and honest for that. Or had I been simply too smug and sure of myself?

I was frightened at the thought of losing her. I tried to reason myself out of my state of mind, but my reason would not respond to the reins.

My reason became cold and clear and remembered a dozen little things. The far-away look in her eyes during the past few weeks. The rapt expression of her face. Sometimes I'd had to voice a question or statement twice. It was as if her thoughts, her interests were elsewhere at the moment.

I recalled the night a week ago when I'd called for her at the Bath Club. She'd come into the club room with its long bar and bamboo tables and chairs, and when she'd seen me, sudden fright had flared in her eyes. She'd been out on the terrace, and when I'd suggested going out there, she had pleaded a headache and rushed me home.

Who had been concealed by the warm darkness of the terrace? Whom had she been with out there?

I ripped the next to last cigarette out of the package, lighted it from the one I'd smoked down. Bitterness had crept into my reasoning now. I had probably raised a brow myself at the situation some time or another. A man enwraps himself in the task of giving his wife an ever higher standard of living, leaving her lonely, more and more leisure on her hands, free to draw the assumption that she is unloved.

With Bill Farnsworth and his wife it had been that way. And I recalled a remark I'd made to Vicky the night Bill's wife had walked out on him, *"Can you really blame her? How about him. After all he couldn't expect her to become nothing more than a hot-house plant. She's a flesh and blood woman."*

Vicky was that, very much so. A flesh and blood woman.

A light tap sounded on the jamb of the study doorway. I glanced up. Old Shoffner said, "Anything else I can do before I turn in for the night, Mr. Townsend?"

I shook my head. He was looking at me closely, and I colored a trifle and stopped running my fingers through my already tousled hair.

As he turned to go, my voice stopped him. "I suppose Mrs. Townsend is pretty busy with the garden these days?"

He hesitated. "She works at it."

My gaze held the attention of his salt-and-pepper stubbled face. "Come in, Shoffner. Sit down."

"I'm really tired, Mr. Townsend. Been hauling muck for the flowers."

"You can spare another moment. I don't get to see much of her, Wendel. I hardly know how she spends her days. Is there anything I could get, a gift to please her? Does she ever talk of anything she feels she missed?"

He remained rigid in the doorway, twisting his dirty cap in his hands. "She doesn't talk to me much, Mr. Townsend."

"I'd thought she would. She's always so full of chatter, and out there gardening, I figured she might talk quite a lot. Her birthday is next month. I'd like to get her something very special."

"She hasn't said anything about it. I'm afraid I can't help you, Mr. Townsend."

I stood looking at him. He had a rather grim, seamed face, and I suspected that he knew the trend my thoughts were taking and recognized that I was offering him the opportunity to tell me anything I might need to know.

"She probably stays busy with her friends," I suggested.

Shoffner nodded, and I said, "She knows a great many young matrons her age. I suppose they call for her in the afternoon to go shopping."

"Yes, sir."

He was looking more uncomfortable with each passing moment. I waited for him to add anything he knew about the people who called for her when I was away. Perhaps the man who'd been on the Bath Club terrace had never called here, but Shoffner's reluctance, the cold bead of his washed-out blue eyes was answer enough. He knew something. But he was not going to get mixed up in anything. He was thinking of his job and how hard it might be for him to find another at his age.

"I'm really very tired, Mr. Townsend."

"All right, Shoffner. Goodnight."

He went away from the study and I heard the rear screen door slam behind him. I sat down again at the desk.

CHAPTER 2

Mind over Mayhem

It couldn't be true, I told myself.

Vicky would never be unfaithful to me. Damn it, I almost wished that Thelma Grigsby hadn't phoned tonight.

I tried to concentrate on my work. I had done a ratty thing, trying to pump old Shoffner. Bringing out the family skeleton before a servant. Spying on Vicky, who was a part of me, without whom I never could live.

I realized that I was exhausted. Conflicting feelings of shame and then anger—when I thought of a stranger on that dark terrace—beat at my mind. I would never give Vicky up; not as long as I thought there was any chance at all of continuing life with her. She must know that. She must realize the depth of my feeling. It seemed incredible, come to think of it, that she, who was so very kind and thoughtful, could do anything to hurt me.

I rose from the desk. I thought, *You'd better stiffen your spine, Townsend, and start thinking like a man. Vicky started life with you without too many material comforts. You had a small inheritance. You've invested wisely and well, thanks to politics, and the inside dope you've had. You could even take a year, two years off, and coast, putting Vicky first in your life. Quit working so hard, chewing so hard at the muzzle. Even if some joker has caught her in a bored, lonely mood, you can win her back.*

The clock in the foyer began striking eleven. I went out of the study, crossed the sunken living room with its square, modern furniture that Vicky had chosen.

I was feeling better as I started up the stairway. I was glad I had lived this night with its introspection. I must admit that things hadn't been right between Vicky and me for several weeks now. We'd grown distant. I would stop the drift in that direction; for tonight I'd experienced the sodden fear that would only be the beginning of my feeling should I ever lose her.

I was almost at the top of the stairs. The upper hallway was hot and very dark. I fumbled for the light switch; and then I sensed that I was not alone. A rustle of cloth, a whisper of breathing, and I knew another presence was in the hallway with me.

I was not afraid at first; no time for that. Only jarred to a sudden immobility. The instant of my indecision was my undoing. And then terror!

The gun crashed and a tongue of flame lashed toward me. It was quite close. A searing pain shot through my head and I had the swift sensation of a sickness like vertigo multiplied a thousand times. There seemed to be nothing beneath me except black nothingness. I fell, loose jointed and with a complete lack of control over my limbs. End over end, elbows bumping, legs flying like strands of rubber, I jolted all the way to the foot of the stairs, to the parquetry of the entry foyer.

I jolted to rest with my limbs at awkward angles. I could feel no pain now. I could, in fact, feel nothing, except the wild terror that came with this feeling nothing.

I tried to move, and could not. I was wrapped in a blackness, a helplessness that made of my body a lump of cold clay. Then I heard the footsteps coming down the stairs, and I seemed to know that they belonged to a man. A light fell on my face, and I guessed that my eyes were open; for I could see the light like the haze of a faint moon almost obscured by clouds.

The light moved. He had moved. I heard his breathing, like two skeins of silk being rubbed together. I supposed that he was giving me a quick examination by the light of a flashlight. What he witnessed must have satisfied him. The light vanished, and after a considerable time I decided that I was again alone.

As I became accustomed to this numb lack of sensation, some of the sickening fear of it left me. I was feeling no tiredness; no pain, as if in the next moment I might swoop off to some world beyond the stars. The images of my thoughts were possessed of that same peculiar weightlessness that had taken my body.

Was this the experience of death? The question did not seem at all surprising to me right then, but very concrete and real. I doubt that I would have been surprised had several beings of this strange world floated forward to bid me welcome to their company.

I was human, and therefore concerned first with myself. Next followed a flood of questions regarding the man who had shot me. I didn't doubt that the murder had been a deliberate one. He had known I would turn out the study light, cross the living room with its dim night light and walk up the stairs.

Had it been a burglar? I dismissed that possibility. The smart second story man never enters a house with the male head present and visible—as I had been through the open study window. Neither does the smart housebreaker carry a gun. The risk of a much stiffer sentence—even the chair—if caught armed is too great.

There was still the remote chance of course that he'd been a very dumb second story artist, but in that case he would have bolted and run. Instead this man had been cool, in full possession of his nerve as evidenced by the fact he'd followed me down to make sure he'd done the job right. His examining me before taking flight was proof enough that he'd been waiting in that upper hall for the express purpose of murdering me.

But why? Doug Townsend had few enemies—and those Lew Whitfield and every policeman in Santa Maria could also claim. I'd only been a part of every investigation I'd worked so far. If some minor hood had finished his sentence I had done nothing to provoke him to return and commit murder. True, there was young Loren Sigmon, whose crime I'd eyewitnessed. But he was safely in jail. So there seemed little possibility that my work or anything connected with it was the motive for my murder.

I experienced a fresh fright at the detached manner in which my mind could view the situation. This was me! Put a few tears into it! This is personal, Townsend.

Personal, but still a problem in criminology, and my mind went ahead in its own fashion, as if, being released from body, it was for a time released from all emotional hedges also. Coolly, my mind went about the business of sorting out motives for murder. There are only two, provided the murderer is not insane. Passion, and gain.

Passion was most probably out. I had quarreled with no one, insulted no one; I had not been sufficiently vicious to drive anyone to murder.

Was a killing for gain to be any more seriously considered? Wealth of course is a relative matter, and it was possible that my earthly possessions, a good home, two cars, several decent investments that were putting money in the bank, were great enough for someone to value them higher than my life. But those things of course would all go to Vicky once this inert hulk at the foot of the stairway was buried.

There was only one possibility left, a mixture of the two motives. Passion *and* gain so interwoven that the motive became a single driving force. A desirable woman, plus the estate of the deceased.

Can hell hold any greater torture? The desirable woman. Vicky. The deceased. Doug Townsend.

In desperate agony I wanted to be done with this reasoning. But my mind, with a grim, macabre relentlessness clung to that one idea, for there was no other with any substance.

Perhaps he had been plotting this very act that night I'd been so close to him, when only the curtain of darkness on the Bath Club terrace hid him from me.

Fresh light came, a shimmering in a fog. Footsteps moved toward me, around me. Someone had heard the shot and hurried to the scene…

I couldn't see him. Just one flick of my eye muscles would have put him in a line with my vision, but the muscles were dead, powerless and the vision was dim and distorted.

I experienced a great need for his presence. He was human—he was living. Don't go away! Look at me and tell me that this is not death!

A door slammed and fresh footsteps whispered into my foggy world. They stopped then came forward with a rush. "Doug! Oh, Doug!"

It was Vicky. Thank heaven, in that moment the sound of her voice was too dear for me to think of murder and its motives. Whatever the man had done, Vicky had had no part of it. Vicky would never be a party to a thing like this.

Right then I could have forgiven her of anything. I had never needed her more. The presence of living human beings had driven a fresh awareness of my present state through me. A fresh terror.

Surely she would drop by my side. Her hands would touch me. Yet the moment lengthened and I heard a voice, Shoffner's. "Easy, Mrs. Townsend. You look pretty green. I heard something that sounded like a shot and ventured to come in just a few seconds before you got here. Don't you think we'd better call a doctor and the police?"

He must have helped her to a chair. She moaned softly and the moan mutated into weak, soft sobbing.

"Yes, the police. How could he have done it?" And then she whispered brokenly, "Oh, Doug—how could you?"

If I had hoped there was a limit to the depths of torture, I knew better now. For a moment her words brought only a stunned, blank nothingness to my mind; then the insinuation behind them began to sink in. I didn't understand. Desperately I thought, *Darling, if I could look at your face at this moment, would I see something there I've never beheld before?*

The last prop beneath my world was shattered completely. I might possibly have accepted oblivion right then; but oblivion failed to come. If this were death, then death was far from oblivion.

Only minutes passed before they came. The doctor. The police. My coworkers. I don't know how many of them there were. At times it seemed the room was filled with the babble of many voices; then again there was the silence of emptiness.

Lew Whitfield came, of course. I sensed it was he when I heard the elephantine pad of footsteps on the foyer carpet. He stood over me during one of those silences before going down the two short steps that led to the living room.

The vague outlines of his heavy-jowled face came through to me. I could fill in the details of his expression, the pain in his eyes as they seemed to sink in the fat rolls of their sockets, the bitter passing of color from his ruddy cheeks, the sorrowful drooping of his heavy lips.

"My God," he said, like a prayer, "this is terrible." His words might have been inane, considering the situation, but I knew the meanings behind them. The days we'd worked together, the trust between us, the feeling of being on the same team. Those were the wonderful things Lew was talking about.

"He looks pretty gory, doesn't he, with his right temple all torn and bloody. His eyes, glassy and staring—as if looking at hell itself."

"He doesn't look like Doug Townsend," Lew agreed with tears in his voice. "Where is Vicky?"

"Out in the kitchen. A matron is feeding her coffee."

"She find him?"

"No, the yardman heard the shot and came in the house just before she got here."

"I can't believe it," Lew said. "I just can't believe it. How much more have you got to do here?"

"We're about finished, photos all taken, statements down. It seems like a clear-cut case of suicide. His wife told us he kept the revolver upstairs in their bedroom when he was off duty. He must have gone up, got it, and came back down. Maybe he was planning to do it in the study, or the kitchen, or out in the yard someplace. Or maybe he was only thinking about it, toying with the idea, and the impulse became suddenly overwhelming. The gun is in his hand, and he does it right here in the foyer. We've found only one set of fingerprints on the gun—his."

I knew the scene as well as if I'd been able to stand away and look at it. I'd been through the scene before, in a different role, of course. A far different role. The body inert in death. A photographer, a lab man, a cop or two in uniform and a couple in plain clothes. Most of them smoking nervously, until the air was thick and blue with the smoke, ashes scattered on the carpet. All of them prowling like restless shadows in the knowledge that they were human and this dead thing had been human too. Nervous neighbors on the lawn trying to gawk through the windows, shushed away by the patrolman assigned to that duty. The phone screaming, and the sound of weeping.

But always the dead one was the center of the scene, the hub around which the prowling took place, the subject of all the questions.

That flat, droning voice which had been speaking with Lew spoke again: "Charlie Markham is out of town. So the autopsy will have to wait. Of course Mrs. Townsend's own doctor came over as soon as the servant called. We have plenty already to establish the time of death. The shot, heard by Shoffner at about eleven. The wound still oozing blood when Mrs. Townsend came in. The body still warm when the doctor got here. The doctor hoped for a second that Doug was still alive. But there was no heartbeat, no response of his eye pupils to light. Death must have been instantaneous."

"All right," Lew sighed. "Send the body on over to the funeral home. Markham will be back early in the morning, in a few hours. We'll do the autopsy then."

There was a tired finality in Lew's voice, a deep touch of sadness. The case was closed as quickly as it had begun. His friend was gone. In two or three days the funeral would be held. The rains would wash the grave and the massed flowers would wither to nothing. Would there be rest for me then?

That reasoning part of me which refused death was overcome with bitterness and despair that bordered on madness. *He* was safe. His plan had been successful. Only a little while now and he would have to meet her in the darkness over a terrace no longer. Let the rains wash the face of the grave and the seasons change, and he would be able to call openly on Doug Townsend's widow.

My mind writhed in agony. To know that he bad not only robbed me of life, but of everything else that had given that life significance as well—even Vicky—the very completeness of his triumph was the most refined torture of all.

Soon he would know how complete his triumph had been. He could stop his restless pacing, his sweating, his watching the clock and hearing it tick, wherever he was waiting for. He had made one mistake, I knew now. He hadn't meant for me to catch him in the upper hall. He would have preferred to arrange it better. He'd had to fire before he was ready. But his luck had held. He had been close enough to me so that there must be powder burns on the torn flesh of my temple. His quick examination of me had shown him there was still a slender chance his plan for making it suicide would succeed.

Yet he wasn't sure that his luck had held, and during these present long minutes he must be enduring an agony akin to my own.

They must have moved me. I was aware of no movement, no sensation in any part of me. Light came and went, fuzzy, distorted. A voice said, "Watch that end of the stretcher. You almost dropped him."

"Hell, he wouldn't feel it. It wouldn't matter to him."

An engine came to life. An ambulance, I supposed. The purring of the engine stayed close to me, and I guessed that I was taking a ride. To the city morgue…

I wondered what he was like. Tall, good-looking. It would take somebody like that to attract Vicky. A good dancer. Not necessarily a smooth talker, but a good one. Vicky was always fastidious in her conversation. He would have a good face, too, and a smile open and honest. A mask, shielding the workings of his mind and the morbid plotting in his heart.

My thoughts whirled back to Vicky. A thousand memories of her came through to me. She'd been working for a living when I'd met her, a secretary in a lawyer's office. Her employer had been defense counsel on a case to which I'd been attached. Vicky and I had met over a dry mass of legal briefs. But she had been almost illegally beautiful and I'd taken her to lunch, and after that the world was a different place for me.

I'd looked at her with eyes that made everything about her perfect. She'd grown up right here in Santa Maria. Her mother had never been well and her father had never made quite enough money out of his trio of fishing boats. Yet it had been a wonderful life, she'd said. A barefoot kid in jeans and T-shirt, a kerchief binding the mass of gold that was her hair. More tomboy than girl when she was small, scampering about her father's boat with sun and spray in her face.

She'd finished school and worked part time to get her business course. Then her job for a couple of years before I'd met her.

"Really a very dull and uninteresting life," she said once with a smile. "I wish I were made for better things."

"You are!" I'd told her fervently.

And she had been. She had a good mind. She never ceased bettering it by good reading. She had a natural sense of good taste—a flair for clothes. She took to an ever higher mode of life with simplicity and a naturalness that was amazing.

Could this woman have been a part of a plot to kill me? Had some foreknowledge of the plan caused her immediately to label my death as suicide? Had the sudden, wild turbulent emotion of a love affair killed the

Vicky I'd known, leaving in her place a creature beyond my normal understanding?

I thought of husband-murders from the time of Ruth Snyder. Quiet women, delicate women. Women who had trod the marriage path with gentleness. But one day the monotony had become suffocating. The routine and dull respectability had become unbearable. And the smoldering fires had erupted, all the more violent because they had been buried so long and so deep within here.

Let me finish dying. Let this be over. There must be an end even to this horrible torture...

The purring of the engine ceased. A man grunted. Light came again, like milk splashed in water. There was a fresh mumble of voices.

"The D. A. says leave him on a slab until Charlie Markham gets back in town and can make an autopsy."

"Looks terrible, doesn't he?"

"Oh, I've fixed 'em for the casket when they looked worse. Fixed a farmer once who'd used a shotgun."

"Well, you're the undertaker. Me, I wish I'd never studied medicine. I don't like this interning."

"Oh, undertaking's all right. But right now I want to get back to bed. I'll undress him and throw a sheet over him. I'm glad that Markham won't start the autopsy 'til morning."

Time passed and light faded again. I lay naked on the slab and each marching minute brought the autopsy closer. My mind crawled away from the knowledge of that experience. The deadly quiet about the autopsy table. Then the click of a scalpel, the gleam of it...

My mind stopped working for a terrible moment.

CHAPTER 3

The Death of Me

The slab on which I lay was cool. That fact in itself was not surprising. Santa Maria's leading undertaking establishment was also the town morgue, as is often the case in small cities. And the stone slab supporting me was just as cool as the air conditioning of the place had made it. Yet it was not the workings of my mind alone that told me the slab was cool. I was aware of the coolness. I could feel the coolness.

Alone in this dark, silent house of death, my mind screamed a question. How could this be? What was happening to me? The dead do not return.

I lay there with a fresh urge to move a muscle, to flick an eye. I was powerless to do that; yet I could feel the coolness of the slab against my calves and buttocks.

How much time passed I have no way of knowing. I was too caught up in the grip of a new, fearful knowledge to think of anything else. With the coming of day, Charlie Markham would arrive. The autopsy would be performed on a living man!

Every post mortem that I'd ever witnessed came marching across my thoughts. The slash of the knife, the removal of the vital organs, the splitting of the scalp, the sawing of the skull...my thoughts became a wild, silent screaming.

A pain began to ooze from the right side of my head through my brain. A tingling touched my toes. Still I could not move or bring my eyes in focus.

Light began coming back into the room, slowly, grayly. Dawn. How much longer until Markham came? I almost wished he would hurry and get it over with.

Then I gradually realized that the ceiling over my face was of plaster— I could see it. And I could feel the clammy sheet clinging to me from my waist downward. The pain in my head was excruciating now; so great that it brought a gasp from me. A gasp—which meant that my lungs were functioning normally.

My hands were like two dead weights as I tried to move them. I tried again and the effort succeeded.

My heart was pounding now, rocketing blood through every artery, bringing a singing sensation through the pain in my head.

It took me perhaps five minutes to sit up. I was dizzy and almost fell from the table. I clung to my senses until the dizziness had passed, pulled my feet around, and felt them drop to the floor. The pain in them, through my toes, was almost unbearable as I tried to stand.

I next took cognizance of my surroundings. The room was bare, the table in its center, two doorways leading from it.

I drew the sheet around me, stood up, and fell to the floor. I spent several gasping moments in a prone position before I was able to clutch at the leg of the table and crawl to my feet again.

Like a baby tottering through its first steps, I made my way to the doorway across the room. It opened into a hallway, and I closed it again. The second door opened into a small washroom. My clothes were there on hangers.

Before I tried to put my clothes on, I looked at myself in the mirror of a medicine cabinet on the wall. I almost retched at the grey-faced man who stared back at me. Blood had run down the side of my head, matting my hair. There was a heavier, uglier clot on my right temple. I bathed it gently in the corner wash basin. It was too sore to stand washing thoroughly, but I got most of the blood off.

I looked again in the mirror. Color was seeping back to my cheeks now. The wound was a nasty gash in the flesh and the bullet had torn its way along the bone, but had not penetrated the skull.

I slipped into my clothes, weak, gasping. I stood a moment before leaving the room, gathering strength. I was seething now with a fierce hatred that sent ripples of heat out through my being. I didn't know how it had happened. I didn't know why.

I knew only that I was back in the land of the living. I had returned—to find my murderer!

Gray dawn hung over the alley behind the funeral home. I reached the mouth of the alley. The streets were still deserted except for a passing milk-man and a whistling boy with a bag of newspapers slung across his shoulder. Santa Maria was still drugged with sleep. The gulf breeze was cool and fresh across my face. Save for the extreme, blinding pain in my head, I was feeling better by the minute. The last thing I'd done before leaving the washroom had been to find a compress and tape it over my temple.

In my thoughts a plan of action was forming, he must not know that I was after him. Secure in the belief of his success he would be emboldened, until the moment came for me to strike.

Somehow a way must be found to keep hidden my disappearance from the funeral home, the fact that I still lived. That would take some doing. There was one man with the power to swing it. Lew Whitfield.

Normally I could have walked the distance from the funeral home to Lew's house in ten minutes. Today that movement required a full thirty minutes. I hurried as fast as I could. I knew that my absence from the funeral home might be discovered at any moment and an alarm raised. I passed few people. Dock workers. Fishermen. I got a glance or two from some of them, the kind of glance they might give a man who's been out all night on a drunk and got in a fight.

I was reeling on my feet when I arrived at Lew's. His large, old frame house loomed against the red eye of the rising sun like a hulking barn. For three years Lew had promised himself to paint the place next summer.

I walked around the side of the house to his study window. The window was open against the Florida weather, as I had guessed it would be. The screen, however, was locked. My head was spinning, and it took me a few seconds to figure a way out of that. Then I remembered the pen knife in my pocket. I used it to cut a small hole in the screen through which I could slip a finger and throw the hook latch.

I pulled the screen out, crawled over the sill, and collapsed on the floor of Lew's study. I was going again, back into that nether world of shadows. I clenched my hands and almost screamed aloud. I was slipping—slipping. The shadows were heavier. Sweat broke cold on my forehead. The effort of my exertion had been too much. Over me the shadows came.

The blackout didn't last long. I woke slowly, blind with that ache in my head. I could hear footsteps moving about overhead. A child came running down the steps outside the door, and from the back of the house I heard Marge Whitfield, "Breakfast!"

I heard the scramble toward the dining room. Then the house was silent as the family ate.

I pulled myself across the floor, up on the leather couch against the wall. I sat down with a deep sigh. Lew's desk, as cluttered as my own, was across the room from me.

* * * *

Fifteen or twenty minutes passed before Lew came into the study. The door swung open, admitting him, partially concealing the couch. He closed the door. He was alone. He patted his stomach as if his breakfast had been the best; and then he walked to the window and stood looking out at the day, lost in thought. Perhaps he was thinking of the friend he'd lost.

When he turned, he saw me.

He had nerve. His face drained of color and his body went rigid, but he made no outcry upon beholding the apparition before him.

He breathed out explosively, crossed the room, and reached out to touch my shoulder.

"It's really me, Lew. You're not seeing things."

"But how, Doug? How?"

"I don't know myself, yet."

"I'll get Marge, Vicky—a doctor."

"No, wait! No one must know, Lew, until we're ready. Until I say the word."

"But, man, you may be dying."

"You're probably right, but I'll take long enough in the process. I have that feeling. That I won't die until I find him."

He dropped to a sitting position on the edge of the couch beside me. "I don't understand any of this, Doug!"

"You thought last night I tried to kill myself," I said, "but such a thought was the furthest thing from my mind. Somebody tried to murder me."

He found a cigar in his pocket with fingers that shook. Then he dropped one flat word: "Who?"

"I don't know. That is, I don't know his name. I can't think of any-body who would have done it—except maybe the man who's been fooling around with my wife."

"So you know that? Although 'fooling around' might be a little strong."

I cut a quick glance at his face. "You mean you've known for some time?"

"Nothing definite, Doug. Just talk I heard—behind your back."

I felt more than a little ill. "The old saying has some ground under it, then, about the husband being the last to know. You're going to help, Lew. First, you've got to get hold of that undertaker. Next you've got to dig into—her recent past. Find the man. Find out if he's the kind who might commit murder for a beautiful woman who will come into considerable material comforts and money through her husband's death."

He made no move to interrupt as I tried to bring back everything that had passed through my mind last night. I told him of the growing distance between Vicky and me lately. I told him about the incident on the Bath Club terrace.

"Thelma Grigby's phone call only brought the matter to the forefront of my mind. Now we've got to lay a trap for him. He mustn't know that his plan has failed—until it's too late to do him any good."

Lew's heavy face had taken on a greyness. "It might hold water," he admitted. "It's an old story. But what of Vicky?"

"I have to know about her, too," I said slowly. "She was pretty quick to tell the world that I'd killed myself. If she was covering for him,—I—I've got to know that, too, Lew."

"It's a pretty hateful business," he said, rising. "But we deal with hate-ful things every single day in our line."

"Then you'll help?"

"I'm your friend," he said simply. "And I'm the D.A. I don't know whether or not it's ethical for me to hide you, to conceal the fact that you're still living—I don't have a precedent to establish the ethics of the case, do I? But if there's a would-be killer in our town, I want to know it." He hesitated. "It'll take some fixing, Doug. With the undertaker, Charlie Markham—one or two others I'll have to bring into the thing."

"You can do it," I said.

"I'll try."

* * * *

A little later that morning Lew got his family out of the house. I learned then that they'd brought Vicky over for the night. Marge and the kids were taking her home. I wondered what it would be like in that silent, empty house. What thoughts would pass through Vicky's mind as she went from room to room, each with its own flood of memories?

Lew brought me food; then he took me upstairs to a small back room with windows on two sides overlooking his side and back yards. There was a three-quarter bed in the room, a scarred bureau, a night stand holding a lamp, and a single boudoir chair.

Next Lew brought a visitor up to the room, a tall, florid man who wore grey tropicals and a pince-nez. He was Doctor Hardy, and he knew the story and we could trust him, Lew assured me.

I was silent during Hardy's examination; then when he stood up and snapped his bag shut, I asked, "Do you know what happened to me? Can you explain it?"

"Certainly," he said. "You've been deeply depressed lately?"

"For some time," Lew put in. "He's been working too hard."

"And of course you were deeply frightened when the shot rang out and the bullet struck you?"

"Scared to death."

"That's almost my precise diagnosis," Hardy said. "Lying in your foyer last night you were in a state of very acute catalepsy, a nervous condition in which the power of your will and of sensation are suspended. It arises from prolonged depression and acute fright. It's more common, in its less acute phases, than many people would think. Your condition was aggravated by the wound, of course, which came very close to killing you."

"A doctor examined me," I reminded him.

"Of course. But in a state of acute catalepsy no heartbeat was audible. No pulse could be felt. Your eye muscles had completely lost for the moment the power of contraction, of focusing; so your eyes responded to the doctor's light exactly as a dead man's would respond. That is, no response at all. In short, you exhibited several signs of death, and in the moment the doctor is not at all to blame for interpreting your state of suspended animation as he did. We're human, too, you know. We make mistakes like the rest of the race, though often our mistakes are never known—they're buried."

With a smile and a last admonition that I should be in a hospital under observation, Hardy prepared to leave.

I felt a lassitude taking hold of me, and then I slept.

The sun was dying a crimson death in the gulf when I awoke. I was ravenous, but forced to wait until Lew should show up, as he did half an hour later. There were a dozen questions trying to spill out of my mind, but my first interest right then proved to be the food he brought. Once I started eating, I felt as if I would never be filled again.

"I had to ring Marge in," he said, watching me spoon up the last drop of the broth in the bowl. "She's too much the homebody for me to succeed long in sneaking food up here and keeping the door locked. She was shocked, of course."

"And Vicky?"

He hesitated. "We've found the man, Doug."

I tried to keep my voice casual. That was impossible, and the word quivered when it came out of me: "Who?"

"Keith Pryor."

"The water-skiing instructor at the Bath Club."

Lew nodded, and a silence came to the room. I recalled Pryor to my mind. I'd met him when he'd first come to the club three months ago. We'd had him at our table two or three times for drinks. He'd danced with Vicky during a couple of our evenings at the club. He must have been every day as old as I, but he looked more boyish. Slender, but extremely well knit with wide shoulders. A lean, almost hungry face, topped with close-cut sun-scorched blonde hair. With his deep suntan, the brilliant white of his teeth flashed when he smiled, and he had an easy, relaxed air about him. On the whole he was the kind of man who would appeal to every lonely instinct in a woman.

"Have you got anything on him?" I asked.

"Only a little. He's not exactly a gigolo, but he's never made much money and he likes to live high. Two items on his record. A Jax woman had him arrested for making off with some of her jewelry, but in the end broke down in court and admitted she'd given it to him, as he'd claimed, bringing the charges later because he'd walked out on her. An assault charge in Miami. He punched an irate husband in the nose in one of the beach clubs. But the man's wife testified for Pryor. Pure self defense, she said. Nothing at all between her and Pryor. Her husband was just a nasty-minded old man, she said."

"A nice boy. Does Vicky know any of this?"

"Of course not! You listen to me, Doug! You're hurt because she happened to look at another man twice in a weak moment. She's never been alone with him, though they've met at the club and parties. Maybe she was lonely. You've been moody, depressed, you've neglected her."

"Dammit, Lew, are you for her or me?"

"I'm for both of you, son, and don't forget that!" he said in a rough tone. "But I want you to stop acting like the emotionally wounded little boy. You're jealous and mad as hell, deep down, and in a way I can't blame you. But just because Pryor's made a play for her doesn't mean she'd ever be a party to hurting you."

"I hope you're right."

"You're damn right I'm right. Now forget it. I've got things to do. I'll see you in the morning. How's the head?"

"Better."

"Then take some more of those pills the doctor gave you and rest. That's the thing you need most."

There wasn't much time. Every meal I ate, every nap I slept brought the sands that nearer to a finish. We could not keep secret the disappearance of the body from the funeral home indefinitely. The time would come for a burial, for an official statement. Lew knew all that as well as I did. He knew how far he had his neck out.

But there was, for me, too much time. Time in which to think, to picture Keith Pryor gradually making head way with Vicky—perhaps holding her in his arms. To watch them in the tortured eye of my mind standing close together. How many times had she lifted the warm softness of her lips to his? How many words thick with passion had he murmured to her?

I tried to keep the pictures out of my mind.

Lew came to my room the next morning with a downcast expression. She had seen Pryor last night. I knew that even before he spoke. They'd met on a downtown corner, gone to a dine and dance place in a cheaper section of town. They hadn't come in until very late. The shadow that Lew had put on their trail had reported that they hadn't danced much. They'd talked with people in the juke joint, drifted on to another in the raw section of town. They hadn't been at all romantic, the shadow had reported.

Good, I thought with grim satisfaction. Maybe it's going sour between them, with death a black blight on their feelings. Maybe the husband, dead, stands between them now far more than the living husband had.

Or perhaps he was simply playing it smart, biding his time, not rushing her.

I sat there thinking about it a long time after Lew had gone. The pictures of him and her together came back more vivid than ever. I wondered how much more of this waiting I could endure.

The second day passed, and I knew my nerve was going. I was cracking up and I seemed unable to halt the process. Lew wasn't moving fast enough. He had found nothing conclusive. The second night his shadow had lost Vicky and Pryor across town in a section of cheap hotels.

Lew was a worried man that night. He wouldn't take his eyes off my face. He insisted on staying in the room until I had gulped the pills Hardy had given me.

But I palmed them instead and drank the water as if I were swallowing the pills. I lay back across the bed, closed my eyes, and after a time Lew went out. I waited until I heard his footsteps fade downstairs; then I sat up, threw the pills under the bed, and began dressing. I didn't put on my shoes. I wanted no echoing footsteps as I slipped down the rear stairs out of the house.

I stayed in shadows and used back streets. I was still weak, and it took me thirty minutes or better to get from Lew's house to my own. My place was dark, and I didn't go in. I stood in the shadows of a row of royal palms across from the house watching, waiting. Expecting the two of them together.

But she came alone. She swung the green sedan in the driveway, entered the house, and I saw lights flash on. She appeared in the living room window for an instant, going toward the phone alcove. I moved quickly across the street, into my own yard. I could see her through the window. She was across the expanse of living room, talking quickly with someone on the phone. Then a shadow, the shadow of a man, long, distorted, showed briefly against the living room wall. Before I could catch a breath the light in there snapped off, and then Vicky screamed.

I hit the front door. It was locked. I fumbled for a key. A voice shouted from inside, "Stand back, or I'll shoot her." Sweat popped out on my face. I heard a door slam, and I ventured the key into the lock then. Another door slammed, and I tore toward the rear of the house. I heard the surging roar of the engine of the green sedan. I was hearing his words over and over, "Stand back, or I'll shoot her."

I knew him. I'd recognized the voice.

I hurled myself across the yard toward the driveway just as the big car careened out of the drive into the street with a scream of tortured rubber.

I stood there a moment, gasping. Then I forced strength into my shaking legs and charged back into the house.

My hands were shaking so badly I could hardly dial Lew Whitfield's number. His phone screamed twice before anyone answered, and then it was Marge, not Lew. "I've got to talk to Lew," I bellowed.

"He's not here, Doug. He just got a phone call from Vicky. He's on his way over there now."

"He'll be too late. Marge! Shoffner's got her! He barreled away from here with her in my green sedan. Got that? Old man Wendel Shoffner, my yardman, has Vicky as hostage, at his mercy, in my green car. Call headquarters. Tell them to make it an all-car signal. That's an order from the D.A.'s office!"

She got it, she said, and I didn't waste any more time. I slammed down the phone and pushed my reeling body back out of the house. The second car, the light coupe Vicky usually drove was still in the garage. There was a key for it on my ring.

The sedan had disappeared by the time I got the coupe on the street. It had turned west, and I turned that way also. In the distance I heard a siren. Lew would get the call. A dozen cars would get the call. They'd pinpoint my home—and we would get him. But it would all be less than worthless if he harmed Vicky first.

I heard another siren and then another. They were converging on the downtown area. I saw the swarm of cars when I skidded the coupe into Central Avenue. A fire truck rounded an intersection and clanged to a stop just ahead of me. Patrolmen were trying to move the crowds gathering on the sidewalk, and a searchlight threw its yellow tongue up the side of the six-story Parker Building.

I'd stopped the coupe, but I couldn't let go of the wheel when I saw that light snake its way up the face of the building. I knew then that he had her up there and we might never get her down alive.

Somehow I crawled out of the car and was able to stand. I found Lew standing beside his own car. He was snapping orders. To firemen with a net. To the cops rigging a loudspeaker system.

"For God's sake, Lew, be careful!"

He showed only brief, surprise at seeing me. "We're doing that. Doug: If we wanted to take chances, we'd send men up after him."

I could see them now. Vicky and Shoffner, near the low parapet around the building roof.

Shoffner's voice rang out thin and high-pitched: "Go away! All of you go away, or I'll push her over!"

Lew's shudder almost matched my own. "He's cracked. He's gone. Loony as they come. He's Loren Sigmon's father, Doug." I stiffened. I had been the single eyewitness to Sigmon's crime.

Lew said, "He was probably out to get you from the minute he went to work for you. We found some dirt from your garden in your bedroom near the night table where you kept your gun. Ordinarily it wouldn't have meant much to us—either you or Vicky could have brought it in—but to Vicky it suggested Shoffner. She remembered that Shoffner had been working in muck that afternoon, bringing it in for the flower beds. She slipped into his rooms, found some pictures of Sigmon in the old man's things. She went to some of Sigmon's old haunts last night and tonight with Keith Pryor. She was asking questions and must have got a few answers. She phoned me that she was certain of the old man's identity. But before I could get to your house, he snatched her, found himself cornered, the street blocked, and dragged her in the building."

Now she was six stories above the street. This, then, was the ultimate torture...

"You'll never talk him down, Lew," I said. "There's only one way—let him know he isn't guilty of actual murder. I'll have to go up, alone—"

A trooper was standing near me. I slid the carbine he was holding from his hand.

Lew made no move to stop me. He knew that Shoffner might kill me, but he knew too that this was something I had to do. For myself. For Vicky.

The stairs upward were long, silent, manned by patrolmen who sucked in breath when they saw me, a man they'd believed dead. The last flight of stairs was steeper and narrower, leading up to the radio tower on the roof. I saw Shoffner and Vicky the moment I pushed my exhausted body out on the roof. The spotlight limned them, Shoffner behind Vicky, waving a gun, yelling threats.

Shoffner must have been dropping quick glances behind him to make sure no one else was coming on the roof, for he saw me.

"Don't take another step," he shouted, and his full intent was in his voice. "I'll push her!"

"I came to help you," I said. "I don't want you getting yourself into any worse trouble."

My voice brought a little cry from Vicky's throat, and a startled gasp from Shoffner.

"You can't be Townsend!" he said in a thick, fearful voice.

"But I am. Move away from her, Shoffner. And I'll come toward the light. You can see for yourself."

I took another step. A little of the light caught my face. The old man screamed and started shooting. Vicky crawled aside. I hated to do it, but I squeezed the trigger of the carbine. The bullet hit him high in the chest. He stumbled back against the parapet.

And then he was suddenly gone.

The gun slid from my fingers as Vicky stumbled toward me. The boys who came to the roof found us locked in a tight embrace, Vicky's face burrowed into my neck, hard sobs racking her. She was trying hard to tell me something about being a fool, about never having let a pipsqueak gigolo turn her head for a moment, but about having been lonely. But until I'd gone she'd never known what loneliness meant. She'd told Pryor that and he had understood; he had been willing to help her in any way he could in bringing her husband's murderer to bay. Did I believe her?

Her question echoed in my mind. Yes, I believed her. I knew that I would never doubt her again. I led her toward the stairs.

"Darling, it's time," I said, "that we were going home."

DEAR MR. LONELYHEART

Originally published in **Ellery Queen's Mystery Magazine,** *Nov. 1958.*

643 Elm Ave.
Centerville, S. C.
July 9

Dear Mr. Singleton,

I have read your description in the cute little news letter put out by the Orange Blossoms Friendship Society.

I, too, am a lonely person, Mr. Singleton. So please don't think me forward. I'm just ever so lonely, and that is why I'm writing to a man I've never seen before. I'd like to correspond with a mature gentleman, and I am sure it would be like a beautiful light in my dreary existence.

I'm a whole heap younger than you, being an ignorant 23 years of age. But I'm sure that years don't really determine age, aren't you?

I don't find much in common with the boys of my age. They're so silly. And all the 65 year old men in my little town are married.

But oh how I long for real intelligent, mature talk with someone. So I'm not forward, Mr. Singleton. Really I'm not. I'm just real lonely down here in this little town in the sands of South Carolina.

I thought your face, in that little picture in the news letter, was the sweetest, kindest, most intelligent I have ever seen.

Dear me, now I know you will think I'm a forward girl, but really I'm not. My poor old mother says I carry my honesty beyond the point of virtue, and I suppose that's true. I just can't be dishonest. It hurts me inside. So I had to tell you honest how I felt about your picture, and feeling that way, I picked you of all the men in the news letter to write to.

I don't make a practice of this kind of thing. Really I don't. But we're both members of the same lonelyhearts club and that makes a difference, doesn't it? I mean, it isn't just like writing to a stranger, is it?

Your friend (?)
Trudy Bell

P.S. It must be awfully exciting, being the retired owner of a big fertilizer factory. I'm just dying to hear all about you, how you had all those hundreds of people working for you and gobs of salesmen out on the road selling your products.

* * * *

2643 Elm Ave.
Centerville, S. C.
July 14

Dear Mr. Singleton,

I'm ever so grateful you answered my little old letter so fast. After I mailed my letter, I almost wished I hadn't done it. I couldn't help but think that I had written to a strange man. I didn't sleep a wink the whole night through. Honest I didn't. I was afraid you wouldn't understand my writing a strange man, and I was purely fearful you'd think my letter plumb silly.

I feel much better now, thanks to you. I have to be honest. So I'll say that yours was the sweetest, nicest letter I ever had from any body. Not that the mailman breaks his back with letters to me, ha, ha. Especially with letters from strangers. Yours was the first of that kind I ever had. But what I mean is, letters from my own darling mother were never so sweet and understanding as yours. I know you must be a great man, and I'm humbly thankful for your friendship. I was real pleased that you enjoyed my letter so much. I sure enjoyed yours. My, I know you're a strong spirited man to have borne up under all the responsibilities of your business life. Why, the way you started out as a young man with nothing and built up that fertilizer factory reads just like a story book.

I truly feel sorry that you lost your wife three years ago. I know what you mean by that statement that you feel like you've been living "in a vacuum". Loneliness is such a terrible thing. What a shame your wife never had any children. Like you say, you've felt that there is just you on an island of loneliness in the midst of the whole world.

I feel like I know you real well. We have a feeling in common, and I know it was a lucky day for me when I wrote you, if you get what I mean.

I am honestly flattered that you'd want a picture of little old me. I am not bad looking, if I do say so myself. Course I don't claim to be a raving beauty, but these silly boys, with only one thought in their empty heads, seem to think I'm sexy. That's why I want the friendship of a mature gentleman. Not that I'm a prude, but a lady doesn't like to fight a wolf every time she has a date, and it's my one desire to be everything he wants when the right man comes along. I'd die before I'd be anything less.

Oh, how embarrassed I feel, pouring out my heart to you this way. But in you I feel I have found understanding, and I'm sure so fine a gentleman will take my comments as they're meant.

To get back to the picture. I don't have many pictures of myself. I think someone who has a lot of pictures made of themselves is kind of self-centered, don't you? Maybe I'm wrong. Just one of my little old ideas.

I do have a picture taken of me at the beach last summer. It isn't in color, so I have to tell you that my hair is blonde and my eyes are blue. I had to take my dear mother to the beach for her health, and that boy lolly-dallying in the background is my cousin Ruel. He's a sweet young man, always looking after me. It was him that drove me and mother down to the beach. She felt ever so much better after her little vacation.

I really have to run now, for I'm a working girl. I work because I feel young people should have a sense of responsibility.

I'll be looking forward to hearing from you again, Mr. Singleton.

Warmly yours,

Trudy Bell

* * * *

2643 Elm Ave.
Centerville, S. C.
July 19

Dear Amos,

It was so nice of you, Mr. Singleton, to ask me to call you by your first name. I think Amos is the sweetest, nicest name ever. It makes me think of wisdom and gentleness.

I have read your letter over and over. At first I didn't know how to take your remarks about the picture of me in my bathing suit. Then, I have to admit, I got a little thrill by the warmth of what you said, and I decided that I rather liked the compliments. You tease you, I'll bet there are many sides to your fascinating character. A great man, filled with sublime thoughts who nevertheless has a touch of the wolf in him. I do believe that you're one of those rare, truly exciting people that are not often found in this world.

And now, how about a big, clear, framed picture of you?

Your

Trudy

* * * *

2643 Elm Ave.
Centerville, S. C.
July 25

Dear Amos,

No, I don't mind if you call me your Little Bunny. I think it's real cute and it took somebody like you to think up the term. To be honest, it makes me feel cuddly and wanted. Dear me, I'm blushing—but I can't help feeling the way I do, can I? And I don't care—I want you to know how I feel, because I suspect the way you feel, and my life was so drab before I wrote to you, but now it isn't.

I certainly appreciate the picture, and you didn't have to apologize because your hair is white and thin on top. I think your hair is just right. I looked at your picture a long time. And you know what I decided? Honest, I know that my first impression of you was correct. Those small eyes would peer deeply, but they are offset by the cute little pouches your flesh makes along the sides of your jaw. In short, I know you have real character. Nobody could take you in, no, sir! And that is the kind of friend I want with all my heart.

I'm going to place your picture right on my bureau. It will be the last thing I see each night. I'll tell you a little secret. I think your picture is so nice, so much like you, that each night after I get into my nightie I'm going to blow a little kiss to the picture and make believe you're beginning to care for me as I'm beginning to care for you.

Goodbye for now—darling.

Your,

Trudy

P.S. Dearest, please don't think poorly of me if I don't answer your next letter the very minute I get it. I have to take dear mother to Florida for a few days rest. She needs it, but I haven't been able to afford it. We are not moneyed people. I'm just a little old southern girl who has more than money, my virtue and good name. Cousin Ruel, bless his heart, is going to drive us down. He borrowed some money. Oh, I know the value of a dollar and mother says I can squeeze a nickel until the buffalo stampedes, ha, ha. I hate to think of spending money in those hotels, but it's all for dear mother.

* * * *

2643 Elm Ave.
Centerville, S. C.
August 15

My darling,

I write this with tears in my eyes. If there are stains on the paper, it's from the bitterest tears I have ever shed.

How could that person have said those things about me? When the old gentleman overheard my name, he introduced himself and said a man in his home town was corresponding with a girl named Trudy Bell. What a small world, he said.

Well, I tried to treat him real nice. And he isn't such a friend of yours as he lets on. His dirty old eyes practically took my clothes oft there in the hotel lobby, if you want the truth. And he tried to date me up. So that's the kind of friend he is to you.

And if he said me and a boy friend was lolly-gagging and burning up the town, he was wrong. This "boy friend" was Cousin Ruel. He stayed pretty close to me because I'm just a small town girl and he said I needed protecting and I'm glad I have somebody like that. And if that old man said his inquiries revealed that Cousin Ruel was a shady small time gambler and punk and not my cousin at all, I can just say that he was speaking a falsehood. And if he said further that I didn't have a mother in evidence, he just didn't see her, that's all. Dear mother stayed in her room most of the time and rested. And wasn't that the purpose of the trip? I think that nasty old man was taking a lot on himself. He wasn't doing all that snooping just for friendship for you either. He was mad plumb through and through because he practically drooled all over me and I wouldn't even give him a date. I'm not interested in people like that.

My heart breaks as I think of the evil he might have done us. In you, dear Amos, I truly believed a dream had come true. I guess if I never hear from you again, I'll at least have a short memory to treasure all my life. I just can't write any more.

I can't believe that you'd listen to that old man. But I guess you've known him longer than you have me. And the only thing I'll ever feel for you, Amos, is what I have come to feel. I can say that at least I loved once in my life. Maybe it sounds strange. I've never seen you. But oh, I feel I know you. Even with this one weakness of listening to malicious gossip, I love. I love you more than ever, because a little weakness makes you human. You seemed so perfect and strong and I was afraid I could never confess how I felt. But now that it's all over, I can say it and I'm glad I have.

Goodbye, dearest one, and tell that old man I forgive him. I guess when a devil possesses you, you just can't help yourself.

Once your
Trudy

* * * *

2643 Elm Ave.
August 19
Centerville, S. C.

My own Sweetheart:

Again I write with tears in my eyes, but now they're tears of Joy. I have read your last letter until the sweet handwriting has just about been erased from the paper, ha, ha.

I had never expected to hear from you again, after what that old man said. I was going around like a half dead person, then your letter came, then the skies opened up, then I felt so good I wanted to run out and hug somebody.

I'm glad I followed my honest feelings in my last letter and forgave that old man and told you truthfully how I felt about you. I wasn't trying to do anything but be honest. And I'm sure glad I was. You say that a girl who could forgive the old man and expect never to hear from you again must be honest. Well, I was.

No, please don't feel like you have to give that poor old soul a piece of your mind. He didn't dishonor me. It was him that was dishonored. Let's just let him be and maybe one day he'll see what kind of person he is.

And don't you worry none about what you said. I can't forgive you, for there is nothing to forgive. I know I would feel bad if somebody told me a lot of black, dirty lies about you and I guess I would say a few things, too.

I'm going to tell you a teensy secret. You have stirred feelings in me I didn't know I had. I think about you all the time. The more so, when I thought I had lost you. If you hadn't written me again, I hate to think of it. I guess little old me would have just up and died. I'm going to move your darling picture—to my bedside table. So it'll be the first thing I see when I wake up every morning, just like it'll be the last thing I see before I fall into the land of dreams each night.

Take good care of my little old heart, darling.

Your slave,

Trudy

* * * *

RECEIVED YOUR TELEGRAM STOP WILL COUNT THE MINUTES UNTIL YOUR TRAIN GETS HERE STOP A WALL OF FIRE COULDN'T KEEP ME FROM MEETING IT STOP DEAR MOTHER IS STAYING AT SISTER IN GEORGIA SO YOU WON'T BE ABLE TO MEET HER STOP BUT I'M A BIG GIRL NOW AND I GUESS MY WAY OF ANSWERING THAT CERTAIN QUESTION YOU HINTED AT WILL BE ALL RIGHT WITH HER STOP PLEASE HURRY STOP PLEASE. LOVE TRUDY.

* * * *

Pine Tree Lake, N. Y.
September 2

Dear Cousin Ruel,\

Why don't you come up and see us? Amos says it will be all right. We are living in a cottage, all alone. Our nearest neighbor is six miles away.

We have a big lake practically in our front door, and it certainly is quiet and private up here.

The lake is real big and deep. Amos don't swim much, but he insists on going in the boat every time I go on the lake. Isn't that wonderful devotion, to risk his life possibly just to be with me? If there was to be an accident he couldn't save himself, much less me. Why, I'd need somebody's help to reach the shore, and as for Amos, why, he can hardly swim at all.

But we don't want to think about things like that, do we, Cousin Ruel? You just come up here as soon as ever you can.

Amos is reading this over my shoulder and says any relative of mine is more than welcome and for you to feel more than welcome.

Sincerely,

Trudy

RIVALS

Originally published in **Manhunt, October 1958.**

In the deck chair Lissa stretched her long, slim legs before her and wondered why she loved Carl enough to kill for him.

He was at the helm of the speeding cruiser, his yachting cap at a rakish angle, his white t-shirt stretched tight across the muscles of his shoulders, back, and upper arms. He wore white trousers to match the shirt and white duck shoes to match the trousers.

As the cruiser sliced through the salty green water of the Gulf, Lissa studied Carl, knowing she would find no reason for her decision in the outer man. He was not a really handsome man. His features were all too pronounced and coldly blunt. His lips were heavy, his eyes almost cruel. He was a very dark man, and very hairy. The long black hair gleamed in the brilliant sun on the backs of his hands and arms.

Lissa felt the animal magnetism of the man even as she sat looking at him. And he became handsome. Feeling the inner power of him, his features took on a softer cut. But still, he was remote. And perhaps there lay the reason. He was a world unto himself. Lissa had felt that the first moment she'd met him. He could be completely selfish. He could make the slightest concession or gesture of tenderness to a woman seem like an act of earth-shaking importance. Somehow, he could make a woman weak with gratitude just for a gentle touch of his hand.

He was also very wealthy. But that was only a part of it. He had been born with money, and with his physical strength and the money to back him up, he could afford to be an arrogant, overbearing man.

But I could be his without so much money, Lissa thought, although it's nice to live in a world of luxury.

He was generous, but he handed out his money only because there was so much of it. But his kind of generosity didn't underline her reasons for committing murder.

He despised just about all people. He saw their weaknesses, where he had none. He met a great number of people who groveled before his money, and he had never groveled to any man.

He possessed no great humanitarian traits to inspire a woman to the supreme act for his sake.

The question was a knife in her mind now. Why do I intend to kill Jocelin?

Because he's mine.

There the crux of the thing lay. There'd been a steady parade of women, like toys, in Carl's life. He could have his pick. He'd never married and probably never would. Women like Jocelin were always seeking him out. He looked upon them with a mingling of cynicism and contempt; and they were too stupid to realize it.

No woman had ever interested him for long.

Except me, Lissa thought.

He's mine.

I simply intend to keep him.

That's all there was to it.

She lifted her gaze to Jocelin, who lay on her stomach on the foredecking.

You have about one hour of life left, dear.

Jocelin was a strikingly beautiful woman even in the Gulf Coast resort city of Sarasota where beauty, spawned in luxury, is little more than commonplace.

Jocelin was tall, slender, and dark. With the figure of a Venus, the face of a madonna, and the morals of an alley cat. She was the kind of woman who lived enwrapped in her sleek inner satisfaction. She petted herself with a self-delight and self-assurance that was unholy.

Right now she was wearing a white bathing suit that was startling against her deep tan. She turned slowly and sat up, almost as if she had felt the weight of Lissa's gaze.

The eyes of the two women met and a thin smile came to life on Jocelin's full red mouth. She looked at the golden blonde beauty with a sneer for something that was second rate. A little gleam of triumph was in her eyes.

A small red explosion took place inside Lissa's head as the silent communication of rivalry and hate continued.

Lissa was trembling with hatred.

Never had she hated anyone so much.

And there was the second part of the reason. Killing Jocelin was going to be a pleasure.

Under the bright sun and kind beauty of the deep blue sky the cruiser cut its way past Longboat key. There in the distance, solid and pleasant, stood the pastel houses and private docks with bobbing cruisers. The surf whispered lazily against the pure whiteness of the beach. The cruiser turned in a long arc away from the key, its prow showering glittering jewels of spray, its wake a path of silver. A swooping pelican gliding over the cruiser spread his webbed feet and came to a skiing contact with the water. He folded his wings, shook himself, and bobbed contentedly, as if the beauty of the whole scene were plucked out of heaven itself.

Lissa felt the wave of redness leave her brain, and her vision cleared. Her head still pounded a little at the temples.

She broke the interlocking of gazes and glanced at Carl. A pulse jumped in her throat. He was looking at her, then at Jocelin, as if the two-way silent conversation of hate had become a three-way communication. His eyes were narrow and cold.

"Fix me a drink," he said.

"Yes, Carl," Lissa said, getting out of the deck chair.

Jocelin smiled faintly and patted a yawn with the back of her hand. "I'll have scotch on the rocks, darling."

Lissa was trembling when she went into the small, gleaming stainless steel and chrome galley below deck. "I'll have scotch, darling," she mimicked as she raged inwardly. "Enjoy your scotch, you cheap pig. Enjoy every last moment you've got left."

Lissa fixed the drinks and carried them up on deck. As she came up, the breeze, light as feathers, ran its fingers through her hair and touched her fevered cheek lightly.

The breeze helped. So did the drink.

She wouldn't have another. She must have a completely clear head and all her resources for the act ahead.

It would be very simple.

Lissa had the agility of a tawny amphibious animal in the water, and an ability to hold her breath that would have brought admiration from a pearl-diving South Seas native.

Once they were in the water, Jocelin simply couldn't match her.

"Here you are, darling," she handed Carl his drink. She could feel the weight of his eyes on her. She gave him a smile. It brought no change to his face.

With a forced lightness, she turned and rounded the flying bridge of the cruiser to pass a drink to Jocelin.

"Is it poisoned, darling?" Jocelin asked softly, not loud enough for Carl, at the helm, to hear.

"Of course it is," Lissa said.

Jocelin laughed, sipped the drink, and said, "Why don't you give up? You haven't a chance, you know."

"I don't care to discuss it."

"Why not? You'll have to sometime—unless you are capable of bowing out with grace." Jocelin looked at her over the rim of her glass. "Don't be such a greedy minx, Lissa. You've had him far longer than anyone else."

"Long enough for it to become an unbreakable habit," Lissa said.

Jocelin sighed. "It's really going to be quite painful for you, poor dear."

Uninterested in any reply Lissa might make, Jocelin turned forward, lay on her stomach, propped on her elbows, her drink held in her two hands.

Lissa looked at the dark tanned back and felt dizzy for a moment. It's going to be sweet, she thought, so very damned sweet.

She didn't return to her deck chair. She stood on the foredeck a moment, little droplets of spray catching on her tight blue bathing suit like rhinestones.

She held the thought of the future moment in her mind. It had been easy to arrange it. Jocelin had been more than willing to go when Lissa had suggested the jaunt last night.

Lissa turned, went to the bridge and stood beside Carl. He was remote, giving no indication he knew she was there. He stood solidly on his rather short muscular legs, handling the boat with the touch of a master, like a man who feels stronger than the sea itself.

She wished he would say something. Anything. He said nothing, and the old burn began to grow in her. It was a devil inside her. It lashed her senses and seethed within her flesh. It made her willing to do anything to have him admit she was there, flesh and blood. A desirable woman. A human being.

She laid her hand lightly on his arm.

He looked at her. "Having fun?"

"I always do."

"That's one thing I've always liked about you, Lissa."

"Boredom and me," she said. "We don't mix."

She went aft and sat down, feeling buoyed up, as if from a victory.

Carl looked back long enough to take a sighting from two landmarks. He turned the boat a little, until he had the angle he wanted between the tall, white water tower, a tiny bulb in the distance on its spidery stilts, and the final channel marker. Then he headed the boat into the open Gulf and the land fell below the horizon.

They were quite alone on the endless, swelling, falling sea. The other boats had gone further north today, to the waters off Mullet Key, where mackerel had been reported running.

No friends around. No other eyes.

Just the three of us.

Carl throttled down the cruiser's twin Continentals. The engines putted softly and the boat rose and fell with the gentle sighing of the Gulf.

"I guess this is it," he said.

Lissa's heart throbbed with fear and anticipation.

Jocelin had come aft and put on a face mask. "Sure I can get a giant snapper?"

"No guarantee," Carl said. "But you've got a good chance. A lot of snapper and sheepshead around the old wreck down there. Really monstrous sheepshead."

"I'll leave them for Lissa," Jocelin said, the veneer of a smile on her face as she glanced at Lissa.

Sheepshead, Lissa thought. I know what she means. Lissa can have the sheep.

Side by side they stood on the aft decking, over the baitwells. The baitwells were always empty. They'd never been filled since Carl had bought the boat. Carl had only contempt for tackle fishing.

Carl stayed at the helm, keeping the drift of the boat corrected.

"One shot only," he said. "Then I'll show you how to haul the granddaddy of all snappers out." Lissa stood inhaling through her mouth, deeply and rapidly, charging her blood with oxygen. Jocelin went into the water like a sleek blade. Lissa counted four seconds and followed her dive.

As she shot down through the clean green world of water, Lissa saw Jocelin ahead of her.

Ten, fifteen, twenty feet down. Lissa felt the pressure on her eardrums and the little needles that reached out into her brain. A small fish backed off and stared at her.

Below were the shadowy outlines of the old wreck. She lay on her side, covered with moss, half buried in sand, one broken mast sticking out like a finger, yawning holes in her decks and planking. She'd been a proud one, sailing these waters when Florida was young.

The driving flippers on her feet drove Lissa closer to Jocelin. Jocelin was intent on the wreck below, as if determined to get in the first shot and bring the first snapper to surface.

A sheepshead, enormous for his breed, drifted up out of the old hull through a hole in the deck. He was big game, but Jocelin ignored him, and Lissa stayed close behind Jocelin.

The big snapper came drifting over the prow of the wreck. He floated gently, in curiosity. He backed away with slow movements of his fins as Jocelin glided to a standstill in the water.

Jocelin fired, missed, and the big fish wheeled with, great speed and was gone in the greenery of water and waving seaweed.

Now, Lissa thought.

She fired.

Straight into the old timbers. The missile struck and embedded its barbed steel head deeply. Lissa snapped the line tight around her left wrist.

Now that she was anchored to the bottom, she threw herself against Jocelin and clamped Jocelin's slender neck tight in the crook of her right elbow.

We shall see who is stronger…

Jocelin froze, stunned by Lissa's attack. Then she came to explosive life. She twisted her body. She clawed at Lissa's arm. She was a thrashing fish. Much bigger game than a sheepshead.

Lissa felt the struggling body grow limp. Jocelin made a last feeble attempt to pull Lissa's arm free of her throat. Then Jocelin was draped over her arm, arms, head, and legs dangling, her hair a black cloud floating about her face.

A ringing had begun in Lissa's ears, but she couldn't surface yet.

With the line, she pulled herself and Jocelin down to the rotting hole. Where timbers had broken jaggedly, she wedged Jocelin's ankle until it was secure. Jocelin bobbed against the wreckage like a figurehead that had come to life only to go down with the ship she had adorned.

Lissa felt the blood boiling in her veins. Everything was growing dim and far away. Hard steel spikes were being driven through her chest.

For a moment, she was lost.

She almost opened her mouth to suck in a great gasp of air.

Panic hit her, and cleared her head.

She freed her wrist of the line and started up. She could see sunlight shafting down into the water. It seemed so very far away…

Her face broke water, and air burned into her lungs. She closed her eyes, gulping greedily.

If I'd been five feet further down, I never would have made it. I haven't the strength left to swim a single stroke. Now Carl will help me into the boat and I shall tell him about the accident.

She opened her eyes and looked around. Then she screamed. Her wild gaze followed the wake of the boat. She saw Carl look back and give her a tired, bored wave. Then Carl and the boat were gone.

SALESMANSHIP

Originally published in Ellery Queen's Mystery Magazine, *November 1958.*

Howard Alden's day started on a miserable note. At breakfast he had to tell Clara, his wife, that they couldn't afford a new coat for her, much as he admitted she needed one.

It wouldn't have been so bad if she had burst out with something mean. Instead, she just sat there and looked at him as if he were a nonentity, an absolute zero.

Clara was a brunette, slender and beautiful. Howard was very much in love with her. It gave him a hard inner pain to have her look at him like that. He writhed inwardly when the villagers looked at him that way, but for Clara to give him such an appraisal was an unendurable torment.

She pecked at her oatmeal and sipped at the chickory she had brewed for breakfast.

Howard tried to think of something to say. She hadn't always looked at him like that. In fact, the way she had once admired him was the one thing in life he had to treasure.

He was a man in his mid-thirties, middle-weight in size, trim, sandy in coloring, and not bad-looking. He had met Clara ten months ago during a business trip to Atlanta and they had married after a brief courtship.

He had brought her back to Pine Needle, which nestled in the barren Georgia foothills, without the courage to tell her the whole truth about himself. She had come to the village knowing only that he was the one mortician in the county, as his father had been before him. His profession put him, in her mind, on a level with the mayor, the leading merchant, and the chief of police.

She'd had to learn the hard way that he was the most poverty-stricken man in town. The dirt farmers had their chickens and hounds, but Howard Alden had only a dreary undertaking parlor and ramshackle house, both heavily mortgaged, and a yellowed sheaf of bills his dead father had never been able to pay.

Clara had envisioned an old plantation-style home with servants, but she found herself cooking on an ancient gas stove and polishing silver plate that had worn to the base metal.

She had first wanted to redecorate the gloomy house. Howard had borrowed all the money he could, yet the best she could manage were some new draperies, a cheap living room suite, and a table-model television set...

"Clara," he said, his taste for breakfast gone, "if you'll just be patient I know I'll collect some of the money due me."

"Collect from whom? The poor share croppers stuck in this Godforsaken county? The people you bury at two hundred dollars a funeral—on credit? And darn few burials at that. Most of the folks around here are too poor to die." He didn't answer—he had no answer. Sometimes he felt he didn't know much of anything about life, or about women. He knew only the occasional dead who came his way. He wished he could change for Clara's sake, but he didn't know how.

Clara avoided his off-to-work kiss. He left the house with something squeezed tight inside of him. She had not mentioned it, but he knew she was brooding on going back to Atlanta. And thinking about her life here in this bleak Southern county, he couldn't really blame her.

His jalopy of a car rattled to a stop at the lower end of Main Street. There was little activity in town—a few dusty pickup trucks parked along Main, a couple of men swapping talk at the feed store, a few old-timers sitting on nail kegs under the unpainted wooden awning of the hardware store. They whittled irresolutely, argued dogs and women, and crusted the curbing stone with tobacco juice.

Howard sighed and went into his place of business. Once the gold leaf spelling out *Alden Mortuary* on the front window had no missing letters. Once the walnut benches in the chapel and the foot-pedal organ had been glossy and new. Once the front office had been something more than a gloomy clutter of shabby furnishings.

Today the place held only the old sweet sick smell of dying flowers— and death.

Howard opened the windows to air the office, then went out to the diner on the corner. The diner had been converted from an old street car an enterprising soul had brought in from Atlanta.

The usual crowd was in the diner. Bayliss, who owned the dry goods store. Sheriff Loudermilk. Bill Suggs, who trained horses and hunting clogs for the vanDeventer family.

Suggs was an overbearing man, but it was said that old vanDeventer liked him. This was enough to give Suggs considerable prestige in Pine Needle. The vanDeventers owned practically the whole county—most of the farms, the cannery, even the local telephone exchange.

Maddy vanDeventer, beautiful, young, and blonde, had been educated at a fashionable girls' school in North Carolina and had traveled in Europe.

If Pine Needle had a princess, it was Maddy. The old man prized her slightest whim above the welfare of the entire human race.

Howard ordered a cup of coffee from the hefty, sweaty girl behind the counter. He sat listening to Suggs, Loudermilk, and Bayliss plan a fishing trip. They had acknowledged Howard with the briefest of nods, not quite friendly enough for Howard to take the liberty of joining them. It was unspoken knowledge that he was too poor and too unimportant to be included in any fishing trip.

Howard sat down at the next table and tried to appear as if he weren't listening. They were going all the way over to Santee in South Carolina. There were bass there half as big as a man's leg. It was going to be a rather expensive trip, by the time food and liquor were included. It was the kind of trip men talked out—long and detailedly. They wouldn't leave for ten days yet, but a trip like this took a lot of planning and discussion.

And Howard just sat at his table and tried not to let the warm comradeship of the three other men make itself known to his senses. But he couldn't help the pictures that came irresistibly to his mind: the car piled high with equipment, screeching to a stop before his house in the early dawn. Bayliss yelling, "Get a move on, Howard! You waitin' for them bass to have grandchildren?" And Clara kissing him and telling him to be careful as he hurried from the house, loaded with rod, reel, creel, boots, and spare clothing. And Suggs flapping him on the back as he got in the car, thrusting a bottle into his hand, and saying, "Smoothest bourbon you ever drunk, boy. Right out of the old man's private stock. Take a shot of that to settle your breakfast."

Over at the next table Bayliss laughed heartily at something Loudermilk said, and the minute of fantasy was gone. Howard sat alone.

The pay phone on the wall at the end of the counter broke in on Bayliss's laugh like a sudden scream. The sloppy waitress shuffled back to the phone and unhooked it. "Yeah?"

Then she turned, holding the receiver. "For you, Sheriff."

Loudermilk uncoiled his hawkish six feet and strode to the phone.

Bayliss and Suggs continued talking. But they broke off when Loudermilk gasped, "Maddy vanDeventer! Where?"

The Sheriff listened a moment. Then he snapped, "I'll be right out!"

He turned from the phone, his face colorless. "Maddy vanDeventer's dead!"

Nobody else in the diner said anything for a long moment. Then Suggs croaked, "Where? How? By the devil, there ain't never been a sweeter, more considerate, nicer girl born than Maddy vanDeventer, even if she is rich. She just can't be…"

"She was found a few minutes ago," Sheriff Loudermilk said. "She slipped and fell off her cliff." Howard knew that this simple explanation was sufficient to make the occurrence clear to every inhabitant of Pine Needle. Near Maddy's home, the vanDeventer mansion, there was a wild cliff with jagged rocks at its base. Maddy enjoyed taking long walks on top of the cliff in the cool of the evening. Apparently she had taken one walk too many.

Loudermilk, Suggs, and Bayliss rushed out. Howard sat staring at the bright hot day outside.

The waitress said something to him. She was so excited she was scratching the rolls of flesh along her ribs. He looked at her and said. "Huh?"

"I said I'm closin' up. I want to get out there."

"Yeah," Howard said. "I guess I better be getting back to business myself."

He had his undertaking parlor aired, swept, and dusted when Sheriff Loudermilk brought the girl's body in.

She was so young and beautiful. And then Howard, laying her out on the slab, touched the back of her head where the blood was clotted and the bone crushed, and she wasn't beautiful at all.

Simply pathetic.

She had been wearing jodhpurs, flat-heeled oxfords, and an open-throated nylon blouse when she had gone down the cliff. The ripped and torn clothing was no problem. The bruises and scratches also presented no great difficulties. The head, however, was going to be a really tough job.

Face drawn, Sheriff Loudermilk wiped his forehead with a blue bandanna. "She wasn't missed until this morning. Her daddy knew she was out and thought he heard her come in last night—but it was a servant walking around upstairs. She always sleeps until ten or eleven o'clock, so the poor old man thought she was safe in her own home until a couple boys came to tell him what they'd found at the bottom of the cliff. They were on a berry-picking trip."

"Where is Mr. vanDeventer now?" Howard asked.

"He's coming down here," Loudermilk said. He gave the body a brief glance. "I reckon it's a clear case of accidental death. She didn't have an enemy in the world."

The bell attached to the front door tinkled.

"I'll bet that's her daddy now," Loudermilk finished. The Sheriff trailed Howard as the undertaker went from the rear of the building to the entrance. The caller was vanDeventer.

The old man usually presented a rather dashing appearance, for all his years. He was slender and in good health. His white hair fell in snowy, glistening waves across his head. His blue eyes were sharp and clear, his lean, tanned face firm.

But now Howard was shocked at vanDeventer's appearance. He seemed to be a bag of dried sticks from a quaking aspen. His face was blotched with spots of color the hue of a sick liver.

"Please sit down, Mr. vanDeventer," Howard said, pulling a chair from the wall.

The old man sank into the chair and leaned his head on one elbow. Loudermilk hovered in the background as Howard came around and sat down beside the old man.

The girl's father pulled himself together. "I came to discuss..."

"I understand," Howard said.

The old man looked around the office, sat in thought, then said at last, "Perhaps a bigger establishment would be better. Perhaps an Atlanta mortician..."

Howard looked directly at vanDeventer and suddenly there was steel in Howard's eyes.

He spoke quietly but firmly. "Mr. vanDeventer, I am the only man alive to whom you can entrust this precious duty. I admit that Atlanta offers bigger establishments, but I offer you—and Maddy—much more. They would lay her away with the precision of a machine. I shall do so with the skill of an artist."

He rose and stood over the old man, his face kind but unyielding. "Two generations of Aldens have buried all the departed of this county, Mr. vanDeventer. The Aldens as well as the vanDeventers are of this land, this soil."

"You almost convince me, young man."

"I need only to point out the facts, sir. Consider me first as a craftsman. I grew up in this business, sir. I know all the old ways, the fine ways. I take no short cuts to streamline my effects. I am the most capable mortician in this whole state of Georgia.

"Next, consider me as a man. I knew Maddy—her generosity, her beauty, her graciousness. I can impart to her a full measure of her divine naturalness. I shall approach my task, sir, with the deepest sense of duty.

"Add to all this the deep knowledge I have of what you, sir, would want. When this land has become ancient, her memory will still remain a landmark. Is that not your true desire, Mr. vanDeventer?"

"You read my heart, young man."

"I would suggest, sir, a crypt of the purest marble from our own Georgia earth. If I may be permitted, I would deem it an honor to go to the quarries myself and personally choose every stone, supervise every inch of its cutting."

"You would do that, young man?"

"Humbly," Howard said.

"Then spare no expense," the old man said, rising.

"As high as twenty thousand, sir?"

"As high as fifty thousand. The years left me are few, and of what use is my money now?"

The chauffeur was waiting outside to help the old man into one of the vanDeventer cars. Howard stood at the window and watched them drive away.

Behind Howard, Sheriff Loudermilk said, "We'll get the inquest over quick, so's you can get on with it, Howard. Just a formality, that's all. Ain't no doubt she died accidental, purely accidental." Loudermilk went out. Howard spent the rest of the day seeing to preliminaries, such as pricing caskets in Atlanta and comparing them with prices quoted over the phone from Montgomery.

When he drove down Main Street at dusk he sensed a change that had come over Pine Needle. Sidewalk loungers waved to him, and he knew they were talking about him as he drove on.

When he got home, Clara met him with a kiss. Her smile was bright and warm.

She had cooked his favorite dinner, porterhouse steak with mushrooms. He hadn't eaten a dinner like that in a long while now. It did more than warm his stomach. It told him their credit at the butcher and at the grocery was once more A+.

"Howard," she ventured, "do you think we might have a weekend in Atlanta sometime? After the vanDeventer funeral, I mean?"

"I don't see why not," he said expansively.

Right after dinner the phone rang. The caller was Bayliss, who owned the dry goods store and was Pine Needle's leading merchant.

"Say, Howie old man, think you'll be free for a few days after the vanDeventer funeral?"

"I might be."

"Sure hope so. Me and the boys got to have you on that fishing trip. Wouldn't be a real trip without you, son."

"I'd like to go," Howard said simply, really meaning it. He wasn't going to permit himself any resentment. Yesterday he had been nothing; today he was a leading citizen. The profit on fifty thousand in a pauperized village like Pine Needle made a lot of difference. That was all right with Howard. He was glad it did.

"Me and Loudermilk was talking a few minutes ago," Bayliss said. "You know, this town needs enterprising young blood on our town council. We can chin about it on the trip. And I reckon I'll see you in the diner tomorrow?"

"Sure, a man's got to have a spot of coffee to keep him going."

"That's right," Bayliss laughed heartily. "Specially a real live wire. Loudermilk told me—and the whole town's talking—what a real spunky job of selling you did on the poor old man. Real salesmanship, boy!" Salesmanship, Howard thought after he had hung up. He stood by the phone and a faint shudder passed over him. But he controlled it quickly.

Selling the old man hadn't been so tough. He hadn't figured for a moment it would be.

The really tough part of the job had been that moment last night when Maddy realized it was he who was shoving her over the cliff.

JURY OF ONE

Originally published in **Alfred Hitchcock's Mystery Magazine,** *October 1959.*

I knew right away that the district attorney wanted this Mrs. Clevenger on the jury.

Pretending to listen to my lawyer question a prospective male juror, the D. A. studied Mrs. Clevenger, sized her up out of the corner of his eye.

There was a dryness in my throat, a fluttering in my stomach—I was on trial for my life. Murder was a capital crime in this state, and they didn't use anything merciful and clean like a gas chamber. They made you take that last long walk and sit down in a chair wired for death.

It was a nice spring day. The tall windows of the vaulted courtroom were open, letting in a soft, lazy breeze. Speaking quietly and without hurry, the lawyers had been going about the business of picking a jury for a day and a half. The fat, bald judge looked sleepy, as if his thoughts were of trout streams. The whole thing so far had been casual, almost informal. I wondered, considering the difference this day and half had made inside of me, if l was going to be able to sit through the whole trial without screaming and making a break for one of the windows.

To get my mind off myself, I swiveled my head enough to take a new look at Mrs. Clevenger. She was well into middle age; her armor of girdles and corsets reminded me of a concrete pillbox. Her clothing, jewels, and the mink neckpiece draped carelessly over the arm of her chair all added up to a big dollar sign.

I looked at the heavy, blunt outlines of her face which even the services of an expensive cosmetician had failed to soften. You didn't have to know her; just looking at her would tell you she was rich, arrogant, selfish, merciless. Nothing, quite obviously, mattered to Mrs. Clevenger, except Mrs. Clevenger. And as she cast a passing glance in my direction, her eyes were beady and cold. There was no doubt about her being the kind of person who would have her way, no matter what.

I didn't like the way she glanced at me, but the D. A. did. He was the sort who could impress women easing past their prime. He had a tall, rangy, athletic build, a rugged face, sandy hair worn in a crew cut. He'd spotted Mrs. Clevenger already as the key juror, the one he would turn those open, warm, brown eyes on, the one he'd address his quiet, reasonable remarks to—if she were chosen. Win her, and he would have the jury. Win her, and the rest of the jury might as well try to move a mountain.

My lawyer finished his examination of the male juror. "He's acceptable to us, Your Honor," he said.

The judge stifled a yawn, nodded, plunked indolently with his gavel, and told the juror to step down.

Mrs. Clevenger was the next one to be up for examination. Mentally, I squirmed to the edge of my seat.

My lawyer came to the defense counsel table. His name was Cyril Abbott. His given name fitted him very well, perfectly. He was lanky, had a thin face which made his nose look like a big afterthought, carelessly stuck between drooping lips and narrow eyes. A gray thatch of unruly hair completed the rube picture. But if you looked closely into his eyes, you saw he was a tough old fox with wisdom garnered from countless legal battles.

As he shuffled some papers, Cyril Abbott said, "How you feeling, Taylor?"

"Not so good," I said.

"Relax. Everything's under control so far."

"It's getting Clevenger on the jury that's got me worried," I said.

* * * *

I was more worried on that point than I was about the witness.

The witness had been one of those fluke things. The killing had looked perfectly routine, just another job, though a little out of my usual line.

It was the only time I'd taken on anything outside the Syndicate. I'd been with the Syndicate quite a number of years. I guess I'd grown to take the job for granted. I was never touched by the law. Few professionals are. We're given an assignment, flown into a strange city. Our man is pointed out to us. We choose an immediate time and place. We perform our service and are whisked out of town.

The Len Doty job had seemed simple. A scrawny, down-at-the-heels crook, he'd arrived here recently and taken up residence in a fourth rate hotel.

I'd studied Doty's movements for two days. A thin, harried, nervous man, he'd seemed to have a lot on his mind. He'd been under a strain, as if something big was imminent in his life.

I was the imminent something, only he didn't know it.

I'd tried to approach this job with the same lack of feeling I had on Syndicate jobs. But here I'd been doing my own planning, and not enjoying the security you had when you were a cog in a huge machine.

By the end of the two days, I knew I had to get the job done. I was feeling a growing nervousness. I didn't go for solitude. I wanted to be back in the big town, having a drink with men I knew or stepping out with a particular woman who was gaga over my tall, dark ranginess.

I'd kept the thought of fifteen grand—what Doty was worth dead—in the front of my mind. What could go wrong? It was the same as all the others, nothing to connect me with Doty. He'd die, and I'd disappear. The case would eventually slip into the local police department's unsolved file. There may be no perfect crimes, but the records are full of unsolved ones, and the record was good enough for me.

I decided on the time and place. Both nights, late, Doty went from his flea-bag hotel to a greasy spoon far down on the corner for a snack before retiring.

The block was long and dark, with an alley at its midpoint connecting the street with one that ran parallel to it. It's always wise to choose an alley that's open at both ends.

The parallel street was a slum section artery, crowded with juke joints, penny arcades, hash houses. In short, the kind of street to swallow a man up.

I knew the Syndicate big-shots had a rule of planning they tried never to break. Keep it simple.

I kept it simple. The plan was to shoot Doty with a silenced gun in the alley, walk to a garbage can, ditch the unregistered, wiped-clean gun, continue to the crowded street of joints, mingle, catch a city bus to the downtown area. There, I'd return to the good hotel where I'd registered under an alias, take a cab to the airport, and return to the big city fifteen grand richer.

Doty came from his hotel at the expected time. In the mouth of the alley, I listened to his footsteps on the dark street.

When he came abreast of the alley, I said, "Doty."

He stopped.

"Come here," I said, "I want to talk to you." I let him glimpse the gun.

He began to shake. He looked around frantically.

I pushed him twenty feet into the alley. He pleaded for his life.

The sound of the gun was a balloon popping. Doty's knees gave way, and he fell dead.

At that moment, the witness had screamed, long and loud as only a frizzy-headed blonde, in cheap clothes and makeup, can scream. She and her boy friend had decided on the alley as a short cut from one of the amusement places on the parallel street to the tenement where she lived.

Her boy friend was having none of it. He took off on the instant. The girl was right behind him, but just the same she'd glimpsed my face.

Two more balloons had popped in the alley, but in the darkness the shooting was bad. I'd missed her. Then I'd violated another Syndicate rule.

I'd panicked—run straight out of the alley almost into the arms of a beat cop who'd heard the screams and was charging up for a look-see.

The cop was no sitting duck. He was big and fast—and armed.

I dropped the silenced pistol and held both my hands up as high as they'd go.

The Syndicate of course had never heard of me. I'd put myself out on the limb. Still, I had dough to hire Cyril Abbott. First day he'd come to jail to see me, he'd asked how much the job had paid. I'd had sense enough to say ten grand. He'd taken the whole ten and told me not to worry.

It was like telling me not to breathe. Maybe a lawyer as foxy as Abbott could cast some doubt on the blonde's testimony. After all, the alley had been pretty dark. I'd faced the street glow only briefly. And everything had happened awfully fast.

* * * *

The big question—to me—was whether or not this overbearing old lady Clevenger qualified to sit on the jury.

The D. A. buttered her up with those boyish, friendly brown eyes. "Your name please?"

"Mrs. Clarissa Butterworth Clevenger."

"You're an American citizen?"

"Of course."

"Do you have any moral or religious convictions against capital punishment which would disqualify you to sit on a jury in a capital case in this state?"

"None whatever, young man."

I reached for a handkerchief to wipe my face. In my mind I reviewed what little I'd heard of Mrs. Clarissa Butterworth Clevenger. She had lived here twenty years, meeting and marrying one of the town's leading citizens when he was on a Florida vacation. Abbott had mentioned that she'd been boldly, strikingly beautiful in those days, before time, luxury, and her inner self broadened the beam and altered the surface. Her husband had been fifteen years her senior. Three years ago he'd died in a private hospital after a long illness.

The D. A. gave her a considerate smile that silently said he disliked putting a lady of her position through a nonsensical routine. "Do you have any opinions already formed regarding this case, Mrs. Clevenger?"

"None."

"Do you know the defendant, Max Taylor?"

She looked down her nose at the D. A. "Hardly."

"Of course. But this is all necessary, Mrs. Clevenger."

"I quite understand. Get on with it, young man."

"I think we need go no further," the D. A. said. He turned toward the judge. "Your Honor, we find the juror acceptable."

The judge nodded. "Counsel for the defense may question the juror."

Cyril Abbott shuffled a few steps toward the Bench. He stood with that country bumpkin slump and scratched his gray tangle. "Your Honor, I guess the District Attorney has asked the important questions. I don't see any grounds for disqualification of the juror. The Defense accepts her."

I stared at Abbott's slouching back for a moment. Then I sagged in my chair and let a hard-held breath break from my lungs.

As Abbott turned to face me. I'm sure he controlled an urge to wink. For a second I was almost sorry I'd lied to him, hadn't given him the whole fifteen grand.

I don't know what Mrs. Clevenger was before she married old man Clevenger, when she made that trip to a dazzling vacation land in a tropical clime. I don't know what Len Doty had on her when he came looming out of her past. It must have been plenty to cause her to spend a young fortune seeking out a trustworthy name—my name—and making the arrangements to get rid of him.

I'd never know that part of it, and I didn't care. I did know that there was only one thing she could do now, if she didn't want me singing my head off.

I knew how great it was going to be, getting back to the city and telling the boys how I'd been tried with my own client on the jury.

LIFE SENTENCE

Originally published in **Manhunt,** *April 1960.*

In my official capacity I've escorted many men to state prison, each handcuffed to me during the train ride. Several of them have been murderers. This one was in that macabre category, and the thing that interested me was that I couldn't imagine him killing anybody.

As a matter of fact, his was the goriest murder of all. He had taken a heavy meat knife and chopped his wife so thoroughly that she was buried like a mass of hamburger.

His name was Hervie Taylor. He looked as if he should be on his way to keep books in an electric appliance store. This was precisely the job he'd had. If you'd noticed him at all against that background you'd have felt instinctively that he would never go far. He was an excellent bookkeeper. This, coupled with his natural colorless attributes, kept him in his dim corner writing his careful rows of figures while the world went its laughing, crying, loving, brawling, lustrous way.

He was a considerate little man, doing his best to keep from being an inconvenient appendage attached to me by steel. Some of them can't help worrying their hand against the handcuff. Others want water. A few try to bury our hands in the seat to hide the cuff. Last one I took up before Hervie Taylor had to go to the bathroom every five miles or so.

Hervie sat beside me watching the scenery stream past, beautiful farming country of low. Rolling hills and green meadows, white houses and red barns. In this, he was different from the others. There are several stock reactions. Hatred for the beauty of the countryside. Bitterness. Nostalgia. Inner torture, if the man being taken away had a masochistic streak. Even hope, in a few.

Hervie Taylor simply sat and looked at the scenery.

He was a man of fifty, small-boned and not given to excess flesh. He had brown hair that he wore neatly parted. The hair had faded a little, but there was no gray in it. His eyes were dark brown, keen and intelligent. You'd never guess his age—or his crime—simply by looking at him. There was still the suggestion of boyishness in his face. A lively eagerness in his eyes that the monotony and cares of the years had not altogether extinguished.

He was of course going up for life. Perhaps he was thinking about it, now that each click of the wheels carried him that much closer.

"Do they have good food?" he asked.

"Simple, but substantial," I said.

"Not a lot of sticky, sickening stuff or creamed mess on toast, I guess."

"You guess right," I said.

"It was the only mess Jassie knew how to cook, wanted to cook, or cared to eat," he announced.

Jassie was—had been his wife. You've seen couples like them, a little guy with a woman who had spread, flabbed, and grown to three times his size. There'd been a lot of Jassie to chop up.

"I lived with Jassie thirty years," he said idly.

"That's quite a time."

"Jassie never should have strung it out," he said. "She changed. Or perhaps I did. Or maybe it simply took me a long time to get to know her."

He must have loved her once, I thought.

As if suspecting the thought, he said, "She was a cute kid when we got married. Only having a husband made her feel secure, I guess. She had a man. She didn't need to fix up any longer. She let herself go to seed in a hurry."

"Some women are like that." Mentally, I added: Only you don't kill them for it.

"We never had children," he said. "We—ah—never did very much of the necessary prerequisite to having children. Jassie didn't want them around. Too much trouble, she said. I wanted a gang of kids. So the wife and I could sort of grow up all over again with them. Fellow with kids has got a good excuse to do lots of stuff like pitch a baseball in the back yard or tinker with a bike or take in a circus and eat hot dogs. Jassie didn't like any of that. She had to have a man who'd come in, cook supper, wash the dishes, and sit in the living room with her. Sometimes she started snoring on the couch—she had a wet, blubbery little snore. Still, she liked to have her husband sitting there with her. It was his place, she said."

"Fellow like you," I suggested, "should have become a Boy Scout troop advisor or had a Sunday School class of boys."

He looked at me as if I weren't very bright. "I tried both of those things. It made Jassie ill."

"*Ill?*"

"Yes. She'd have to call the doctor. She wouldn't get better until I had loaded the house with chocolate creams and was staying with her again." He sighed. "It got worse as time went on. She'd time me from the house to the store and back again. If I missed my bus, I'd have to explain every minute I was late."

"Sounds pretty dull," I conceded.

"You've no idea," he said. "For a time, I tried to make friends. You know, have somebody drop into the house and play bridge or have a little dinner. The experiences were horrible. A couple would drop in and Jassie wouldn't stir. I'd have to cook the dinner and explain her illness. Newly made friends usually dropped in only once, the house was usually…well, dirty, unmade, you know. Sometimes the dirty dishes and garbage container made it smell. Anyway, Jassie would never return a visit. As time went on, she got worse, of course." He looked at me calmly and I got a mental picture of Jassie, spreading over the couch as the years spread over her. Jassie so helpless, demanding every moment of his time, hemming in every second of his life.

"After a long time," he said in a tone more introspective than he'd used before, "I realized I must leave Jassie. I had no money. We never had any money. I didn't make much, and she knew the amount to the penny. She didn't know how to handle money. We arrived at every payday flat broke. Week by week—sort of like a motion picture that's going nowhere.

"Although I lacked money, I did get a chance to go in business. A man who knew my work offered me the same starting salary and a small interest if I would go into a new venture he was starting.

"Jassie wouldn't hear of it. It was risky. I wouldn't be able to work set hours. Sometimes I'd have to work nights or on weekends. The business was bound to fail. Everything must go on just as in the past."

"Did the business fail?" I asked.

"Most ironically," Hervie Taylor said. "The man who took the place I was offered absconded with considerable funds. He was later caught and punished, but the damage to the business was done. He'd spent the stolen money. I'm certain," he added solemnly, "the story would have been different had I entered the venture. I would have worked hard. I would never have touched the first penny."

I believed Hervie Taylor on that point. Until he'd chopped up Jassie, his record had been without blemish.

"Please understand," he said, "how this affected me. Here was a business ruined and gone in which I might have found delight, interest, even excitement. So for the first time I left Jassie."

"First time?"

He nodded. "I slipped my clothes out of the house and moved to a hotel. I left her a note saying I would send her money each week. Believe me, I had no intentions of living a dissolute life. But I did have a glorious evening, just able to walk the streets. Jassie came to me. She begged. She wept. She implored. She just now realized how much she loved me, she said. She'd do better."

He looked out the window for a few moments. "Women," he said, "have emotional weapons they use against men sometimes, some women. You can't feel this weapon, you can't name it. It's like an invisible net and the more you struggle against it, the more you feel like a monster and brute. Do you know what I mean?"

"Well," I said, "I've never had your experience."

"You haven't a Jassie," he said. "I went back to her. And for a little while she was different. She even cooked a steak or two. It didn't last, this new Jassie. Before long she was back in her rut, only more so."

"You left her again?"

"Yes. This time she came with the tears, the imploring, the promises. They didn't work. The next, evening a seedy looking guy with the photostat of a private detective's license in his wallet came to see me. He said that Mrs. Taylor was his client and I was through mistreating her. His threat was veiled, but I understood. I returned to Jassie."

"That was the last time you left her?"

"Oh, no. She hemmed me in worse than ever. I simply couldn't stand it any longer. This time I would really run away, go to another city, change my name."

He paled a little, remembering. After a moment, he said, "She caught me slipping out of the house. Know what she did? She whipped the literal hell out of me. That's what she did. I mean, she used her fists. She knocked me down and kicked me and dragged me to my feet and knocked me down again. This went on for a considerable time. I really don't know of anything more shattering that can happen to a man. I despised myself. She despised me just as much. For years she had counted out my pocket money to the penny. Now she even told me what to eat for lunch. It was never much. I've never known the human heart could hold so much hatred as I felt for Jassie."

"You didn't run away again," I said.

"No. I knew it would be no use. A week later, after I'd cooked supper one night, she called to me to bring her food to the living room so she could finish watching one of her interminable TV programs. A strangely nerveless feeling came over me. I found myself with the knife in my hand. Funny…when the knife disappeared in her, she gave a little squeak for all the world like a fat, gray mouse."

We rode a little in silence. We were almost at the prison now. Hervie Taylor sat at his window to catch the first sight of it.

"Relax," I said. "There are no whips or sadistic guards in displace."

"Relax?" He turned to look at me. "But I understand it's a model prison. Weekly movies, a machine shop, a prison brass band, a nice library, even a baseball team."

"That's right," I said.

His reply was brief, simple, and straight to the point. A beatific smile brought out the boyishness in his face. He looked out the window toward the distant grey walls of the prison. "Freedom," he said.

MONEY, MURDER, OR LOVE

Originally published in **Alfred Hitchcock's Mystery Magazine,** *June 1961.*

The call came in shortly before I was due to go off duty at 7 A.M.

York stuck his head in the squad room. "We got a job, Nick. A kid just found a stiff in an alley off Kilgo Street."

We went downstairs to the garage and got in one of the black, unmarked cars. As I drove across the city to Kilgo Street, York kept up a barrage of talk. He's been a cop almost as long as I have, twelve years, but he's never got used to the idea of death. He talks to cover his nervousness.

He talked about his wife and kid, as if really interested in selling me on the idea of marriage. He talked about the weather and of Sergeant Delaney's gall stone operation. He talked of anything except the violation of a human life.

The city was awakening, and for this brief moment it felt vital and clean, qualities that never extended to the street we were headed for.

By the time we reached Kilgo Street, York had run out of extraneous talk. "Well," he muttered, as I stopped in the mouth of the alley, "I guess he can't be much. Some bum. Who else would get himself killed in a Kilgo district alley?"

We got out of the car. The beat cop—a heavy, porcine guy intended by birth, reflexes and mentality never to rise far—came forward to meet us.

Hemmed in by scabby brick walls, a Kilgo Street alley is a particularly unpleasant place to die.

The beat cop grimaced. "He's back there."

"Touch anything?"

"No, sir."

"That kid find him?" I asked, pointing toward the skinny youth pressed against the wall.

"Yes, sir. He was short-cutting it through the alley, on his way to work at the produce market."

I saw York had that pale look about him. So I said, "Take over with the kid."

"Sure, Nick," he said quickly.

In our society, few people find their natural place. York should have been an insurance salesman. Instead, he'd needed a job years ago and the civil exams had been open. It's the little fates that put us where we are.

I walked back to the dead man and stood looking down at him. He was not big. He was slender, wiry, with a narrow, cruel face. I guessed that he had been arrogant and vicious when he hadn't had his way. He looked to be about thirty-five.

The strangest thing about him was the fact that he didn't belong in that alley. His clothing—suit, shoes, shirt, tie—had cost about what I draw for working a month.

I kneeled beside him. He'd been shot under the heart. Most of the bleeding had been internal. He hadn't lived long after the small bore bullet had struck him.

I touched his pockets, turned him slightly. His wallet had been jerked out of the hip pocket of his trousers. The wallet, soft, hand-tooled calfskin, was ripped. It had been cleaned of money. There was a driver's license, a club membership card, a diner's card, and a picture remaining in the wallet.

I had to look at the picture first. Even in that pocket-sized image, she was that kind of woman.

I stood up, holding the wallet York had been wrong. This was a big one. The dead man was Willard Ainsley, according to the driver's license. And Willard Ainsley was a financier and playboy. Worth so much, if you believed the newspapers, that it was a remote, unreal figure to a man like me. Seven or eight million. No one knew for sure. In that category, it seemed to me that a million more or less wasn't terribly important.

The gun that had killed Willard Ainsley was nowhere around. There were two parallel lines in the cinders of the alley, marks his heels had made. He'd been killed elsewhere and dragged into the alley.

On the sidewalk, the beat cop was breaking up a gathering crowd. A siren growled the approach of the meat wagon and lab boys.

* * * *

Ainsley had lived with his wife in the penthouse of the Cortez, the sumptuous apartment hotel overlooking the lake.

I was on overtime, but I wasn't sleepy. The doorman didn't want to admit me. The desk man endured the shock of having a policeman on the premises. I pocketed my identification, told him I was seeing Mrs. Ainsley, and asked him not to announce me. For York it would have been an ordeal. I didn't much care.

On the top floor, I crossed the wide, carpeted hall and knocked on Ainsley's door. It opened as I knocked a second time. I lowered my hand.

"Ramoth Ainsley?"

"Yes," the woman said.

"Mrs. Willard Ainsley."

"Yes. What is it?"

I pulled out my wallet and showed her my I.D. She gave me a cool look. "Nicholas Berkmin," she said. "Come in, Mr. Berkmin."

I followed her down a short, wide stairway to a large, sunken living room. Tall glass doors across the room opened on a terrace, as green as a landscaped park. The terrace offered a view of the lake, sparkling in the early sunlight Ramoth Ainsley paused near the concert grand and turned toward me. She wore a simple, silken dressing gown over her pajamas. It suggested the lines of a beautiful, supple body. There was strength in her face, and the wallet photo had failed to catch the texture and richness of her black hair.

She was lovely and fashionable, like many rich women. But she had an indefinable quality that money won't buy. Call it a sensuous vitality. You sense it on rare occasions when a woman, possessing it, enters a room or passes on the street.

"I assume," she said, "that something rather drastic has happened."

I nodded, and she said, "To Will?"

"I'm afraid so."

"Has he been hurt?"

"No," I said.

She continued to look at me. "He's dead."

"Yes."

"How?"

"It appears that someone killed him."

"I see." Her lips framed the words, but didn't speak them.

I took her arm and guided her to a chair.

"Do you expect me to faint or have hysterics, Mr. Berkmin?"

"No," I said. "But I must say you are taking it very well."

"Is there any reason why I shouldn't?"

"I don't know."

"Well, there isn't," she said. "I'd like—would you please hand me a cigarette from that box on the table?"

I opened the ivory box, extended it, and when she had the cigarette between her lips, I picked up the lighter and struck it for her.

"Thank you." She inhaled deeply. "When did it happen?"

"Last night, I think. We know very little yet. He was found by a boy on Kilgo Street."

"Not a very nice place to end up, is it, Mr. Berkmin?"

"Do you know what might have contributed to his ending up there?"

"No."

"It looks as if he was robbed. His wallet had been stripped of money. Did he carry much?"

"He considered five or six hundred dollars pocket change."

"There are a lot of people who wouldn't consider it that."

"I suppose."

"What time did he leave here last night?"

"Right after dinner. Seven-thirty or so."

"Did he say where he was going?"

She didn't answer right away. She smoked, then looked at the ash on the tip of her cigarette. "We'd had an argument. He slammed the door on the way out."

"Did you argue often?" I asked.

The cigarette ash broke and fell to the carpet "You'll find out everything anyway," she said.

"We try to."

"We were on the point of splitting up, Will and I," she said. "You see, I come from one of those old families with a hallowed name and social connections. And for the last generation, we've been worse than on our uppers. How we've managed—Anyway, I let myself be talked into marrying Will. I believed that I could—well, develop some feeling for him in time. I didn't know then how domineering and cruel he could be." She rose and got herself a second cigarette. "I'm sure you understand these things, Mr. Berkmin."

"You've told me quite a bit," I said. "Do you remember what the fight last night started over?"

"He accused me of an indiscretion."

"Was he in the habit of storming out?"

"The cruelest thing that he could think of—at the moment—that's what he did."

"Did you expect him back later in the evening?"

"I didn't know. And I was certainly too angry to ask him what his plans were."

"And you heard nothing more from him?"

She shook her head.

"Did he have many enemies?"

"More than his share."

"Any who'd think of doing away with him?"

"I don't think so."

"I'll need the names of his business associates and his attorney," I said.

"I can supply those."

"I'll also need you downtown."

"Right now?"

"It would be better to get the identification over with," I said.

She nodded and started out of the room. Then she paused. "Murders like this—killing and robbing in an alley—are they always solved?"

"Not always."

She went out of the room, and I stood there with the feeling that her husband's murderer had a silent cheering section.

I slept for awhile and went back on duty at four-thirty. I wanted this case.

A list of facts was in. Willard Ainsley had been killed with a .32-caliber bullet. It had been removed from his body and turned over to ballistics. Death had occurred at about eleven the night before. Gumshoeing had turned up no one in the Kilgo district who admitted to having seen Ainsley around that time.

I checked the reports on Ainsley's business associates. None had seen him since late on the afternoon of his death.

His attorney, Bayard Isherwood, was possibly the last of his acquaintances to have seen Ainsley alive. They had met in the elevator of the building, where they both had offices. Each had been on his way home. They had exchanged greetings. Ainsley, Bayard Isherwood had stated, had seemed on the point of bringing up a business matter, but had said that he would see Isherwood the next day. Isherwood had dined alone in his bachelor apartment. He had then attended a concert, alone. And he had retired immediately upon returning to his apartment.

Bayard Isherwood was the senior member of the city's most sedate and respected law firm. There was no doubting his statement, nor the statements of any of Ainsley's associates.

I closed the file and went over to the Cortez.

There were several people, a dozen or so, in the Ainsley apartment. I supposed it had started as a sort of wake, people dropping in on a sympathy call. It now had the earmarks of a party, as the memory of good-old-Will was washed clean with drink.

Mrs. Ainsley led the way to a den off the main hallway and closed off the noise in the living room. She stood with her back against the door. "How are you progressing, Mr. Berkmin?"

"We're punching," I said. "Bayard Isherwood says your husband was concerned with a business matter, so much so that he made a compulsive mention of it during an elevator ride, without saying what it was. Do you know what it might have been?"

"No." She moved from the door and rested her hips against the edge of a desk, studying me.

"It probably isn't important," I said. "The case looks cut and dried. Robbery and murder. It may break if we pick up a punk spending beyond his means."

"Really?"

"Or liquor loosens him up and he starts bragging. Or he tells his girl and they have a fight and she makes an anonymous phone call out of spite."

Suddenly, a shiver crossed her shoulders. "You're a very good cop, aren't you?"

"I like promotions," I said, "and the bigger paychecks."

"But you don't like being a policeman?"

"Not particularly."

"You're a rather strange man."

Her words seemed to hang in the room, forming a quick, strange bond between us.

She looked away from me, found a cigarette on the desk, and lighted it.

"Thank you for coming," she said.

"Why don't you call me Nick?"

She ventured a look at me. "Okay, Nick. I hope you catch your punk and get a nice promotion."

* * * *

The break came twenty-eight hours later. I was again on duty early. Fresh routine reports, masses of detail, were on my desk. Included was the fact that three phone calls had emanated from the Ainsley apartment the night of the murder. One had been to Bayard Isherwood, who'd been out at the time, ten o'clock. The others, between ten and eleven, had been to friends. In both instances, Ramoth Ainsley had asked if the friend had seen her husband that evening.

I pushed the reports back, wondering where we went from there. It was then that York came into my office, his breath short, his face very red.

"We got the gun, Nick!"

"Yeah?"

"Punk kid named Jim Norton hocked it this afternoon. Thirty-two revolver. The pawnbroker reported it. Ballistics checked the gun. It's the one that killed Willard Ainsley, all right."

I stood up. "Where's the kid?"

"That's the catch. When Simmons and Pickens went over to pick him up, he bolted. He's teetering on the roof of a six story tenement on Kilgo Street, threatening to jump."

I'd been through this kind of thing twice before in my years on the force. The youth looked like a skinny doll pinned against the night sky by spotlights. The fire department had roped off the block and unfolded the big net. Uniform-grade police had cleared out the rubberneckers.

I skidded the black car to a stop at the barricade. York hung back, needing all of a sudden to tie his shoe laces.

I knew most of the men on duty. I learned quickly that half a dozen men were inside the building, including a priest. They'd opened the skylight trap and reached the roof. Now they were stymied. Every time they moved a muscle, the kid got ready to jump.

A weeping girl was huddled in the shadows at the base of a building.

"Who's that?" I asked an assistant fire chief.

"Kilgo Street girl. Her name's Nancy Creaseman."

"Norton's girl?"

"Something like that."

"Why didn't you get her out of here?"

"Chief told Norton on the loud speaker she was down here. It may have kept him from going off. She's made no trouble."

I walked over to the girl. There are thousands like her in any large city. Thin, malnourished body. Mousy brown hair. Eyes shaded with long-continued anxiety. Wrong colored lipstick, attempting to hide the thinness of the pinched face.

"Nancy," I said.

"Yes, sir."

"My name is Nick Berkmin. I'm the homicide man in charge of the Ainsley case."

"Jimmy didn't kill him, Mr. Berkmin."

"How do you know?"

"He couldn't."

"Has he ever been in trouble before?"

"Not with the police. He's not the kind. I tell you."

"Willard Ainsley," I said, "was carrying a lot of money on him."

"Jimmy wouldn't, he wouldn't he wouldn't!"

"Take it easy," I said. "I'm not saying he did it. But we don't want him doing anything foolish now, do we?"

Her anxious eyes lifted toward the spot of light in the night sky. A sob burst out of her.

"Where did he get the gun, Nancy?"

"He found it."

"Where?"

"In a gutter, around a corner off Kilgo Street. He didn't do anything with it at first. Then he went and pawned it."

"Why didn't he tell us that? Why did he break and run when the police came?"

"He's scared of the police, of everyone. He overheard them asking his mother where he was, if she'd seen him with a gun. Then he got scared, lost his head, and ran. Please help him, Mr. Berkmin!"

She grabbed my hand and clung to it with her sweaty, thin, sticky fingers. "I know it looks bad, but Jimmy didn't do it. You've got to help him. You see, he got hurt—"

"Hurt?"

"Weeks ago. He had a job, delivering for a drugstore. Some guys caught him one night, took his money, and beat him up. He's had these blind spells ever since. It's why he's so scared."

I got my hand loose from hers. "I'll tell you what, Nancy. You go up there, on the roof, and talk him down. I'll see that he gets a break." Now it was her eyes clinging to me. Her weeping stopped. She squared her shoulders and started across the street.

* * * *

I called Ramoth Ainsley from my office. She agreed to see me. I drove over, brought her down to my car, and we got in.

When she saw the direction I was taking, she said, "I was under the impression we were going to your office."

"Isn't this nicer?"

"I'm not at all sure," she said.

"I wanted a chance to talk to you in private."

She sat in cautious silence as I drove through the clean luxury of her neighborhood. I drove far down the lake shore to an undeveloped area. There, I picked a side road, turned off and parked. "We might put the case on ice," I said.

"Really?"

"We've got a kid in a cell right now who was in possession of the murder gun. He says he found it, where someone had thrown it after wiping it clean. It isn't registered, but there are people who will sell unregistered guns—for a premium."

"Do you think he killed Will?"

"We have a case. We can make a monkey of him in court, with his statement about finding the gun. He had blackouts, and conceivably might not remember mugging somebody. There are ways of wrapping a thing like this up. Fact is, it probably would be best for the kid for me to wrap it up quick. A jury wouldn't go hard on him. He'd get needed hospitalization and treatment—and I promised his girl the best break for him."

She moved restlessly in the car seat "You've got something on your mind, Nick."

"Yes, I have. You're a very beautiful woman."

"Thank you."

"One who'd do most anything for enough money."

"Now wait a—"

"I'm not being critical," I broke in. "Only analytical. By the way, why did you try to call Isherwood shortly before the time your husband was killed?"

"I didn't, Nick. Why are you asking me—"

"I thought so," I said. "You see, a call was placed from your apartment to Isherwood's residence. Only it was Will calling, wasn't it? You didn't know he'd made that call, did you? But now I can wise you up. He was in another room, using the phone a good two hours *after* the time you said he'd left the apartment. The call places him in the apartment very close to the time of his death. Why'd you want us to think he'd left earlier—unless he was in the apartment up to and including the time of his death?"

Her lips seemed to redden. The shift of color was actually in her face, not her lips. "Nick! What are you saying?"

"That you had motive. He was about to throw you out, separate you from all that nice money, wasn't he?"

"What makes you think I'd even considered killing—"

"First thing started me wondering was the matter of the car. Kilgo Street is a long way from your neighborhood. If Will had driven to Kilgo and got himself bumped off, why hasn't his car been found in that vicinity? The kid in jail hocked only an unregistered gun, he didn't peddle a hot car.

"When you've been a cop a long time, you get to wondering how a thing might have happened, if a detail strikes you wrong. You wonder if a beautiful woman gets herself a little gun as a last resort. You wonder if she, finally, feels she has to use it. You wonder if she has sneaked her dead husband down the service elevator from their swank apartment, driven him all the way to a crummy place like Kilgo Street You wonder if she stripped him of money there to make it appear he'd been robbed. You wonder if she then drove herself home, her plan completed, satisfied that nothing could possibly connect her with a dump like Kilgo Street and the death of her husband."

"Nick, honestly, how could I, a woman—"

"Looked pretty good, didn't it the whole plan? But you're strong, athletic, well-kept, and he was a small man. There was a service elevator to help get him downstairs. It was late at night. You envisioned little risk of being seen, and you weren't. The whole setup looked great and you saw no reason why you couldn't carry it off."

She hesitated a long time before she spoke. "Nick, you can't prove any of this…"

"I'm in charge of the case. I can prove that kid guilty, if I want to. I got the power to close this case, but quick. On the other hand, there's a limited number of places where you can buy an unregistered gun. I know these places. I know how to make people talk. Believe me, baby, I can make them talk when I want to. If I took you to those places one by one, I'm sure I'd get an identification sooner or later. Of you. As the buyer of an unregistered gun."

"Nick—"

"Shall we start? Pay a call on one of those places?"

"Nick, please…"

"You killed him," I said.

"No, Nick."

"Okay. Let's get started on this detail of a gun."

"Nick, you can't do this to me!"

"You killed him," I repeated.

She slid toward me. "Nick," she said, "it was self defense. I swear it!"

"Self defense—with the purchase of the gun a prior act?"

She put her arms around me. I felt her shiver. "Nick, will you give me a break?"

"I guess that'll do it," I said. I held her away briefly and reached under the seat I clicked off the switch of the compact, portable, battery-powered tape recorder. Her eyes got large as she watched me put the tape carefully in my inside coat pocket

"You tricked me," she said "You didn't know—"

"I suspected," I said. "But I needed proof. Now I've got it. It's the finest insurance I can think of."

"Insurance, Nick?"

"Sure. I'll see that that tape's put in a safe place and fix things so it'll reach the right people—if anything ever happens to me."

She began to understand.

"You," I said, "are a beautiful woman worth six or seven million dollars. What's my future on the cops compared to that? You'll mourn, and I'll work awhile before I resign. For appearances' sake." Her eyes showed that her mind made a lightning fast survey of the situation. She saw no way out. And so, recognizing the inevitable, she accepted it.

She linked her arm in mine and rested her head on my shoulder. "You're right, Nick darling. We must think of appearances, mustn't we?"

OLD MAN EMMONS

Originally published in **Alfred Hitchcock's**
Mystery Magazine, *February 1962.*

The feeble outcry from the old man's bedroom penetrated Charlie Collins' slumber. His senses swam back to consciousness. Then a light flashed on and he was aware that Laura was getting out of the twin bed next to his.

"I thought I heard father," she said.

"I heard something myself."

They threw back covers, slipped into robes, and hurried to the bedroom the old man had wanted when he came to live with them, the corner bedroom, the one with lots of windows, cross ventilation.

The old man's bed was empty. He had made his way into the adjoining bathroom. He seemed to be through with being sick, and stood shivering.

Charlie and Laura rushed to him.

"Father," Laura said, "you should have called us."

"I did. You wouldn't answer," the old man said accusingly.

"We came the second we woke," Charlie said.

The old man fumbled for the drinking glass in the porcelain rack beside the medicine cabinet. Charlie grabbed the glass, rinsed it, filled it with water.

The old man washed his mouth out, gargled noisily, his mouth a sunken, wrinkled hole in his face. His skin held a grayish cast. A bundle of dried sticks inside the old-fashioned nightgown, the old man was a terrifyingly cadaverous comment on the mortality of human flesh.

"I'll get the doctor," Laura said.

"I don't want the doctor," the old man said, pulling away from them belligerently and shuffling toward his own bed, across the room.

"It must have been those pickles at dinner," Charlie said.

"I've eaten pickles before! I know what made me sick!"

Charlie and Laura looked at each other, then at the old man wavering toward the bed.

"What, sir?" Charlie asked.

"I know," the old man said ominously. "I got a good stomach. I don't get sick easy. I know what caused it."

The old man crawled into bed and pulled the covers over his head. Laura touched Charlie's arm. They slipped out of the room. In the hallway, she whispered, "You can't do much with him when he sets his mind this way."

"How about the doctor?"

"I'm sure he's all right, Charlie. It was those pickles. You go on back to bed. You've got to work tomorrow—today. I'll listen for him."

Charlie didn't think he would get back to sleep. He lay and smoked, thinking of Laura in the chair she'd drawn close to her father's door.

He'd thought he had a full awareness of the circumstances when he married Laura. An only child, she'd cared for her father a long time, since the death of her mother. She'd explained that she wanted to keep her father with her, and Charlie had said okay. It wasn't, after all, as if they were a pair of teenagers running away to get married. Both were in their thirties.

Charlie's first wife had accidentally killed herself nearly ten years ago, rushing home from a bridge game late one icy afternoon. Laura had never married, never had much chance to know men, for that matter.

She and Charlie had met prosaically enough in a supermarket. They were, he guessed, prosaic people. Laura was no raving beauty, though she was well built and had a pleasant face framed in brown hair. Charlie was a tall, pleasant-looking man, a little on the thin side, who looked as if he worked long hours at a desk in a large office, which was exactly the case.

The old man's strenuous objections had marred what should have been one of life's more perfect moments. Charlie had regretted this more for Laura's sake than his own. He'd figured he understood the old man and was old enough himself to overlook the shortcomings of a close, demanding in-law.

But now, after only a few weeks of marriage, Charlie wasn't so sure. There was a point where churlishness became too barbed for comfort, where a martyred air of being persecuted permeated the whole house.

Charlie napped finally, awoke too quickly, and dragged through the day. Driving home, he hoped Laura'd had a chance to catch a nap this afternoon. She'd looked plenty bushed when he left the house this morning.

Old man Emmons was in the living room, cackling toothlessly at a TV run of an old W. C. Fields comedy. Charlie spoke cordially, and the old man speared him with a look from his cavernous eyes. "You back?"

Charlie let it pass. "Where is Laura?"

"Gone to the store," the old man said. "Can't you keep still while the movie's on?"

With a sigh and shake of his head, Charlie passed through the house, crossed the rear yard and entered the garage. He was outfitting a woodworking shop, using one side of the garage. The place was chilly. He turned on the butane heater and began to tinker with a drill press, setting it in position and bolting it down.

He was spending more and more time out here, he realized. The thought caused him to drop his wrench, sit on a saw horse, and light a cigarette. He wondered if he were already in the process of becoming one of those hobbyist husbands, shunted out of his own house by an in-law.

He threw the cigarette on the floor and ground it under his heel. Damn it, that old man was going to have to change his ways, and that's all there was to it.

Charlie went back into the house. The living room was empty. Laura was home—there was a bag of groceries on the table just inside the front door.

Then Charlie heard their voices, hers and her father's, in argument, from the old man's bedroom.

"He hid my pills, I tell you!" the old man said.

"No, father," Laura said patiently, "they were right there in the cabinet where you put them—behind the soda box."

"You're working hand in glove with him!"

"Father..."

"I can see it now! He's turning you against me."

"No, father. We both love you and want you to be happy. We want to take care of you."

The old man snorted in disbelief as Laura came into the living room, picked up the groceries, and started toward the kitchen.

"I'll hurry dinner up, Charlie. I was late getting to the store."

Laura's worn look caused Charlie to put off what he'd intended to say.

"I'll give you a hand," he said.

The right emotional distillation didn't again take place inside of Charlie, and he didn't speak his mind during the following week.

Then on Tuesday Laura called him at the office. The old man had fallen down the basement steps and would Charlie please hurry home?

He explained briefly to his boss, ran to the parking lot, and fought traffic out to the development Laura met him at the door.

"How is he?" Charlie asked.

"He's all right." She passed the back of her hand over her forehead. "I guess I shouldn't have called you, Charlie, but when I heard him go tumbling..."

"I know. What does the doctor say?"

"That my father is a very lucky man, or indestructible." Her face twisted, giving it a strange expression Charlie had never seen before. "The doctor just left."

"Is he coming back?"

"Not today. He wants me to bring father into his office tomorrow morning, just for a check-up."

She'd need the car, then. That meant riding the bus to work. Schedules out here put Charlie either fifteen minutes late or forty-five minutes early to the office.

He sighed. "Well, I guess I better look in on him."

"Charlie—"

"Yes?"

"Don't get him...I mean..."

"I'm the soul of patience," Charlie assured her, a touch of bitterness in his voice.

Charlie opened the old man's bedroom door softly and stepped inside. The old man had his eyes closed. His bones made creases in the covers and that was all.

As Charlie neared the bed, the old man opened his eyes and looked at him.

"How are you, sir?"

"I'll survive," the old man said softly. "I'll survive a long time."

"We hope so. How did it happen?"

"I fell down the basement steps."

"I know. Laura told me that on the phone."

"I could have been killed."

"But you weren't, and we're grateful for that. The doctor said you're fine."

"Could have been killed..." the old man said, as if Charlie hadn't spoken. "All because there was a carton of old shoes on the steps. Right near the top."

Charlie tried to understand the old man's feelings. "I meant to take them down last night."

"But you didn't," the old man said in that soft voice that sounded like a whisper from an eternal tomb.

"No, I... Laura asked me to... Listen, what am I explaining every detail to you for!"

He caught the glint of warped satisfaction in the old man's eye. He felt awkward and foolish. His quick anger drained to be replaced by something else.

"You hate me," the old man whispered.

And it was true. For the first time, Charlie knew it was true. The old man seemed to have a profound knowledge of it.

"You're a little upset," Charlie said through stiff lips. "You know we care greatly for you."

He turned and went out. He found refuge in the shop, turning on a lathe and letting the chips fly.

Finally, he realized that Laura was calling him from the house. He switched off the lathe, turned off the heater, and hurried across the backyard. He had no right to act childishly toward her, to pity himself because he lacked the manhood to be the head of his own house.

He waited until late that night, until he was certain the old man was asleep and wouldn't come creeping in. He cut the legs for a cocktail table without his mind being on the task. When he came into the house, he washed his hands in the kitchen, thinking of what he would say.

Laura was on the end of the couch, feet curled under her while she watched TV. Charlie felt a great reluctance inside of him as he approached her. The word "showdown" came to his mind, frightening him a little.

He eased down beside her. She looked at him and smiled. He really did love her, he thought. Under different circumstances, with some kids around...

"How's the table coming, Charlie?"

"Fine."

"Can I have a look tomorrow?"

"Sure, if you want Laura..."

Thundering hooves and banging six-guns filtered into the space between them.

"I wanted to talk to you," he said, his collar feeling tight.

"About father," she said "Yes, I guess so."

"You want him out."

"I'm afraid I do," he said.

"Why be afraid, Charlie?" she asked, almost gently.

He stared at her, again with that feeling of strangeness.

"I'm not afraid, Charlie. I'll be glad when he's dead."

"Laura..."

"Why deny it? You feel the same way. I'm not surprised. He taints and kills everything he touches."

"Then we'll put him in a home?" Even with her attitude, which had surprised him so, the words sounded callous, cruel.

"No, Charlie, we won't put him in a home. I knew from the beginning this was something we'd have to discuss."

"But if we keep him here..."

"That's what we're going to do, Charlie."

"But you just said..."

"That I'd be glad when he's dead? I mean it. We're going to keep him right here, right with us, until the day he dies."

"I see," he said glumly, although he didn't see any solution at all.

"You think I'm choosing between duty to a father and love for a husband, Charlie?" She stirred with a faint rustling sound of her clothing against the couch upholstery. Her hand reached to touch his cheek.

"I love you, Charlie. And I don't feel any duty toward him. His miserliness and meanness killed my mother and ruined my childhood. If the question were so simple, there wouldn't be any problem."

"I don't think I understand, Laura."

"Of course you don't. You've never been told that he's a rich man."

"Rich?"

She leaned toward him slightly. "He's worth over a quarter of a million dollars, Charlie."

"But that gloomy old barn you lived in before we were married!"

"I know. But it isn't so strange or unusual. Not as extreme as those cases you read about where some recluse dies in filth, with a million dollars glued under the wallpaper or tucked under the mattress. My father's a miser and always has been. I didn't know he was worth so much myself until my mother died. There were some papers I had to sign. I made inquiries, and when I found out—well, Charlie, right then and there I began waiting for him to die. I'm his only heir, you know. It will all come to me."

The walls seemed to tilt a little, and the TV was a crazy, animated painting by Dali. Charles wiped his hand across his face. It came away wet. The discovery of the old man's wealth was not the real shock. This new side of Laura—that's what took him a moment to absorb.

"You think I'm evil, Charlie?"

"No, I realize…I mean, years of living with him wouldn't endear him to anyone…"

"He's never suspected my feelings. Isn't that a greater, more laudable sacrifice than acting out of pure love?"

"Yes." Charlie said, his voice hoarse and quick. "Yes. It is, Laura."

"If we throw him out, there is the chance a nurse will marry him for all that money."

"Yes, there is a strong chance."

"Or out of spite, he'd will the money to some charity. I know he'd do that, Charlie."

"I'm pretty sure of it myself, knowing him."

"So we don't have any alternative, do we?"

"Not that I can see."

She smoothed the hem of her dress over her knees and stared thoughtfully at the carpet.

"A quarter million, Charlie."

"I can't imagine that much honest-to-goodness money."

"Trips around the world. Good clothes. Thumb your nose at the mortgage company. Think in those terms, Charlie. When he is at his most trying."

"I'll do that."

She raised her eyes slowly to his. "We'll earn the money, Charlie."

"I guess we will."

"We must always be kind to him. As long as he lives."

"Yes. Kind."

"Are you afraid, Charlie?"

"Of taking care of an old man until he dies?" he laughed softly. "No, I'm not afraid, Laura."

Charlie felt five years younger when he woke the next morning. He hummed while he shaved. His undreamed-of good fortune caused him to look at himself in the mirror "Old pal," he said to his image, "you're going to be a rich man."

A feeling of love and respect for the old man surged up in Charlie. *When I spend that money*, Charlie thought, *I want it free and untainted. I want you to know that its mine by right. I want to remember that I eased your last days, Father Emmons.*

* * * *

The old man noticed the change. Two days later when Charlie brought him a box of his favorite sugar stick candy, the old man's eyes seemed to sink in even deeper depths, cloaked with caution.

They were in the old man's bedroom, the nice, sunny room. "Charlie," the old man said, "what are you up to?"

"I don't know what you mean, Father Emmons."

"This business of holding a chair for me, of calling me father, of bringing me stuff like this candy."

"Why, I…"

"And no accidents, Charlie, for the last couple days."

"Accidents?"

"You know what I mean," the old man said softly. "Nothing in my food to make me sick. No hiding of my pills. No boxes on the basement stairs."

"Just accidents, that's all," Charlie said. "I hope you like the candy."

"Here," the old man said suspiciously, "you eat a piece of it."

Charlie stared at him. Then he took a stick of candy from the box.

"Not that one," the old man said, grabbing the candy away. "I'll eat this one."

He pulled a piece from the box and thrust it at Charlie. Charlie took a bite while the old man watched him closely.

"Is the candy good, Charlie?"

"Sure, but if I had your…"

"What was that? You meant to say something, didn't you, Charlie. If you had my what? My what, Charlie? If you had my what?"

Charlie swallowed. "If I had your taste, I'd try some better candy."

"I like this candy," the old man said.

He remained standing there, just staring, until Charlie finally said awkwardly, "well, it's pretty good candy at that."

He went to his own room and closed the door. He leaned limply against it. The first misgiving since his talk with Laura came to him. Already he suspects that I'm planning something…that I know about his money…that I'm going to kill him.

Kill him.

Charlie put his hands over his ears, went in the bathroom, and took two aspirin. Through the small window, he saw the old man puttering in the backyard, nibbling at his stick candy.

Charlie was in the living room trying to concentrate on the newspaper when the old man came back in. The old man stood holding his candy. He was stringy inside his heavy sweater and baggy pants. "Have some candy, Charlie."

"No, thanks, I—"

"It's real good."

The overture seemed genuine enough. Charlie took a stick of candy, and the old man went to his room and closed the door.

Charlie carried the candy to the kitchen and dropped it in the garbage can.

"Dinner in a few minutes, Charlie," Laura said, busy at the stove. "Sure," he said absently.

He stepped out of the kitchen, crossed the yard, opened the shop door, and clicked the light switch.

The small room was full of butane from the heater's open pet-cock. The electric spark and the butane produced a chemical reaction that sent the garage mushrooming into the twilight sky. A piece of the garage knocked down an antenna across the street. A woman in the next block went hysterical when she heard the explosion and screamed something about the Russians. Charlie had barely time for one last thought: "Old Man Emmons had it all worked out. Blast him, but he's blasting me right out of his money!"

PRECIOUS PIGEON

Originally published in **Manhunt,** *April 1963.*

The motel was an old one, located on a once-busy highway that had been by-passed by the new city expressway.

The number of cars in the parking area indicated occupancy of about half the units. I slid my car to stop beside a four-year-old Chevy.

It was a hot, humid autumn evening, the last growl of summer. In the drab unit at the far end a baby was crying fretfully.

My own reaction to the surroundings was one of sharp distaste. I knew how Constantine must be chaffing, anxious to get on the final phase of the task we had planned. Constantine was living, I knew, only on the hope of escaping this and similar places forever.

I assumed he had been watching for me through a crack in the blind. The door of his room opened even as I approached.

I stepped inside and he closed the door quickly. He looked me up and down with envy and impatience in the dark eyes beneath the shaggy brows.

"Anyone see you, Cary?"

I shook my head. "We are total strangers, totally disconnected."

"Good." He turned toward the bureau, a great mass of man, swarthy, oiled with sweat. Something about Constantine always made me think of steam. Steam in the close confines of a dark room. "Drink?" he asked.

"No, thanks."

He helped himself to a drink from the bottle of dark rum atop the bureau. He always drank such liquids, heavy and dark, sweet brandies, wines, thick liquors.

His glossy, moist eyes were hooded by their heavy lids. "How was the honeymoon?"

I shrugged.

"Now she dies," he said.

He saw a reaction in my face. He laughed, a sound heavy and thick. "Still the man of tender feeling."

I didn't let him ruffle me. "From the beginning," I reminded him, "this job has consisted of two distinct phases."

"Quite so, Cary. I am perfectly willing to complete the second division of labor, sparing you the details. By the way, how much is she actually worth?"

"Slightly more than two million dollars."

A delicious shiver ran the length of his massive frame. "Two million… divided equally…we are millionaires, Cary."

"Not quite. Not yet."

"But soon—as soon as the precious pigeon dies." He was growing more excited. He breathed as if he were smothering. "A million dollars… Ah, the thought of it! All my life I've waited and watched for this one, Cary. The big one at last…" Then a horrendous thought struck him. "There are no other heirs named in a will?"

"She is very young to think of making a will, Constantine."

He trembled. "Don't tell me—"

"No, no," I said. "There is a will—now. She suggested it herself, insisted on it."

"Ah, you are clever, Cary!"

"I am named sole heir."

"You—and me." Laughter shook him. He slapped his hands against his sides. "How little she dreams that her will covers both of us."

"She has no idea."

The laughter subsided to a smile that wreathed his face, pushing the flesh so that his eyes were almost buried. "Incidentally, Cary, I suppose you've thought of cutting me out?"

"Why do you say such a thing?"

"You are human, subject to all the vagaries of the human mind and emotions. It's natural for the thought to occur to you. Do you deny it?"

"No, I can't truthfully say that I do."

"Good." He slapped me on the shoulder. "I'm glad you didn't try to pretend. Cary. It would be impossible to cut me out, you know."

"I recognize facts and limitations when I see them," I said.

"Excellent. You will not forget them, either. It was I who spotted the lonely, plain, precious pigeon after her parents died. My mind evolved the idea. My money financed you, Cary, so that you could meet her, woo her, win her."

"I know."

"While you were squiring her about, I lived in flea traps and ate gruel."

"Must you…"

"I must remind you, yes," he said. "I must impress one thing on you, Cary. My life has been the story of near-misses, of petty crime that didn't quite pay, of deals that failed by a hair to jell. Of rotten prisons. Of waiting in cheap places like this one," his hand made a gesture that despised the room, "until you returned with her. Until the moment when she dies and we become rich.

"So I warn you, Cary. I impress the truth of myself upon you. I gamble everything on this one. I am old now, and tired. Nothing will be left if I fail. Do you understand? We are inexorably bound together, Cary. We shall be accessories before, during, and after the fact. Think for one moment of cheating me, and I will destroy you."

"Even if it means destroying yourself as well?"

"Even so," he said calmly. "For I welcome destruction, if I am to have nothing. I fear destruction far less than you, Cary—and therein lies all the insurance I need. Are we clear on this point?"

"Quite."

"Good. Would you care for a rum now?"

"Yes, I think I need it."

We drank.

He burped softly. "Have you a plan?"

"That's not my phase, is it?"

"Touché." He smiled. "You've met important people through her, I'm sure."

"A few. She hadn't many friends."

"I suppose not. A plain girl slipping beyond the age of marriage, saddled with sick parents... But we need important people for your alibi, Cary."

"I've joined a club or two," I said. "Does she mind? Does she keep a close rein on you?"

"Not at all. She's very understanding. She insists on my having an evening out occasionally."

"Then we shall make it soon, provided she remains home when you have these evenings out."

"She usually reads."

He nodded ponderously. "And this Thursday evening—as she reads—a prowler will enter your home at ten o'clock. He will kill her and make off with a few items of value. These items I shall drop safely to the bottom of the river. After it is all over, you will take your grief to New York. There, in a few days we shall meet—total strangers. Nothing to tie her death to either of us. Nothing to link us to a scheme that required two phases.

"The casual meeting of the two strangers in New York will develop gradually into a firm friendship. Only we will know the friendship to be irrevocably cemented by our mutual past and the gradual division of two million dollars. I think we shall use foreign banks and a dummy corporation to affect the transfer. Do you agree?"

"You have it pretty well airtight, I think, Constantine."

He rolled a swallow of rum lovingly down his throat. "Now—as to details. How about the servants?"

"Two. An old couple. They have quarters over the garages and usually retire early."

"Excellent. Does she have friends who might visit her that evening?"

"I doubt it. I can't guarantee that part of it, Constantine, but the odds are very much against it."

"If the odds show against us, we'll simply postpone it a few nights. And that leaves only one thing—a way to enter the house."

I felt my face go even paler. He noticed, and his eyes despised me briefly. "You need not risk the apparent loss of a key or anything you'll have to explain, Cary. I must be able to get in, get to her before she can raise an alarm. Before I leave, I can make it look as if entry was forced."

"A window..." I mumbled.

He nodded. "Simply leave one unlocked."

"Dining room," I said. "Dining room is away from the garages...on the sheltered side of the house...fourth window down the west side of the house..."

I moved toward the door.

He caught my arm. "Don't you want to know how I shall do it, Cary? Whether she'll be strangled or struck over the head?"

"Not my phase, Constantine..."

I pulled away from him, ran, and collapsed in the car.

She cooked dinner herself Thursday night. She said she enjoyed cooking and did so often. I wished, however, she had made a less intimate gesture that evening.

She seemed to savor the feeling of our being alone together in the house. She really didn't like servants. She was, I thought, too basically kind to order other people around.

"Cary..."

She looked almost unreal as I faced her across the candlelight.

"Yes?"

"Do you know what?" she laughed with delight. "I was a stranger today."

"Stranger?"

"I went unrecognized. At least—almost. I ran into Jean Carraway at The Hub while I was shopping. She hardly knew me. Honest and truly. Said marriage had worked wonders for me. Have I really bloomed, Cary?"

"Oh, I don't know. You always had the basic stuff, the bone structure, the figure under those plain dresses you used to wear."

She reached across the table and touched my hand. "It goes deeper than that, Cary. If I have changed—bloomed, as Jean said—it was because of you. Cary…even if… If I should die tomorrow, I have lived. At last, I have lived…" What gave her the powers to have such a premonition?

I had to get out of the house quickly. My part was almost over. It remained now only for me to make sure that I was in the company of unimpeachable witnesses at ten o'clock, when phase two would take place…

A large cloud obscured the moon when I returned. Except for a single light upstairs in her bedroom, the house was dark.

I let myself silently in the front door. Passed like a shadow through the foyer.

Near the walnut-paneled staircase, I heard a slight sound. The massive bulk of Constantine loomed before me.

He realized I was there. He turned. From the hall table, I had picked up the heavy, antique marble figurine.

I struck him twice on the head before he knew what was happening. He fell across the table, smashing it. I bent over him quickly, striking my lighter. He was dead. The bone in his head was crushed.

Light spilled into the upper hall, and her voice, quick with anxiety, came to me.

"Cary…is that you?"

"Don't come down here, darling!"

I ran quickly up the stairs; she was tall, slender and strangely and exotically beautiful in her negligee, the book she had been reading still in her hand.

"A prowler, darling…" I gasped. "A total stranger… Surprised him… scuffled…grabbed the first thing that came to hand…"

She touched me tenderly. "My poor Cary!"

"It's okay…all okay now…think I killed him…call the police, will you?"

As she called, I was filled with the enjoyment of looking at her. If I had given meaning to her life, she had returned the gift fully.

And that was the thing I never could have explained, a thing Constantine never would have understood.

That I would fall in love with her.

FALSE START

Originally published in **Alfred Hitchcock's Mystery Magazine**, *October 1964.*

In our suite at the Diamond Shores on Miami Beach, Gervasi packed the money, two hundred thousand dollars of it, in an innocent-looking overnight case.

He snapped the case closed and lighted a cigar. Trim and excellently tailored, his careful Florida tan contrasting with the snow white hair, Gervasi looked like the titular head of a very wealthy old family.

He handed me the overnight case. "Call me immediately from Dallas, Nick."

"It goes without saying," I said. I paused at the mirror to adjust my necktie as Gervasi and I strolled toward the door. I had an excellent tan of my own. The face in the mirror was clean-cut with friendly eyes of brown. If Gervasi looked like the titular head, I gave the appearance of the bright young scion who would one day traditionally fill his shoes. Actually, there was no blood relationship between us. Merely the relationship in business, in the similarity of desire to have the best in life that big money can buy. Perhaps this was the strongest kind, after all.

Gervasi opened the door, laying his other hand on my shoulder. "Have a good trip, Nick."

"Thanks. I will."

I crossed to the elevator and rode down to the plush lobby. Through the tall glass doors I saw my car pulling up under the outside canopy.

Johnny, the bellhop, leaped out of the car and held the door for me when I came out. He'd already brought my twin suitcases down and stowed them in the car trunk.

He glanced at the overnight case in my hand. "Would you like that in the trunk also, Mr. Ramey?"

"You needn't bother."

I handed him a dollar, and he thanked me with a short bow. I got in the car and Johnny closed the door gently but firmly. He stepped clear of the car, just a hotel fixture, like the plumbing.

The morning was a monotony of endless miles of flat terrain. I was impatient to get through with the Texas trip and back to Miami for the opening races at Gulfstream. But I kept my foot lightly on the accelerator, never exceeding the speed limit. I certainly didn't want a nosy, rube cop stopping me.

Shortly after mid-day, I drove into a sun-baked town in central Florida which offered no likely place to have lunch, so I continued driving.

On the northern outskirts, I saw a fresh, new motel with spacious, land-scaped grounds, swimming pool and restaurant. I turned in and found a spot in the crowded parking area near the restaurant. I guessed that this was the favorite eating place for the local business gentry.

I carried the overnight case inside. With the case securely wedged be-tween me and a wall of the booth, I lunched on an excellent shrimp creole.

With the overnight case firmly in my grip, I paid the check, went out of the restaurant, and moved the short distance to my car. With my free hand, I was reaching in my pocket for the car keys when a hard object jabbed me unpleasantly in the back. It felt exactly like the business end of a gun barrel, an item with which I'd had previous experience.

"Easy! I'm not resisting," I said with dry-throated candor. My gaze flicked to the surrounding cars. All were empty, their occupants inside eat-ing, talking insurance and real estate and fishing and bird hunting.

"How about we use my car, Mr. Ramey?" the man behind me said.

The voice was vaguely familiar. I turned my head slowly, looking over my shoulder. I saw—really saw—the face of Johnny, the bellhop, for the first time. It wasn't a bad-looking face at all, even features, dark hair grow-ing to a slight widow's peak over a high forehead. But the dark eyes were too calm, too quietly determined to quench the acid of alarm that was sting-ing through me. The face reminded me a great deal of my own.

The eyes went a shade colder. He was carrying the gun in his jacket pocket. He nudged me with it "This way, Mr. Ramey."

The primary moment of nauseating surprise had passed. The eruptions of the shrimp creole became less violent. I made a casual move to drop the overnight case into my car.

He laughed thinly. "No, Mr. Ramey. We'll take the case along—and keep the other hand in the pants pocket until the gun is safely out of the shoulder holster."

"All right, Johnny," I said pleasantly. "We'll do it your way, for the moment."

"I won't need many moments, Mr. Ramey."

"You may not have many," I reminded him.

Herding me toward a five-year-old Ford a short distance away, he said, "I've thought about it, waited for it a long time. I'm willing to take the gamble. It's a big country. I can lose myself easily."

He reached cautiously around my body, lifted my gun. A prod from his weapon forced me into the car on the right-hand side.

"Now slide across the seat," he instructed. "You'll drive, while I have a look at the case."

I started the car. It was as clean inside as a new one. The engine hummed with vibrant, leashed power. It was evident the car had received meticulous care from hands with an aptitude for mechanics.

"Drive north," he said, resting the overnight case on his knees, while he held his gun steadily on me.

I eased the car onto the highway. Traffic northward on the two-lane macadam was just about nonexistent. Insects hummed over the palmetto fields. In the distance, tall pines and cypress stood lonely and gaunt against the backdrop of glaring, tropical sky.

"I assume," I said, "that you located me simply by following me."

"Right," he said. "I had the horse waiting near the employees' entrance at the Diamond Shores. All I had to do was fall in behind you."

"Maybe you were spotted."

"You kidding?" he laughed. "Who sees the coming and going of a bell-hop? It'll take awhile for even the bell captain to realize I'm not around the hotel. You know, it was good of you to drive sensibly this morning."

"Watchfully, too, Johnny," I said on a hollow note.

"Sure," he grinned, "but not for an old car that showed behind you a time or two. Guess you figured it was a farmer's car."

My reply was a bleak silence. The truth is, I hadn't noticed the old Ford at all. Nobody who was questionable to Gervasi and me in Miami, or anyplace else, drove an old Ford.

"Don't let it get you down, Mr. Ramey," Johnny said in enjoyment "We all make mistakes now and then."

"A good point for you to remember, Johnny."

"Thanks, I will. But up to now I haven't made any. I had plenty of time to change from the monkey suit in the back seat of the car, while you were having lunch. It was really simple. I just sat on the rear bumper of the car next to yours and rested until you came out."

"It will get less simple, Johnny."

"Oh, sure." He patted an imitation yawn.

My hands were in hard knots on the wheel. A drop of sweat crept into the corner of my eye and began stinging and making me blink. "Johnny, you're very young to start out like this."

"Younger the better."

"You ought to think of the years ahead."

"Now you dig, pops," he said warmly. "Now you're getting with it I've thought of nothing else for a long time."

"You're a nice, clean-cut young man, Johnny, with a future. Unless you..."

"This?" he said in mock horror. "This? Coming from you?"

"Why not from me, Johnny?"

"Oh, nuts!" he said, slouching slightly against the car door. "Now don't start boring me."

"What do you think you know about me, Johnny?"

"I don't *think*. I know. I know that I know! Most all of us know."

"Most all of us, Johnny?"

"You wouldn't dig. You've never been a hotel employee. We're not quite real people. Never really there. You know? Like unseen hands keeping a big, luxury palace afloat. Like spooks with a world all our own, the bellhops, cooks, waitresses, linen women, maids, maintenance men. We eat together, talk together, party together, live together. We got bitter enemies and bosom pals in our own ranks. You know?"

"I don't think I ever really thought anything about it, Johnny."

"Who does?" he asked. He was silent a moment; then he laughed softly. "Sometimes we know more about you than you know yourselves. Waitresses overhear those bitter, whispered arguments of elegant people at dinner. A switchboard girl knows the origin of a secret phone call. A swimming pool attendant knows why a wife swims every afternoon while her husband is looking after his stocks. A bellhop delivers hangover medicine or more liquor to a falling-down, talkative drunk. Now do you know, Mr. Ramey?"

My vision reddened slightly. Gervasi and I were going to take a certain hotel apart, if and when I got back.

"How did you find out what's in the overnight case, Johnny?" I asked thickly.

"I don't know. Not yet."

I gave him a quick frown.

He returned a smile. "I know about you and Mr. Gervasi," he said. "I know about the phone calls to certain people in Dallas. I know you've hung onto the case like you were a bleeder and it held your spare blood. Finally, I know that you, personally, Gervasi's top dog, are making the trip. It all adds up to something very big. Big enough for me."

"I have to admire your nerve," I admitted, although with reticence.

"Not nerve," he shook his head slowly. "I'm not so long on nerve. Just hungry, Mr. Ramey. I ache with the hunger. I wake up at night thinking about it I just can't live with it any longer. I'm hungry, Mr. Ramey, for a place in that world I and the other spooks help keep afloat."

"And you think the case is full of bread?"

"I'm absolutely sure of it," he said. "Bread in one form or another. Bread I'll never again have the chance to pick up so easy. What is it Mr. Ramey? Drugs? Hot jewels? Dough for a big gamble that's been rigged? How about the key?" He snapped his fingers. "Give me the key, Mr. Ramey."

"I don't have a key, Johnny. Gervasi has one. There is another in Dallas."

"Okay," he said. "That makes sense. So I'll have to blow the lock with the gun."

"Johnny, there's two hundred thousand in that case."

His face went blank for an instant. Then a laugh of pleased surprise ripped out of him. "Even better than I thought!"

"Johnny…"

"Oh, no!" he said. "No deals. You're not buying me off with peanuts. I'm a pig, Mr. Ramey. And my risk is no greater if I take it all."

"We'll hunt you down, Johnny."

"Where? Hong Kong? Paris? Rome? Rio? Don't talk crazy and spoil the picture I've always had of you, Mr. Ramey."

"There is something I must say…"

"Please, please," he gestured with his hand. "You're spoiling that picture of a man who set his sights and never let anything stand in his way. Why, Mr. Ramey, you've been my idol, my inspiration! I wouldn't think of harming you, unless you forced me. I'm not dumb enough to kill somebody and get the cops after me. After all, their organization is a little bigger than yours. They make it tougher for a man to hide."

"When you take the money at the point of a gun…"

"When I take the money," he said, "I'm damned sure you and Gervasi won't go to any cops. If your deal was honest you wouldn't be taking the risk of transporting the money this way."

"You got it all figured, Johnny."

"I sure have. And we've talked more than plenty. I want to open the case. I want the fine, slick feel of the money against my fingers. I want to go someplace private and count it a couple dozen times before I start spending it."

He held the overnight case as if he were hugging it. "There's a side road turning into those pines up ahead," he said, giving the road a long look. "Take it."

"Johnny…"

"One more peep, Mr. Ramey, and I'm going to start not liking you."

I slowed the car, turned the wheel. The shadow of the swaying, scraggly pines sent a shiver down my spine. We were on a sandy, rutted trail that led toward the distant swamplands, a little-used logging road. The narrow state highway fell behind. Now it was hidden from us by the piney woods. The world became very desolate, as if it were empty, deserted except for the two of us.

His breathing was thinning out, beginning to rasp slightly. "Stop the car, Mr. Ramey."

I braked, opened the door. He let the overnight case slide to the floor and moved across the seat behind me.

I timed the passing seconds with the sensitivity of raw nerves. There was a rustle of clothing as the gun came down, aiming at the back of my head.

I slipped to one side, lashing out with my foot, and dropping to the sandy carpeting of pine needles.

A meaningless sound caught in his throat. My heel had caught his knee-cap. He thudded against the car.

Spinning and lunging toward him beneath the gun, I glimpsed his pain-contorted face. He forced the throbbing knee to support him, shifted his position, and the gun was swinging down again.

I slammed into his middle, grabbing for his wrist. I had it momentarily, but he was sweating. He slipped loose as we fell.

I tried to turn on him a second time. I had lost the advantage of surprise. He took a side step. A fresh look of viciousness was in his face. Halfway to my feet, I suddenly covered my head with my arms. The impact of the gun barrel made my right elbow feel as if it had dissolved.

I stumbled backward, concerned only with defense now. He danced in and out, in and out. The third or fourth blow with the gun knocked me cold. I'm not sure which. Johnny had ample time for a clean getaway.

* * * *

I suppose an hour or more passed. The fog began to clear. I rolled over on the pine needles and sat up. The trees around me did a dizzy dance. I groaned, and cradled my throbbing elbow, lowered my aching head, and finally tried to brush away the swarm of sweat bees that made life right then even more hellish.

Another thirty minutes passed before I staggered onto the highway. I looked up and down the road, aching for the sight of a car, or a farmer in a truck. The road was devoid of all movement, except for the shimmering heat waves that made the road look like black water in the distance.

I started walking. A southbound car passed at last, but swooped by without even slowing for my frantic, waggling thumb.

I was on the point of passing out again when I reached the motel. I needed a doctor, but that could wait.

In an outside phone booth. I placed a call to Gervasi. He wasn't in his room. I guessed a faceless bellhop had to page him.

His cultured tones reached me at last, "Gervasi speaking."

"Nick Ramey here."

He took a breath. "You couldn't be anywhere near Dallas yet. What went wrong?"

"I lost the stuff."

He let the breath out. "Are you—confined?"

"No."

"Can you return under your own power?"

"Yes," I answered him bereftly.

"Then it wasn't the police?"

"No, Gervasi. It was a punk bellhop who followed me from the hotel."

"A *what*?"

"Look," I groaned, "I'm nearly dead. I'll give you the details later. He got the money. He got away. I did the best I could, and I won't apologize."

He gave himself a moment for it to sink in. When he spoke again, his voice was less strident "I know you always do your best, Nick. Did he take the car?"

I looked across the motel parking lot where my car was still parked. "No, just the money. All of it. He didn't give me a chance to tell him, either. He kept shutting me up."

"Then you'd better get back here as fast as you can, Nick."

"You don't have to tell me." I was practically weeping. "Better start winding up things right now. That bellhop is going to have Federal men like a dog has fleas, when he hits the first bright spot and starts scattering two hundred grand of counterfeit dough…"

A HEAD OFF HER SHOULDERS

Originally published in **Dime Mystery Magazine,** *August 1949.*

Maxie Bemelmens' penthouse was like a huge nerve center in a state of morbid, quiet excitement. Atop a fifteen-story apartment hotel that Maxie owned, the penthouse was everything a penthouse should be, down to the last shrub growing on the terrace. I stood at the French doors, listening to myself breathe. Now and then the phone tinkled and Leon Myart's smooth voice murmured into it. He was talking to the nerve-ends, men out scouring the city, putting little pieces of information into a pattern.

Myart said, "He want to see you, Hilliard."

I looked at the closed door across the room. "I hate to go in there."

"I know, but you'd better go on in."

I went in the room. It was a kind of den. There was Maxie pushed back in a big club chair with that sad, sour, dead expression on his face. His thick lips looked grey. I wanted to yell at him to snap out of it. I have never seen anything like it happen before.

Right near Maxie's chair was a large plush couch. On it lay a figure. The silk dress clung enough to show the lines of the body and the hands were at the sides in calm repose. But Melissa's face was missing. In fact, her whole head was missing, severed just above her shoulders.

"Steve," Maxie said, "get Cecil Calhoun. Bring Calhoun here for the job."

"Calhoun, the sculptor?"

"That's right. He's one of the best in the country. Promise up to fifteen grand if you have to."

He reached for a bottle. I saw that he was blind drunk. "Here's the address, Steve."

I took the piece of paper and went out. Men were on guard at the top and bottom of the elevator shaft. Archie was the one on guard at the front entrance to the building. While I waited for the car to pull around Archie chatted with me. "Nothing showing down here," he said.

"Myart's narrowing the time element down fast now," I said.

"I don't like that Myart," Archie said. "Colder'n a snake's belly in zero weather." He rolled his eyes up. "Maxie still in there with her?"

When I nodded, Archie looked worried. "It ain't right," he muttered. "It ain't normal. Couldn't you talk to him, Hilliard? Get him to tell the cops about this thing, the way he should?"

"He'd let the cops dog Melissa's murder the way he'd give his dough to charity."

"Nothing good's going to come from it," Archie said. "Somebody is really gunning for Maxie this time, sending him that trunk with Melissa in it that way. Maybe," he added hopefully, "it ain't Melissa after all?"

"It's Melissa, all right. Whoever did it wanted Maxie to know right off that it was Melissa. The shoulder of her dress was pulled down enough to show that birthmark."

Archie fogged smoke out of his nose and shook his head. "Somebody sure hates Maxie!"

"And Melissa," I said.

Oldham pulled the car up to the curb then and I crossed the sidewalk. I got in and handed Oldham the piece of paper with Cecil Calhoun's address.

The address turned out to be an old gingerbread house. A card on the bell button read: "Out of Order." I knocked.

When nothing happened I knocked again. A woman's voice, husky and impatient, called out, "All right, all right. I'm coming!"

The door was jerked open. She was very good looking in a tall, rangy way, the kind of dame you imagine on an archery range or gracing a sleek saddle mount or floating down in a perfect swan dive from a high board. She had long auburn hair that glinted in the sunlight. Her mouth was red and wide, and her eyes were a liquid brown, capable of great expression. She was wearing a smock stained with clay and paint, and there was a clay smudge on her cheek where she'd brushed the back of her hand.

"The Calhoun residence?" I said.

"I'm Cecil Calhoun."

"I hadn't expected to find a woman."

"Neither did my father," she smiled, "and unfortunately named me before I was born. Would you come in?"

She closed the door behind me and crossed the room to get herself a cigarette. The flash of her bare calves and ankles was easy to watch. When she turned she caught me peeking. It didn't fluster her.

The living room was filled with old furniture and cluttered to the point where you knew she didn't care much for housework, or for a lot of servants getting in her way. She cleared away enough magazines from the sofa so I could sit down.

"My name is Steven Hilliard," I said. "I represent Mr. Maximillian Bemelmens. There is a job of sculpting he wishes you to do. But it must be done immediately. You'll work in his penthouse. Anything you need will be supplied."

"Well, really, I—"

"You can check Mr. Bemelmens in Dun and Bradstreet. He wants only the best, but there can be no delay whatever. A certain young lady will have to take a trip shortly, and Mr. Bemelmens wants—"

"A keepsake? A reminder?"

"You could put it that way."

"A bust?"

"Just—the head. But you'll have to go see Mr. Bemelmens now. He instructed me to offer fifteen thousand." I wondered why I'd quoted that top figure right off the bat.

Those eyes of hers expressed pleased surprise. She gave me a careful scrutiny, seemed to decide that I was not too long out of college, one of those young men in a solid business firm who wore a Windsor knot in his tie. It was evident she didn't read the papers too much or she'd have known a little something about Maxie.

"I'll shuck out of this smock," she said.

I relaxed. I had thought I would have more trouble. I watched her leave the room. The smock couldn't quite hide the rhythm of her hips as she walked.

* * * *

When we got back to the apartment hotel she didn't notice the guards scattered through the building. I wouldn't have noticed them myself if I hadn't known where to look. We rode the elevator up to the penthouse.

Myart was over at the cabinet that unfolded into a bar, gesturing and mumbling at Dominick and Todd when I ushered Cecil Calhoun in. I wondered what Dominick and Todd had found out.

Myart spun at the sound of our entry. His narrow eyes pulled together, and I said, "Cecil Calhoun."

He looked as if he didn't much like the idea of a girl, but he said, "Maxie's waiting."

I crimped my lips tight on a breath and steered Cecil into the room where Maxie sat. She looked at him and at the thing on the couch and turned back toward the door fast. She looked a little green. She said, "You'll pardon me."

I caught her wrists, my back against the door. Her gaze flashed up into mine. I could feel the warmth of her, the lithe strength of her body. I wondered how expressive those eyes would get in soft darkness alone with some guy she thought a lot of.

"I really am in no serious need of fifteen thousand dollars," she said. "Now if you'll excuse me…"

"*Sit down!*" Maxie said.

She gave me an angry look and sat down.

"Can you sculpt a head from photographs," Maxie asked.

"I suppose, with enough shots from enough angles."

"You'll have enough. I've got dozens of them, from all angles." For an instant Maxie's sour, dead gaze lingered on the thing on the couch. "I won't bury her like that," he said. "She's got to have a head. You make a head of wax and I'll pay you fifteen thousand and then you'll be free to leave."

She looked about the room as if seeking a way out. "I suppose this is one job any sculptor would never forget," she said at last, squeezing a wry smile across her lips.

"Give her the rumpus room," Maxie said. "Get it cleared. Bring in whatever she wants."

I steered Cecil into the rumpus room. She saw me looking at the darts in the large cork board on the wall. She said, "You don't think I'm a fool, do you? What good would a few darts do?"

"I'll send the photographs in. Make out a list of things you'll need."

She dropped in a modernistic leather chair. "It's driven him crazy, hasn't it, that thing in there?"

"It hit him very hard," I admitted. "When you think of Maxie you think of a guy with steel in his guts, slapping backs, laughing, taking what he wants. When he opened that trunk that she came in, it aged him a thousand years. He's sitting in there like an old, numbed man."

"More like a plotting, insane spider," Cecil suggested. "She must have been quite a gal."

"Honey, I wouldn't even attempt to describe Melissa."

"She was beautiful?"

"More than just that. Not the intellectual type. I guess the animal type would fit her. She was catty, mean, vicious. She'd fly into a rage and throw things. She'd pout. She'd sell you out without batting an eye, see your soul in hell, and suffer acute self-pity if you even suggested she had anything to do with it."

"Some fools go for that type," Cecil conceded.

"Not me."

"What's your type?"

"You."

"That's flattering, considering the source. You must have had a lot of experience with women."

"Not so much so as you'd think."

"This Melissa—where'd she come from?"

"I don't know, before she came to the city. But she cut a wide swath here. First she married a cheap little bookie. He made the mistake of introducing her to Augie Feldman, who was the biggest bookie in town. After Augie there was a millionaire playboy, an aviator who got famous during the war, and then Roy Meek, who dealt in narcotics. None of them ever stopped loving her."

"She didn't marry them all?"

"No." I laughed at the expression on Calhoun's face. "Only one or two of them."

"After this Roy Meek came your boss?"

"Look, why all the questions?"

"Just interested—and if I'm going to do a head of her I have to know what she was like. There must be some character in the head, mustn't there?"

"Well, after Roy Meek came the boss," I said.

"And what happened to the men who loved her? I mean, she must have left her mark on their lives."

"The millionaire ruined Augie Feldman," I said. "Then the millionaire took to drink when she was through with him. The aviator cracked up—it might have been suicide. Roy Meek landed in prison."

She cut me a look out of the corners of her eyes. "Your boss' doing?"

"You'd better not ask any more questions," I said. "I'll get those photos. You'd better list the things you want."

* * * *

When I went out Myart was talking excitedly with Fisk. A tall, lean, grey man, Fisk was mopping his face. They turned as I entered the sunken living room.

Myart said, "Roy Meek is out."

I drew up on my toes, remembering. The day Meek had gone to prison. The poisonous hatred Maxie Bemelmens and Roy Meek felt for each other. I could still seem to see Maxie standing in the courtroom, laughing, Melissa on his arm, when sentence had been passed on Meek. Meek had turned and his eyes had sought Maxie and Melissa out and he had given them a look. That's all, just one long look out of those washed-out cold blue eyes.

"When?" I asked.

"Two days ago. A parole."

"I've been on it all day," Fisk said. "I finally found the rooming house where he checked in when he hit town. But after that first night he hasn't been back there."

"Get back on it," Myart said. "I'll send Oldham over to help you."

When Fisk went out, Myart paced briskly back and forth, stopped before me, rocking on his toes, hands clasped behind him. In the tone of a man delivering a lecture, Myart said, "The ramifications of this thing can be far reaching and charged with disaster, Hilliard. No one outside the organization must know Maxie's real condition. This, Hilliard, is all the work of someone gone mad with hatred for Melissa and Maxie. I doubt that Roy Meek would have the cold nerve to do it.

"But most important—to me—is the organization. The work must go on. Maxie is expending a hundred dollars an hour, bending every effort of our team to track down Melissa's killer. Dozens of people have been questioned, watched, traced. We've examined her movements in detail until one-twenty-five this morning. There we have hit a dead end, a blank wall.

"In the meantime, doubts and wonders about Maxie will be rising all over the city. I want you to go down to the offices. You'll know what to do. Keep things running. Put up a front for at least today." The phone buzzed. Myart went to it.

I stuck my head back in the rumpus room. "I'm going to be out for a while," I said.

Cecil Calhoun looked up from the table where she was jotting on a note pad.

"Just stay in here and you'll be okay, I promise you."

"And I believe I can believe you, Steve Hilliard," she said.

"Calhoun, I like you."

As the afternoon wore on, an air of dread and doubt, like fingers of darkness, stole across the underworld of the city. I knew it from the people I talked with in the offices, the phone calls that came for Maxie that I had to cover. No one outside the organization knew what had really happened, but you can't turn loose a score of human hunters asking questions without causing people in dark places to talk and wonder.

Calhoun was still in the rumpus room when I got back there. I had a tray of food in my hands. I kicked the door closed with my heel. "Your dinner," I said.

"Is it that late? I hadn't noticed."

She had the face of the dart board covered with glossy photos of Melissa, mostly close-ups of Melissa's soft, golden face. She had ruined the ping-pong table with a clutter of tools and plaster of paris scattered everywhere. Midway down the table what looked like a lump of plaster of paris was showing the outlines of a human face. "I hope you like chop suey," I said.

"Adore it." She sat down to eat. "I've been thinking about you all afternoon, Steve."

"That's flattering."

"I'm really serious. You don't belong here. This Maxie is a crook, isn't he?"

"Let's say the average man has ten fingers. Maxie has a hundred with each finger in a different place. He can push a lot of weight around, Maxie can."

"But you don't belong with him," she repeated. "You need to put that good-looking, smiling kisser in a brokerage office."

"And get up every morning at seven-thirty, jostle my way through the mob to get home at five, read the paper and go to bed? Set myself up so that a Saturday night bridge game is a big celebration?"

"I wish I knew your early environment," she said. "Something has twisted you up. How did you ever get hooked up with Maxie?"

"I inherited it," I said. "An old uncle raised me. He was a side-kick of Maxie's. Maxie has always regarded me as a son. That's why I have the run of the place, why I'm one of the few people he can trust."

She was looking at me with a world of expression in her dark brown eyes. I leaned over and kissed her. She didn't move.

When I took my lips away from hers she said, "I'm sorry you did that."

"Would slapping my face help?"

"Not that kind of sorry. Get out of here, will you!"

I went back in the living room. Myart was on the edge of his chair at the phone. Beads of sweat stood out on his narrow forehead under his patent-leather hair and his waxed mustache had got a little limp. He was saying in agitation: "No!... Really?... Wonderful!"

He slammed the phone down, turned to me. "We pushed through the blank, Hilliad." He laughed in that way of his, that dry, mirthless sound that wasn't real laughter at all. "Until one-twenty-five this morning we had connected Melissa with no one who might have had a motive to kill her. But Boudreau has found a cab driver who remembers taking her to Augie Feldman's place about two this morning. She wasn't seen after that until she showed up here—in the trunk. Get Feldman, Steve. Boudreau says he just went back to his rooming house after eating in a hash house. Boudreau is watching the place. Dominick is downstairs. Take him with you."

Augie Feldman's rooming house was on the lower side of town in a neighborhood of 1890 houses, huge, gloomy old hulks, that had been con- verted from once magnificent private homes. I rolled the car to a stop. Be- side me, Dominick stirred ponderously, breathing through his adenoids. "There's Boudreau," Dominick said.

We got out of the car, drifted to the shadow at the far side of the side- walk. Boudreau said, "He's still in there. Room 10. Upstairs."

"Cover us from here," I said.

The front door creaked and the stairs sighed. Dominick and I stopped before the door of Room 10. We each put a hand under our coats against the pressure of our guns, and I palmed the knob and slammed the door open.

The room smelled. It looked fly-specked and scaly in the light of the one naked bulb. Augie Feldman reared up on the bed, a racing form and pencil in his hands, a cigarette dangling from the middle of his mouth.

I looked at him and remembered him as he had once been, prosperous, sure of himself, heavy on the dough. This quaking, gaunt hulk with the thinning grey hair, slack jowls and fear-haunted eyes was certainly a different man. The big-time bookie was long gone.

He swung his feet to the floor, picked up the overflowing ashtray from the straight chair beside the sway-backed bed and made haste to wipe the ashes, with his palm, that had spilled on the hard bottom of the chair.

"Hello, Steve. Sit down, sit down." He pushed the chair toward me. I pushed it back. I watched a nervous tic develop in his left eye as he sat on the edge of the bed and stared up at us. The room was hot, close, unpleasant. I said, "What was she doing here in the early hours of morning, Augie."

"You mean Melissa," he whispered.

I waited. He said, "She was around here asking about Roy Meek. She knew how it had been between me and Meek once."

"And how long was she here?"

"Not long." The pouches under his eyes looked heavy and purple. He looked; at his hands. "She left about three o'clock this morning, said she was going home."

"You'd better come along and tell it to Maxie."

His gaze darted from Dominick to me. He licked his lips. "I'll get my hat."

We went out of the house with Augie between us. I put him in the back seat of the car between Boudreau and Dominick. When we got back to Maxie's apartment building I got out of the car with Feldman and prodded him across the sidewalk. I would take him up alone. Dominick and Boudreau were both good men, but in a case like this Myart said you could never know for sure, you couldn't be too careful who came into the penthouse.

At the top, Feldman slouched out of the elevator like a man sapped of strength and will. Myart met us in the living room. He looked at Augie with those narrow black eyes and said, "Take him in to Maxie."

* * * *

I opened the door to the den, shoved Augie in. Maxie was standing beside the couch, spread-legged, face slick, a near-empty rye bottle in his hand.

Augie stopped at the sight on the couch.

136 | TALMAGE POWELL

"Melissa," Maxie hissed.

Augie's face seemed to crumble and freeze that way, a thing of grey disjointed angle and shadow.

He stumbled across the room, mouth working, and slipped to his knees. A dry sob racked at his throat.

"You did it!" Maxie said.

Feldman didn't say anything, just stayed there with those dry sobs tearing at him.

"Damn you, talk when I speak to you!" Maxie said. He swung the rye bottle. It hit Augie across the bridge of the nose, brought blood, knocked him over on his back.

I bent over him. "You knocked him out, Maxie."

Maxie wiped his hand across his slack lips. His eyes were burning. Swaying on his feet, he said, "Drag him out in the living room. Then go down and bring up Georgie. If anybody can make him talk, Georgie can. And I want to watch it."

I dragged Feldman out, Maxie shuffling along after me. He closed the door to the den. Myart's gaze flicked at Maxie, darted to me. "He wants Georgie," I said.

"Georgie's covering the service stairs," Myart said. "In the basement."

I rode the elevator down, all the way to the basement. I stepped out in the warm, dry, heavy shadows. My feet scraped and sent echoes over the cement floor.

I moved back toward the service entrance. "Georgie?"

He didn't answer, and I didn't see him. I opened my mouth to say his name again; then I saw him. Georgie was a big mass of flesh near the dark yawning mouth of the service stairs. I dropped to one knee beside him. He was breathing, but as unconscious as a guy could get, a lump like a golf ball on the side of his head. I felt it then, the faint, cold draft of an open window.

I spun around fast, wanting to get the wall at my back, my hand dipping toward my gun.

"Do it and die," a voice said.

I saw his face, hovering there in the shadows beside a boiler. He came toward me, a big gun stuck out in his fist. I tried to swallow and couldn't. I tried to tear my eyes from his face and couldn't.

"You'll take me up, Hilliard," he said, mouthing the words thickly. "You'll take me right up to Maxie."

"Listen, Meek, you can't do it! You'll never get out of the building alive."

"Do you think I care?" Roy Meek said. He was doped to the gills, the rims of his eyes like frozen trickles of blood. But maybe he wouldn't have needed the drug anyway.

"Do you know what it was like?" he whispered. "The same cell every day, every night. I had given her everything, my money, my very life, everything! I lived only to get out, to come back! No other man would ever have the pleasure of looking at that angel face and tawny hair again!"

Roy Meek looked at my face and laughed, so softly it was a bare whisper of sound in the stark basement. "Just take me to Maxie," he breathed dreamily. "One minute with Maxie—and then I'll never be sad again."

He herded me with the gun. I was breathing hard. My collar was limp with sweat. Into the elevator.

The elevator rose slowly. The fifteenth. Maxie's floor. "Open the door," Meek hissed.

I opened the door. He slammed me with the gun, and I stumbled out into Maxie's living room and fell to my knees.

Feldman wasn't in the same place where I'd left him. And I saw that Maxie's knuckles were covered with blood, and dimly I knew that Cecil Calhoun had crept out of the rumpus room. There must have been another tussle between Maxie and Feldman, and she had heard it, heard Maxie knocking Augie unconscious for the second time.

I tried to crawl to my feet. I got one glimpse of Maxie's face, like a blurred, frozen thing. Behind me, Meek was sobbing out laughter. "It's me doing it, rat! Me—Roy Meek!"

Then he began shooting. He shot Maxie four times. Myart had dived behind a couch. I had rolled out of the way, yelling to Calhoun to get down.

Then everything was silent. Meek whirled, leaped into the elevator, slammed the door, and the cage dropped away.

Myart came crawling out from behind the couch. Calhoun was helping me to my feet.

I stood up, shook my head to clear it. Myart snarled, "Get him, Steve! Get the stinking, hopped-up rat!"

Calhoun grabbed my arm, her face very intense. "Have you ever done anything like that before? Like killing a man on Myart's orders?"

"No," I said.

"Then it's not too late."

Staring into her face, thinking of all the blood and violence, I realized what she meant.

I said, "Myart, if you want Roy Meek go get him yourself."

I took Calhoun's arm, and led her out.

* * * *

A week later I was in Calhoun's house, showing her how to grill a steak.

"How's it going?" she asked.

"I've quit fighting the alarm clock every morning."

"That's fine. One of these days you'll own that brokerage house."

After we finished off the steak, she said, "I want to show you something." I followed her into her studio. She turned on a white, bright light. My heart skipped a beat as I looked at the waxen head on the table. "Melissa!" I said.

"I had to do it," she said. "It was inside my mind. It kept bothering me. I had to get it out."

I looked at the head a long time, thinking of Maxie who was dead and whose organization had ruptured at every seam like a rotten apple bursting. And I thought of Augie Feldman and of Roy Meek, whom the cops had cornered after he'd killed Maxie.

I saw then what Calhoun had done with the head; after a few minutes the head seemed to change, and beneath the soft oval face and tawny hair it seemed I could see the real Melissa, a death's head, a grinning skull. I don't know how Calhoun managed to get that in her piece of work, but I knew the head would be around a long time, to remind us, to make us remember…

HEIST IN PIANISSIMO

Originally published in Alfred Hitchcock's
Mystery Magazine, *May 1964.*

Judy put her hands over her ears. "I won't hear another word of it Davie! We're not criminals, you know."

In the moonlight beside the lake, she was a lovely, petite brunette. I took quick steps after her as she flounced her skirt and moved toward my jalopy, which was parked nearby.

"Okay, okay," I said. "Just pretend I never opened my big mouth."

I held the door for her to get in the car.

"The very idea, Davie, the two of us robbing the bank! Why, we come from decent respectable backgrounds. We've never had a mark against us, even when we were in our teens. We're about the last pair of young people anybody in town would associate with a bank robbery,"

I went around the car and got in. "I know," I said. "So forget it will you?"

She sneaked a look at me as I started the car, turned it around, and headed back toward town.

"Davie…" she said in the murmuring tone that indicated a mountain of thought behind a single word. Davie anticipated it.

"Uh-huh?"

"Whatever gave you the thought?"

"Oh, I don't know. Just wishing you and I could make with life while we're still young, I guess. Maybe it was looking at old man Peterson, your boss at the bank, or Mr. Harper at the hardware store. Tomorrow morning, for example, they'll be standing not six inches from the spot where they started standing thirty or forty years ago."

"Both our bosses are nice people, Davie. They've bought homes, raised families…"

"…And seen the same faces, talked the same talk, moved through the same routine day after day. They might as well be vegetables, Judy. One day or a million days adds up to the same for them. Because they've never lived. They've just existed in a kind of vacuum. Now it's too late for them. A few more years of the same malarkey and they'll be planted out in a marble orchard and somebody else will have moved into their same dull spots."

"It's best not to think about those things, Davie."

"Sometimes you can't help it," I said. "Not if there is somebody special that you want special things for."

She reached forward and turned on the car radio loud enough to drown out my voice. But we'd ridden less than half a mile when she turned it down again.

"Now mind you, Davie," she murmured. "I'm not planning on doing anything so crazy, but wouldn't it be wonderful if we woke up tomorrow morning or the next day and had fifty or sixty thousand dollars?"

"That's what I tried to point out, there at the lake," I said. "It isn't like we were turning into pathological criminals. We just do this one thing. We keep right on about our business until the furor over the robbery dies down. Then I tell Mr. Harper one day that I've got an offer of a job in California. We get married. Our friends give us a going-away party. We promise to write, but somehow we never do. You know how those things go.

"A few years from now, we won't even remember what this grubby mill town looks like. Instead, we'll have bought a business of our own, worked hard, and retired by the time we're thirty-five. Then we swim in Miami Beach, or play golf in Pasadena.

"I sure don't intend to squander the money, Judy. Just a break, the opportunity to get started, to make it for ourselves while we're young, that's all I was thinking about. It's no worse than the old financial barons who conspired to take oil lands from the Indians, or who entered political deals to use public domain for railroad right of way." I peeped at her without turning my head, and sighed. "'Course, I guess it was wishful thinking, like we all do at times, and I'm sorry I brought it up."

"It would be nice," Judy said. "Yes, it really would."

"If we had a kid or two, we could give them a decent chance, too." We rolled through the edges of town, toward Judy's house.

Suddenly, she reached and touched my hand. "Don't make the turn, Davie. I don't feel like going in. Let's go to the Jiffyburger and have a sandwich and a malt."

"Okay," I said.

At the drive-in, I found a spot not too close to other cars. We munched on hamburgers without saying anything for a while.

Then Judy stirred in her seat as if her muscles were cramped. "Davie—"

"Uh-huh?"

"It's true that about seventy-five thousand dollars will be in my cage Friday, because of the Landers Mills payday and all their payroll checks."

"I know," I said. "It's one thing that got me thinking."

"Well, I'm certainly not taken with your thieving ideas, Dave Hartshell! But…just making believe…how would you get the money out of the bank without the guard arresting you before you reached the front door?"

I slouched in the seat and took a big pull at my malt straw. "Oh, I'd pull the heist in pianissimo."

"In what?"

"Pianissimo, Judy. That's a music term. It means very softly. I'd take the money so softly the guard would smile as he held the door for me to leave the bank."

She pulled upright, leaned over to have a closer look at me.

"Davie, how would you go about keeping a bank robbery pian-what-ever-it-is."

"I'd prepare the Friday morning deposit from the store a little earlier than usual," I said "I'd bring it over to the bank just like always, in the leather and canvas money satchel.

"I'd pass the deposit over to you, Judy, like any other morning. Only when you got all through, I'd stroll out of the bank with the satchel crammed with the biggest denomination bills in your cage."

She jerked erect, bumping her head on the top of my jalopy. "Of all the nerve, Davie! Asking me to risk my reputation, everything…"

"You wouldn't risk a thing, honey," I said. "All the tune's in harmony, like in pianissimo. We fix up a note in advance, printed with crayon on a sheet of dime store paper, which we're careful not to get any fingerprints on. Except yours. You'll have to handle it."

"Davie, I do believe you've taken to secret drinking!"

"Just an occasional beer," I said. "This note, which you'll carry into the bank with you Friday morning, says, 'Hand over the money or I'll kill you on the spot.'

"After I'm out of the bank a half hour or so and the place starts getting crowded, you let the note flutter to the floor. Then you keel over in a real bad faint."

She was to the point now where she stared at me like she was helpless to move her eyes.

"I faint," she said finally.

"And right at first when you come around," I said, "you're kind of vague. Then it begins to come back to you. You get excited, and scared, and darn near hysterical. Since I'm young, slender, and dark, you ask them if they caught the middle-age, medium-built, ruddy man. Then they have found the note on the floor of your cage, and they say, 'Which man?' And you say, 'He slipped his coat open to show me a gun he was carrying. I put the money in a sack he handed to me. He slipped it under his coat. I tried to raise the alarm, but a terrible, empty blackness was rolling over me.'"

"A terrible, empty blackness," Judy said.

"You're the one girl I know who can really cool it, Judy. Then you leave it lay at that point Not too complicated. Not too much description."

"There's just one thing wrong with it, Davie. You remember the bank robbery a few months ago over in Conover?"

"Sure, That's what gave me the idea of…"

"The teller had to take a lie detector test, Davie. It's routine. They've anticipated the kind of thing you're planning."

"And I have anticipated *them*, doll," I said, feeling pretty good at the moment.

"Have you really?" Her voice was cool, and just a little pitying.

I didn't let the womanish attitude nettle me. Merely patted her small, sweet hand. "That's where Mr. Eggleston comes in," I said. "Eggleston?"

"An old gentleman I met in the Wee Barrel."

"Davie! I've practically *begged* you to stay out of that tavern on your way home from work!"

"This Eggleston is quite a guy," I said, warming to the subject. "Neat, unobtrusive man, with impeccable clothes. Never see him with a gray hair out of place."

"Well, I don't care to know any of the hangers-on in the Wee Barrel." Judy stuck her nose in the air. After a few seconds, it lowered slightly. "When did you fit him into your plan?"

"After I found out he'd once been a metaphysical therapist in Los Angeles."

"Sounds like he was a quack."

"But definitely, Judy. They finally ran him out of town. He's also rigged stock deals, sold salted mines, and headed up drives to raise funds for nonexistent charities."

"You seem to know him quite well, Davie," she said, a note of warning in her voice.

"Yeah, we got to be pretty close friends after he found out my girl friend worked in the bank."

"I guess you'll have to get the rest of it out of your system before you start the car, Davie. And it's too far for me to walk home."

"This Eggleston," I said, "when he was in the business of treating nervous and emotionally troubled people, he used a lot of hypnotism. He's really great with it Judy. You should see some of the stunts he pulls in the Wee Barrel. One night he gave Shorty Connors the post-hypnotic suggestion to stand on his head. And darned if Shorty didn't try to upend himself five minutes after he came out of the trance, just like Eggleston had told him."

"I begin to see the light," Judy said thinly.

"Sure, hon. That silly lie detector machine won't mean a thing. You'll face it under the influence of post hypnotic suggestion. The cops will hunt a non-existent robber and never suspect that..."

"I," she said, "am not the slightest bit interested."

* * * *

She called me at seven-thirty the next morning, a half-hour earlier than usual.

At five-thirty that afternoon, we entered Mr. Eggleston's hotel room together.

Mr. Eggleston made a small bow when I introduced him. "David, she is every bit as lovely as you stated. It is indeed a pleasure to know you, my dear Judy. May I call room service and get you anything? Perhaps an aperitif?"

"No, thanks."

"No need to be nervous, my dear. The process is painless. You will in fact, feel more relaxed than you have in quite a while."

"Let's just get it over with," Judy said, worrying her small handbag in her hands.

"Quite."

Mr. Eggleston crossed the room, partially closed the blinds, and motioned toward a big easy chair.

Judy sat down like she was forcing her knees to bend. Mr. Eggleston stood smiling and quiet before her.

"To be wholly successful, my dear, I must have your total cooperation. Put yourself in my hands completely."

Judy gulped slightly. I thought she was going to back out. But she must have thought of all the money that would be in her teller's cage tomorrow.

Mr. Eggleston's manner was gentle and comforting. He drew a light occasional chair close to her and sat down. From his pocket, he took a shiny piece of metal about the size of a quarter.

"Focus your eyes on the coin. Judy, and blank your mind... Relax completely... Offer no resistance... It is so pleasant to relax..."

He continued to talk soothingly. Judy's lids began to droop.

"You are sleepy, my dear... So gently and delightfully sleepy... Sleep... You are going to sleep... How pleasant to sleep... You are asleep, Judy...deeply asleep...very deeply, Judy."

Mr. Eggleston began to draw away from her slowly. "You are in a deep, deep trance, Judy. You will remain in this trance until I count to three and snap my fingers."

My throat was starting to get a little dry. I evenly shifted from one foot to the other.

Mr. Eggleston glanced at me. "She's a most interesting subject, David. A very wonderful subject. Proof of her intelligence. The moron cannot be hypnotized, you know."

He returned his attention to Judy. "When at last I count to three and snap my fingers, Judy, you will awaken from the trance immediately. Your conscious mind will remember nothing. To your conscious mind it will seem as if you have merely drifted off for a few seconds. But your subconscious will retain everything that is done during the trance to prepare you psychologically and physiologically for what is ahead. Is all this clear?"

"Yes, it is." Judy's voice was so everydayish and normal that I wondered for a second if she was faking the trance. But I knew better. There'd be no point in it. And I remembered how natural Shorty Connors had sounded while Mr. Eggleston had him under.

"Now, Judy," Mr. Eggleston said, "there are a few things we must understand and make clear at the outset. There is nothing magical or supernatural in what we are doing. I can merely assist you. I cannot force you to do anything which you are absolutely determined not to do. For example, I could not force you to remove your clothing in the public square unless you had, in the secret depths of your personality, an exhibitionist urge to do such a thing. Do you understand?"

"Yes."

"If you could stretch a moral point and obtain a great deal of money without injuring anyone, would you do so?"

"Why not?"

"Would you tell a straight-out lie for ten dollars?"

"No."

"A hundred dollars?"

Judy didn't hesitate. "No."

"A thousand dollars?"

Judy hesitated.

"Fifty thousand dollars?" Mr. Eggleston persisted.

Judy rushed the answer: "Any day in the week! Just any old day!" Mr. Eggleston glanced at me with a satisfied smile, which I returned rather weakly while wiping beads of perspiration from my face.

Then Mr. Eggleston returned to his subject: "Judy, since you are a bright and intelligent girl, I'm sure you know the basic principle of the lie detector. When a person tells a lie, he or she experiences a slight rise in pulse rate, heart beat, blood pressure. The graph registers these changes and the operator of the machine determines if a person has told the truth."

"I understand," Judy said.

"Good. The reason for these physiological changes lie in the psyche, the subconscious. Mind over matter, so to speak."

"I understand," Judy repeated.

"But that is a two-way street, my dear. Isn't it? If the subconscious can control the pulse rate, the subconscious can also ignore it. Tomorrow you will tell a lie in police headquarters. Your conscious mind will recognize it as a lie. But to your subconscious, in that instant, it will not matter. That is the whole crux of the thing, Judy. It's simple. Very simple. Your subconscious will not care one whit whether or not you have told a lie on that single subject." Mr. Eggleston's voice became a soft, but insistent lash. "Your subconscious will experience a momentary moral lapse when you describe the man who robbed the bank. Hence, you will exhibit none of the physiological symptoms for the graph to record. Repeat after me, Judy: It will not matter whether I am lying about the description of the bank robber."

"It—will—not—matter—"

"You must accept this thought in such a way as to be comfortable, Judy. Are you comfortable?"

"Yes."

"Good. Now we shall awaken. One…two…three…"

I started slightly when his fingers snapped.

Judy opened her eyes, gazed at me blankly a moment, then looked at Mr. Eggleston.

He was paying her no attention. "David, tomorrow night at ten, I shall call at your rooming house for the five thousand dollars you've agreed to pay me."

Judy said, "I must have dozed off a second. When do we begin with this hypnotism?"

"We have finished with it," Eggleston smiled.

She frowned. "Is that true, Davie?"

I nodded.

"But I don't feel any different," Judy said. "Are you sure?"

"Positively," Mr. Eggleston said. He patted me on the shoulder. "And it's a brilliant idea, my boy, one I might have come up with myself!"

* * * *

I woke the next morning, Friday, with about two hours' total sleep during the preceding night. My stomach was jerky, and I nicked myself while shaving. I had a cup of coffee for an indigestible breakfast.

I walked around the block twice, waiting for the hardware store to open. Inside, I had the bank deposit prepared in record-breaking time. I had to kill several minutes arranging a display of fishing gear for the simple reason that I didn't think it wise to be the very first customer in the bank.

Feeling as if every eye in the grubby factory town was focused on me, I forced myself past the glass and brass doors of the bank. The guard, Mr. Sevier, was looking directly at me.

Normally, Mr. Sevier appears to me as a kindly middle-aged man with an elfin sort of face and tufts of white hair in his ears. Today, he grew horns; his skin was a threatening purple; there was brimstone in his slitted eyes.

"Good morning, Mr. Sevier."

"Nice to see you, Davie." He slapped me on the back as I passed.

Behind her teller's wicket Judy gave me a warm smile. She appeared to have slept quite well, and I wondered if maybe I shouldn't have let Mr. Eggleston put me under also.

I handed the heavy leather and canvas bag to Judy. She opened it checked the deposit.

Nobody paid any attention to my lingering at Judy's window. There was just enough early business to keep the other employees occupied. Anyhow, everyone in the bank knew that Judy and I were collecting pennies in a joint account toward the day we could be married.

With a nod that no one else noticed, she finally returned the satchel to me.

My heart started going like sixty. I felt as if the weight of the bag were pulling me to one side, making me walk out of the bank at a crazy angle.

I was almost at the doors when Judy called my name quietly.

I had to stop right beside Mr. Sevier.

"Don't forget lunch, Davie," Judy said.

"I won't."

She blew me a little kiss. Mr. Sevier chuckled fondly as he gave me a little punch on the shoulder.

I went to the parking lot half a block away and collapsed in my car.

I tugged my collar with my finger, got a lungful of air, started the car, and drove casually to the hardware store. By the time I parked behind the store, I'd transferred the money to the heavy brown paper bag and stuffed it under the seat of the car. I was practically twitching with nervous eagerness to count the money. Driving along with commonplace innocence, the important work taking place with my free hand below window level, I'd caught only glances of the neatly banded money. But I knew there was plenty. I'd never seen so many stacks of fifties and hundreds in one place in all my life—except in the bank. I was certainly grateful to Landers Mills for paying but twice a month, on the first and fifteenth.

I started to lock the car, then decided against it So far, everything was perfect. I'd driven directly from the bank, in plain view of the town. Judy and I were experiencing a routine, commonplace day. I wasn't in the habit of locking the jalopy this time of year. The money was safely out of sight I went into the store.

Fortunately, there were customers to help pass the morning. Even so, I had to make three trips to the gent's room inside of an hour.

Then at ten fifty-six by the clock on the far wall, which had a pendulum behind a fly-specked front that advertised Maney's Merrygrow Manure, the waiting was all over.

Like a well-fed, full-bosomed turkey with a gray topknot, Mrs. Threckle came to the door of the office, spoke my name, and motioned to me frantically.

I hurried to her. "What is it, Mrs. Threckle?"

"Terrible thing…" she gasped, "terrible…a bank robbery…They've got Judy at police headquarters…"

I had to grab the office door framing to keep from folding to the floor like a collapsing letter Z. This part wasn't an act, either. I thought wildly: They've caught her, and she's trying to protect me, going it alone…

"You poor, dear boy!" Mrs. Threckle said. "You must get down there right away. I'll explain to Mr. Harper."

I could think of several other directions more preferable. Then Mrs. Threckle saved me from a nervous breakdown.

"She hasn't been hurt Davie. There was no shooting. They've merely taken her down to get a description of the robber."

Several minutes later, a jalopy full of holdup money was parked in plain view in front of police headquarters. Inside the building there was turmoil. Each time I tried to stop a hurrying policeman, he would jerk his thumb over his shoulder, pointing deeper into the building. "Busy, bud."

Finally I spotted old Silas Garth ambling placidly from a doorway.

Silas has been on the force just about as long as the town has had a charter. He paused in the corridor, more intent on picking something from his teeth than picking up a bank robber.

"Mr. Garth…"

"Oh, hello there, Davie. Guess you're looking for Judy."

"Yes, sir. Is she…"

"Simmer down, son. She's fine. Come on back in the squad room and we'll have a game of checkers until Hoskins and Crowley and that lie detector technician are through with her."

Poor Judy, I thought. Going through hell, that's what.

"What happened, Mr. Garth?"

He shrugged as we walked down the corridor together. "Yegg came walking in, let Judy have a peep at a gun, gave her a second to read the note he shoved in her hand, and walked back out with about sixty-five thousand dollars in a brown paper bag."

"Yowie!" I yelped. "Sixty-five thou... Is there that much money in the world?"

"Shore is, Davie. And I'm feared this hoodlum made it out of town."

"How come you say that, Mr. Garth?"

"Judy—bless her darling heart—was so paralyzed with fright she couldn't give the alarm right away. And when she realized she was in no danger of the gun, she fainted dead away."

"But you said she was fine!"

He laid his hand on my arm. "She is now, Davie. Take it easy, will you?"

"Was she able to give them a description of the robber?"

"General is all. Middle-aged, ruddy, medium height, sort of heavy set. My opinion is, he's an old pro at the robbery game, Davie."

"How come you say that, Mr. Garth?"

The old man started putting checkers in their proper squares on a board that rested on a rickety card table. "We got ways of lifting prints nowadays from surfaces like paper. The note he handed Judy had no prints on it but hers. Reckon he knew his prints would identify him." Mr. Garth shook his head. "Be frank with you, Davie, lots of these yeggs get away with it, at least for one or two outings."

"You don't think they'll catch him?"

"I wouldn't make book on it, son. His chances decrease all the time, of course. Next time out, he may get caught and we'll break our case then."

"Mr. Garth, if you don't mind, I couldn't keep my mind on a checker game right now."

"Sure, Davie." He flung his arm about my shoulders. "We'll go upstairs, son, and see if we can't make it easier on that poor girl."

We went upstairs, and I sought a gent's room while Mr. Garth disappeared into an office. I was pacing the corridor when he opened the office door and came out behind Judy.

She ran straight to me, and I folded her in my arms.

Mr. Garth clucked affectionately. "Judy didn't stretch none of the details of the description, according to the polygraph, Davie. Now you take that girl down the street and buy her a cup of coffee."

I said, "Yes, sir, Mr. Garth!"

* * * *

Judy and I were still slightly delirious when Mr. Eggleston knocked on my door at ten o'clock that night.

He slipped in quickly, and I closed the door. He looked from me to Judy, a smile dividing his lean, hawkish face.

"Well, kids, we pulled it off!"

"We sure did, Mr. Eggleston, and your five thousand dollars is ready for you."

His eyes went frigid. He pulled a short-nosed gun from his side coat pocket.

"Wh-what is this, Mr. Eggleston?" It was the real thing.

"I've waited all my life for the really big one," he said. "Do you think I'd let a couple of hick kids stand in my way? Now get the money!"

"But Mr. Eggleston…"

"All of it! Now! If it hasn't occurred to you, none of us can squeal without implicating himself."

I was unable to move or think for a second. "But if you shoot that gun, Mr. Eggleston, somebody will hear it."

"And you'll be dead. I'm offering you a deal, Davie. Two lives for the money."

"You're crazy," I said.

"No—and don't let the money destroy your sanity, kid. If I shoot the gun, I'll have a good chance of getting away. You won't have any chances, period. I'm willing to make the gamble, Davie. I'm too old, I've waited too long to let this final chance slip away from me."

His cheekbones began to turn white, and he added: "I'll give you ten seconds to make up your mind, David."

I didn't know Judy had risen. Now I felt her pressing against me. She shivered. "Davie…he is a little mad. He means it!"

"Sure I do," Eggleston said cold-bloodedly. "Six…five…four… three…"

"Give him the money, Davie," Judy sobbed, holding onto me wildly.

"In the closet," I said numbly. "The small valise."

Everything around me had a kind of swimming quality. Mr.

Eggleston floated to the closet, the valise floated to his hand. He flipped the catch, peeked quickly inside, pressed it closed with his left hand. The gun still on us in his right hand, he floated out the door.

Judy didn't have to work the next day, it being Saturday. I called the store and reported I was too sick to work.

But I was there bright and early Monday morning. There's no better way to impress an employer than being prompt, when you finally decide you're going to be stuck in a job for a mighty long time.

REWARD FOR GENIUS

Originally published in **Alfred Hitchcock's Mystery Magazine**, *Nov. 1965.*

Cletus Higgins sampled the glitter of Florida sunlight, unwillingly cracking his eyelids as someone banged on the door of his cottage.

"Hey, Clete! You in there? I got to see you, Clete." The voice from outside belonged to Perky Bersom who knew better than to call during the afternoon hour Cletus reserved for siesta.

Cletus turned on his lumpy daybed, making no movement to rise. "Go away," he said.

"Clete, this is urgent," Perky pleaded from outside. "I haven't a minute to waste. Let me in!"

"You are a boorish bourgeois," Clete said, eyes closed, "and I will have no truck with you."

"But I have a commission for you, Clete. You want to make five hundred dollars?"

Clete's eyes flipped open. He didn't exactly spring to his feet, but there was no hesitancy in his action as he rose from the daybed.

Clothed in barefoot sandals, rumpled cotton pants and dingy T-shirt with a slight rip in the right shoulder, Cletus stood tall and lanky. His face was a weathered collection of aquiline features in a nest of wild, fearsome black beard and hair.

Clete made his way toward the door through a clutter and disarray that would have driven even a Picasso to the chore of housekeeping. Canvasses, paints, brushes, palettes, easels were mingled with pieces of junk, rumpled clothing, dirty dishes, bean cans, bread wrappers; it was as if a capricious wind had stirred the contents of the cottage for days on end and then raced off when nothing more could be misplaced.

Perky was all set to rattle the hinges when Cletus yanked the door open. He lowered his upraised knuckles and shoved into the cottage. Under his left arm, Perky awkwardly carried a package, wrapped in brown paper, that was thin but large in its perimeter dimensions.

Cletus recognized stress when he saw it. Normally, an action such as breaking into another person's siesta would have brought a sheepish grin and mumbled apology from Perky. But not today. Instead, he shoved aside some dirty dishes, dropped his package on the table, and knuckled sweat off his forehead. "Boy, am I glad you were home!"

"What's this about five centuries of bread?" Cletus asked. He regarded Perky remotely.

Perky and his wife, Lisa, lived a few miles down the beach, where the real estate was much less overrun with mangrove and palmetto, and considerably more valuable. Cletus had a private word to describe the pair. Images. Images from perfect little molds. Perky was boyishly handsome, and Lisa was lovely. Their beach house was small, but it was a sterile page from a decorator's magazine. They lived within the limits of the income from a small trust fund which Perky's father had set up. They devoted all their time to sophisticated little parties, sailing, swimming, bridge, teas, and chit-chat. They exercised religiously, dieted carefully, and took their vitamin pills punctually.

For some time now, Perky and Lisa, who had met Cletus when he'd had a one-man show in Sarasota, had frequently included the artist in their guest list. Cletus Higgins was unique; he was atmosphere; he was color. Perky and Lisa were as proud of him as they were of the modest, but shiny cabin cruiser bobbing at their private dock.

To Cletus, neither of the pair was quite real; merely porcelain images incubated in the kiln of an affluent society.

Recovering his breath and containing his anxiety, Perky slipped a Florentine silver case from the pocket of his natty slacks, chose a cigarette for himself, and extended the case.

Cletus helped himself to three cigarettes. Two of the butts almost disappeared in the black mane when he stashed one over each ear. The third he thrust between thin lips that were surrounded by a black thicket and waited impatiently for Perky to offer a light.

"You're taking a long time to get down to cases," Cletus said.

"I'm trying to think how to start. It's the wildest thing ever happened to me." Perky snapped a lighter and held it forward, careful of Clete's beard. "It's—I want you to do a portrait. Without a model. From another portrait that isn't all there."

Cletus gave him a look. Perky took a nervous drag on his cigarette. "Maybe I'd better start back at the beginning."

"Sounds reasonable. By all means proceed. You've ruined my siesta with an offer of five hundred dollars for what sounds like an impossible task."

"I'm sure you can do it. You've got to do it, Clete!"

"Really? While I never sneer at bread, five hundred isn't entirely vital to me."

"I didn't mean it that way," Perky said with alarm touching his voice. "I'm relying on your friendship. You're the only person who can help me."

"Then let us explore your woes," Clete said. He scuffed toward the kitchenette and began rattling dirty pots in the sink as he collected the various component parts of a percolator.

Tagging along, Perky talked while Clete began preparations to make coffee in an old percolator.

"I have a cousin, Clete. She's several years older than I. Her name is Melanie Sutton."

"I've heard you and Lisa speak of her," Clete said. "She's the one who's filthy with boodle."

"She can buy yachts like I would buy canoes."

"Hand me the coffee, will you? Not that can. It's full of secondhand grease. That's the one."

"Cousin Melanie's folks are all dead," Perky said. "I'm the nearest of kin, surviving."

Cletus dumped coffee into the basket and set the percolator on the two-burner hot plate.

"We haven't seen Cousin Melanie in several years," Perky went on. "She was educated in Europe, and has a decided affinity for the continent She returns to this country only occasionally."

"I take it that one of those occasions is in prospect."

"She phoned us less than an hour ago," Perky said "She had to fly to New York to talk to some corporation lawyers, and decided it's the right season for some Florida sun. She'll be dropping in on us by the end of the week, which doesn't give you much time, Clete."

"Time for what?"

"I'm coming to that. The minute Cousin Melanie hung up, Lisa and I thought of the picture."

"Picture? What picture?"

"Cousin Melanie's portrait. She sent it to us from Paris three, four years ago. If she paid the artist anything at all, she got rooked. The portrait's an abomination. We never did hang it."

"But now," Clete said, "you decided you'd better hang the rich relative in the choicest spot in your living room."

"You're dead right." Perky frantically lighted a fresh cigarette from his first one. "Lisa and I—well, frankly, the way we have to pinch pennies— Cousin Melanie's money…"

"I'm with it," Clete said, "and I can't blame you for stammering, I suppose. You can't afford to do the slightest thing to offend the rich relative."

"I'd take a chance on swimming in sharky waters if she insisted," Perky admitted.

"So why don't you hang her?"

"We can't."

"Why not?"

"She's ruined," Perky said bitterly. "From the day we got it, Cousin Melanie's portrait has been in the storage room adjacent to our carport. These Florida insects and an audacious rodent have dined royally. Maybe there was some glue or sizing in the canvas that attracted them." Perky shuddered and rolled his eyes heavenward. "If Cousin Melanie ever finds out the manner in which we treated her portrait, she'll draw her own strong conclusions about the way we feel about her. We'll never see the first copper of her money. It will all probably wind up in the hands of some Swiss charity!"

Clete shook stale coffee from a cracked cup and poured himself a helping from the steaming percolator. He carried it into the outer room of the cottage with Perky dogging his heels.

At the cluttered table, Clete ripped string and brown paper from the package which Perky had brought with him. The package, Clete noted, contained two likenesses of Cousin Melanie, a nine-inch by twelve-inch photograph and the desecrated two by three feet painting in oil.

While the face had escaped destruction, the portrait showed obvious signs of careless neglect. A mouse had nibbled the corners. Bug and larvae had burrowed into the board. Moisture and mildew had left stained spots.

Clete surmised that Perky had slipped the photograph from a frame prior to bringing it here. The photo held Clete's attention. Cousin Melanie was not a beautiful woman, but she was patrician, with a finely cut face framed in white hair. The features had that small, firm quality that remained tenaciously young looking, making the hair seem prematurely gray, though it was the real key to her years.

The feature that struck Clete's artistic sense most forcibly was Cousin Melanie's neck. It was amazingly long, delicate, even fragile looking, but it held not a hint of stringy awkwardness. Truly, Clete thought, it was a rare neck, the kind that poets of old rapturously called swan-like.

Perky was literally jittering from one foot to the other. "Well? How quickly can you copy the portrait?"

"I don't know that I can," Clete said. "It's an unholy horror as a work of art, flat, two-dimensional. I'm not sure I can paint so badly."

"But you've got to try!" Perky begged. "She's got to believe that her picture has never been off our living room wall."

Clete dropped the portrait on the table. He gave a derisive laugh that wasn't directed at Perky. Instead, it seemed to be for himself and his cottage and the years that were behind him.

"At least. Perky, our conspiracy has a new wrinkle. Many artists have copied masterworks, but I'm sure I'm the first to copy, for such a purpose, an artistic abortion!"

Perky yanked out a handkerchief and mopped his face and neck. "I can never thank you sufficiently, Clete, old boy."

"Yes, you can. Just write the check. And understand one thing; I guarantee nothing. I'll do my best, but I can't promise to succeed in reproducing a portrait so lifeless."

Perky had more cajoling words of pep talk, but Clete took him by the arm and ushered him out.

Clete sketched in the background, when he'd set up easel and canvas, in a matter of minutes. The rest became a nightmare. By the week's end, he had ruined three canvasses. But in the fourth, he believed he'd produced a copy that would pass the rich relative's inspection. He phoned Perky Bersom and told him to buy a frame.

Then Clete drank a tenth of Scotch and retired to his daybed to sleep around the clock. His exhausted brain purged itself while he slept. Lifeless portraits slipped and wheeled in and out of his dreams. They overlaid and obscured the image of a long, delicate, swan-like neck.

* * * *

The party was one of those small, informal, and entirely happy affairs for which the Bersoms had a long-practiced knack. The aroma of fine barbecue wafted across the patio. Excellent stereo music murmured from the tasteful beach cottage. The landscaping of tropical foliage combined with the background of Gulf and Florida sky to make the spot seem enchanted. Perky and Lisa were the perfect host and hostess. They knew how to choose a guest list, whom to mix.

As he walked from his dirty old sedan, Clete was spotted by Perky who rushed to meet him with a big grin. He punched Clete in the ribs with his elbow.

"Clete, old boy, you're a genius."

"I know," Clete said without superiority. "I take it the portrait passed inspection."

"The minute Cousin Melanie arrived," Perky said, "she spotted the picture. She couldn't have missed it, in the spot I'd chosen for hanging and lighting. She was so overwhelmed by the compliment that she got a little misty-eyed. Clete, old boy, we're in solid with her. Real nice and solid."

"I'm glad I was able to help."

"Help? My friend, we'd be sunk without you! Remind me to put another century of bread in your bank account, as a bonus."

"The worker is grateful for his hire," Clete, said in a slightly insulting tone, "but I sure won't forget to remind you."

"Great." Perky slapped him on the back. "Now, how about a drink? Your usual? And this barbecue is the finest the caterers have ever turned for us."

Clete knew most of the guests, beach neighbors of Perky's and Lisa's. He drifted, passing small talk, sipping his drink.

Fifteen minutes later, Cousin Melanie came out of the cottage, entering the patio from the Florida room. She was slim, trim, youthful despite her years, as her photograph had suggested.

Clete's gaze immediately centered on her neck. Wearing a simple cotton dress, with her neck fully revealed, she turned this way and that in her progress across the patio, smiling and speaking to people. She was obscured now and then from Clete's view as Perky introduced her to strangers. Finally, nothing lay between Clete and Cousin Melanie except Perky's shadow.

Perky was leading her forward. He cleared his throat "And this is Cletus Higgins, Melly, the artist of whom I've spoken."

Clete and Cousin Melanie exchanged helloes.

"Cousin Melly." Perky said, "has an artistic interest."

"How nice," Clete murmured through cold lips. "How very nice."

"I act a bit," she confessed with a smile. "Too often I have to buy a play to find a vehicle, which indicates, I'm afraid, that I'm a very bad actress. But if one has the money, I say, one should make use of it oneself."

"I'm sure one should," Clete said coolly.

Clete's tone brought a briefly worried look from Perky. But Cousin Melanie and Clete were both ignoring him, and Perky drifted with backward glances toward his other guests.

"Tell me about it," Clete suggested.

Cousin Melanie laughed, joining Clete as he seated himself on a redwood bench beneath a multi-colored umbrella.

"There isn't much to tell, really," she said. "In Italy, Spain, France you can always find money-hungry producers. I enjoy acting, even if I am— lousy, as you would say on this side of the Atlantic."

Clete sat as if hypnotized by the hollow of her throat "You seem to have a rare honesty," he murmured.

"Why not? If I get a certain satisfaction from my avocation, who gets hurt? No one. On the contrary, each little play in each little theater makes work for a number of people."

Clete picked up her hands, turning them slowly, looking at them. Then his gaze returned to her neck.

"I'm going to paint you," he said.

She was poised for a moment, her pulse beating like a bird's as she tried to study his face, fathom his eyes. Then she relaxed and smiled. "Are you?"

"A portrait," Clete said, "head and shoulders. A real work, nothing like the atrocity Perky has hanging in his living room."

"And what is your commission for such a work?"

He pushed her hands away almost roughly. "No commission. I thought you would understand."

She was silent a moment. Then she half lifted her hand. "I'm sorry. I am very sorry. When would you like me to begin sitting?"

"Tomorrow morning at ten o'clock. I live several miles down the beach. Perky will tell you how to get there."

Clete got up, walked directly to his car, and drove away.

* * * *

The next morning at ten, red-eyed and pale. Clete looked as if he had substituted small, continual nips of Scotch for sleep during the whole of the night. His mass of beard and hair obscured much of the evidence, and his nerveless control did the rest Cousin Melanie blithely entered the cottage without noticing the clues to his mental state. Instead, the unbelievable disarray of the cottage captured her immediate attention.

"You," she said with a laugh, "have created a room straight from the left bank, here on the sunny shores of Florida."

Clete reached behind himself, flipping the latch, locking the door. "Sit there, please."

She gave him the grin of a gamin on a lark, crossed to a straight chair, and sat down. She was silent as Clete walked around her slowly, three times.

"I didn't believe it at first," he said. "It simply wasn't reasonable. All night long I wrestled with the problem of it."

She began to frown. "What in the world are you talking about?"

"It was as if my artistic senses had gone haywire," he said. "My genius was playing me false. But no! My perceptions are still true."

She came out of the chair slowly. "I think we had better postpone this, or cancel the idea entirely. Perhaps we can discuss it sometime when you haven't been drinking."

"Who are you?" Clete asked.

"I've no earthly idea what you're talking about. Let me pass, please."

"Who are you?" Clete shouted.

Real fright flared in her eyes. She ducked around him and made for the door. Clete caught her before she could reach it. He grabbed her arm and spun her about.

She had an unusual resistance to panic. "You'd better think what you're doing," she said. "Release me and open the door this instant and I won't report you. Otherwise, it will go hard for…"

Clete made an animal sound in his throat, suddenly and without warning twisted her arm. She was wheeled into a helpless position, frozen in a hammerlock. With his free hand, Clete scooped the hair from the side of her face.

"Only a tiny, threadlike scar," he said. "The plastic surgeon didn't have to do much, did he?"

"You're mad!" she gasped. "You shall pay for this!"

He jerked her away from the door and shoved her across the room. She half fell on the protesting daybed and remained there, supporting herself with her hands on the edge of the railing.

"I don't suppose I need to ask you a third time," he said. He loomed over her, hands on hips. "You were probably an understudy, a double to begin with, searched out with her money, through the talent agencies of Europe. Then later, a bit of plastic surgery and you were her identical twin— except for one thing. So the question now is: What happened to the real Melanie Sutton, the rich old babe with the theater bug? How did you kill her? What did you do with her?"

"I don't know what you're talking about! Move aside or I'll start screaming."

"Go ahead and scream," he said relentlessly, "and we'll tell the whole world why. I'll give you three safe seconds in which to scream."

He waited. Both remained silent, the woman crouching on the edge of the daybed.

"Where is the real Melanie Sutton?" he insisted. "At the bottom of an Alpine crevasse? Feeding the fish off the south of France?"

She stirred, finally, "How did you know?"

"Your neck. The conniving, money-hungry plastic surgeon could not very well change the length of your neck, so it is far too short."

"My neck…" she raised her hand slowly to her throat.

"Possibly no one else in all the world would ever have noticed," Clete said. "But I labored over the depicted image of Melanie Sutton for endless hours. When I saw you, I knew instantly, even though it took me all night to believe it, to admit it."

"I should never have come here," she said, "but I had to. The corporation lawyers in New York were faintly puzzled by a thing or two I said and did. I was playing the role of ever-loving elder cousin. They would have become downright suspicious if I'd refused the opportunity to drop by and see my closest surviving relative, Perky boy and his wife. So I had to come. I believed I could carry it off here as well as I did in New York. I'd studied

Melanie Sutton and her affairs from close range for a long time. I knew everything there was to know about her—except that her cousin had you for a friend."

"Now I shall live and paint," Clete said, "away from all this. I am now a painter with a liberal patroness."

She came to her feet almost shyly. "And if I am to be your patroness, how do I know I can trust you?"

"You'll simply have to take my word."

"Your word—yes, I suppose I must. You wish me to mail you your first check today?"

"And once a month thereafter," Clete said, "for so long as you live. A thousand a month will do nicely."

* * * *

The woman was quite composed when she stopped her car in the Bersom driveway. Perky came bouncing out to meet her.

"How did it go, Cousin Melly?"

"Not too badly, but I decided not to sit for any more portraits." She remained behind the wheel of the car, giving him such a sudden, intent look that the smile eased from his lips.

"Perky, I know this isn't talked in polite family circles, but I want an honest confidential answer, just between the two of us. In an acute crisis, to what lengths would you go to insure your eventual inheritance of my fortune?"

The thing in her eyes got through to Perky. His playboy aura seemed to fall away. He became bone and sinew, with the eyes of a hungry, prowling cougar. "I think I would even murder," he said with cool honesty.

The woman behind the wheel looked far down the beach. Then she turned, got out of the car. "My dear boy," she said fondly, "your answer couldn't have pleased me more…"

MIND THE POSIES

Originally published in **Alfred Hitchcock's**
Mystery Magazine, *June 1965.*

No believer in miracles, Mrs. Hester Bennett could not fully account for her husband's new interest in life.

Claude's heart attack had been severe, and without any prior warning. He had been coming up the front walk late one afternoon, an old man with iron gray hair who still retained some of his earthy, brutish handsomeness. He'd staggered, clutched his chest, crumpled, looked as if he'd died instantly.

But he hadn't. Not quite. For endlessly long hours Claude's life had been measured by the successive weak pulse beats which never quite stopped.

Hester had remained at Claude's hospital bedside, never taking her eyes for very long from the gray face canopied by the clear plastic oxygen tent, until the doctor told her the crisis was finally past. A man steeped in bitter solitude had come home, shuffling and looking about the solidly comfortable house as if everything were new and strange to him.

To Hester's queries he gave the same, short answer, "I'm fine!" He took his prescribed rests with the secretive inner rebellion of a small boy. He ate the flat salt-free food stolidly, cramming it into his mouth as if he had a strange sort of derision and loathing for himself.

The rapport built by thirty-five years of marriage was broken. Unable to communicate with Claude, Hester mechanically continued her routine of flower gardening and conscientious housekeeping.

Once, as she was arranging a vase of yellow roses, Claude had entered the living room unknown to her. His voice had startled her. "Why do you bother?" he said. "They'll only die."

He'd turned and left the room without waiting for her answer. And she'd bit her lip, feeling the emptiness and desolation of the house. The attack has left him with traumatic scars as well as physical ones, she'd thought, but they will pass; after all, thirty-five years of marriage does mean something; the scars will all pass.

The passing, when it had come, had been swift, almost as sudden as the attack that had struck Claude a low blow.

He'd returned to the supervision of his small plastics manufacturing plant for want of something better to do. It gave him escape from the house, from windows that seemed to draw his gaze toward a certain spot on the front walk. He came and went, a tall, rawboned giant of a shadow.

And then one afternoon Hester came in from her flower garden and heard Claude humming in the bedroom. She let the basket slide from her hand to the kitchen table. A tremulous expression crossed her faded, wrinkled lips. A light struggled for life in her tired blue eyes. Claude's humming was off-key, but to Hester, it filled the house with a sweeter sound than the singing of the birds who flitted about their bath at the edge of her flower garden.

Controlling the emotion that surged up in her, Hester went casually to the bedroom. Claude was at the dressing table mirror, bending slightly as he knotted a bright, striped necktie, one she had never seen before. He was impeccable in a freshly pressed suit, the iron gray hair brushed against his temples. There was even color in his face, making him look twenty years younger. Something about his appearance and manner disconcerted Hester. She felt drab and old.

"I didn't hear you come in," she said. "Do you want an early dinner?"

His humming broke off. He looked at her reflection in the mirror. He didn't bother to turn, and she had the feeling that the mirrored reflection of her was enough for him.

"I won't be here, Hester," Claude said. "I'm hiring a new man at the plant, a junior exec, and I'll be taking him to dinner. A man reveals himself, you know, in his choice of manner of food and drink."

She didn't know, but she supposed it was true. For thirty-five years she had waxed floors, pressed draperies, seen to the plentiful supply of snowy white shirts, paired socks, and, in accordance with his wishes, left the running of the business to Claude.

Hester drifted to sleep over a book that night, and was awakened by the hissing sound of the shower the next morning. Maudie, the cook-maid, was putting breakfast on the table when Hester went into the nook off the kitchen.

Claude entered, looking fresher and more agile than he had in years. With a nod toward the room in general, he sat down and spread his morning paper.

"Did you hire the new man, Claude?" Hester asked.

"What?" he said behind the paper.

"The fellow you took to dinner."

"Oh. Him. No, I don't think he'll do. Have to keep looking."

"Claude…" she hesitated.

"Yes? Well, what is it?"

"Why don't you bring them home? For dinner. The applicants for the executive position, I mean."

The paper rattled as he lowered it. He gave her a brief look, as if she had gone slightly daft. Then he shook out the paper and turned to another page.

"You might think about it," she said.

"Sure," Claude said. "I will. But it would be a lot of bother."

"I wouldn't mind."

"Well, all right," he said shortly. "I told you I'd think about it." During the morning, Hester kept herself desperately busy plotting a new flower bed. But her thoughts kept returning to Claude's disdainful impatience with her.

In their long marriage, disagreements had been inevitable. But never before had Hester been ridden with this feeling of being shut out, of being a mere nothing in Claude's eyes. The husband she'd known seemed to have passed from her, really, during that frightful heart attack.

Hester looked toward the house, realizing that Maudie had been calling her name.

"'Phone for you, Mrs. Bennett," Maudie said.

Removing her heavy cotton gloves with their earth stains, Hester went into the house. From the living room came the whirr of the vacuum cleaner under Maudie's guidance.

The kitchen extension phone was dangling from its cord, as Maudie had left it.

Hester lifted the phone and said, "Mrs. Bennett speaking."

"You don't know me," a thin, taut, male voice said, "and my name's not important. What I've got to say concerns your husband—and a girl."

"I don't believe I understand."

"She was my girl. At least I thought so, until a well-heeled old leech came along."

Hester clutched the phone in a nerveless hand. The sound of the vacuum cleaner seemed to swell to an intolerable roar that filled the house, reverberated from the walls.

"What are you saying?" she said. "How dare you say such a thing!"

"Okay, lady, keep your head in the sand."

"I don't believe you!"

"So don't. But her name is Marylin Jordan, and the leech is fixing a hideaway for her right now on Taculla Lake. The real cool pad on the point."

"You must have made a mistake," Hester said desperately. "My husband is old and dangerously ill. You're suspecting the wrong man."

"It's more than suspicion, lady. She's a hungry, predatory cat and he's the rat she's been looking for."

"But he—"

"You know the saying, lady. No fool like an old one. Maybe he's just got to burn big before the wick sputters out."

Hester closed her eyes, swayed. "This is the cruelest kind of joke."

"Joke?" the voice became a shallow, humorless laugh. "Maybe so. On the both of us."

The line went dead. Hester lowered the phone slowly and looked at it as if it were a dream substance that would dissolve from her hand.

Stirring finally, Hester turned and walked to the living room. Maudie was rattling Venetian blinds with a cleaner attachment and made no sign of hearing when Hester spoke her name in her soft, normal tone.

"Maudie!" Hester repeated in a louder tone.

An amply-fleshed pouter pigeon, Maudie looked over her shoulder.

"I have some shopping to do," Hester said. "I may be gone a good part of the day."

Maudie nodded and returned her attention to her work.

* * * *

In her light car, Hester drove out of the city without haste. She didn't enjoy driving. And this was all so silly and useless. She really should turn back, she told herself. But the car seemed to have a will of its own. The city limits dropped behind.

Taculla Lake was a full hour's drive, away from civilization, over a secondary road of macadam. While a few families maintained year-round residences there, the lake mainly provided weekend retreats for those who could afford it. The lodges, widely separated to provide privacy, were mostly of an architectural design in keeping with the setting, with vaulted ceilings and long, railed galleries overlooking private docks for cruisers and small boats.

Hester reached the small village above the lake. There was a large store handling general merchandise, a filling station, a glass and brick building, jarringly out of place, that displayed boats and marine gear. And a small log building with a sign on the roof that read: Hiram Hyder, Real Estate.

Hester parked her car on the graveled area beside the real estate office. She got out, crossed the small porch, and entered a pleasant office paneled in wormy chestnut. The lone occupant was a heavyset man of middle age. In shirt sleeves, he was bent over a slightly cluttered desk. With the forefinger of his left hand he toyed with the few wisps of hair on an otherwise bald head, while he checked figures on an adding machine tape with a pencil in his right hand.

As the screen door sighed closed behind Hester, he glanced up, rose immediately, plucked a suit coat from the back of his chair, and put it on.

"Mr. Hyder?"

"Yes, what can I do for you?" He came around the desk to offer Hester a chair.

"I want to inquire about renting a lake house," she said.

"My specialty, Mrs…"

She ignored the hint to give her name. "I have one particular place in mind. The lodge on the point."

"Oh, you must mean the Thrasher place. Yes, that's a rare property to be on the rental market. Don't get many like that. The Thrashers decided to remain in Mexico City and figure the place would be better off with somebody in it." Hiram Hyder spread his pleasantly chubby hands. "Unfortunately, it's been taken."

"That's too bad," Hester said. "By whom? I may know them."

"A Mr. Joseph Smith. He came with his secretary, quite a lovely young woman." Hyder glanced away, cleared his throat, and moved behind his desk. "But I have one other place at the moment that might interest you."

"This Mr. Smith," Hester said. "A big man? Powerful frame? Slightly gaunt? Iron gray hair?"

Easing a covert look at Hester, Hyder's manner became guarded. "An exact description of the man. Why do you ask?"

There was one more question. Claude, she remembered, had taken pride in the uniqueness of his car. "Driving a convertible with a custom paint job?"

"As a matter of fact, yes. Is there something you wish to tell me about Mr. Smith?"

"No, Mr. Hyder, there is nothing I wish to say about him at all."

"About this other place…"

"I'm sure it wouldn't do at all, Mr. Hyder. Thank you for your time. Perhaps I'll call again." She escaped quickly, with a nod, a turn, a flight to her car.

* * * *

When Hester entered the house, Maudie was at the kitchen table sipping coffee and munching on a sweet roll. "Mr. Bennett called while you were out. Twice." Maudie lowered her roll without taking a bite. "You feel all right, Mrs. Bennett?"

"A little tired, a bit dizzy; the sun, the exertion of shopping."

Hester continued her flight, from kitchen to den, where she picked up the phone and dialed Claude's office.

"Where've you been?" he asked.

"Out. Just out…"

"Well, I wish you'd be on the ball when I need you."

She half closed her eyes. Thirty-five years on the ball, she thought Thirty-five years of being in an assigned place and on the ball. "What was it you wanted, Claude?"

"I'm not happy with Jerry Lawter's reports. I don't like the way things are going in the sales office downstate. I'm going down there myself and put some ginger in Jerry and staff. So pack me a bag, will you?"

"Of course, Claude. What will you need? One day bag? Two days?"

"Two days, at least," he said. "I'll be by in thirty minutes. I don't want to drive all night."

"I'll have the bag ready, Claude."

She had the luggage prepared, set at the foot of the bed, when he arrived.

He began stripping off his shirt, preparatory to showering and donning fresh clothing. She saw the excitement sparkling deep in his eyes, the almost frenzied movements of his hands.

"Haven't you anything better to do," he said suddenly and shortly, "than to stand there and gawk at me?"

A coldness washed over her, settling in her eyes. Looking at her, Claude made a movement expressing discomfort, turning away from her. "Sorry," he said. "But you know how it is, things fouled up in Jerry Lawter's office and all. You do understand."

"Yes, Claude, I understand."

She wandered out of the bedroom, through the house. She was at the living room looking out the windows, when Claude paused in the foyer, the packed suitcase in his hand. "Well," he said, a faint note of awkwardness in his tone, "mind the posies while I'm gone."

"Have a good trip," she said.

It was the end of conversation. She heard him go out. From the window, she saw him put the suitcase in the back seat of the car, which he'd parked at the curb. He got in the car and drove off. She stood at the window and watched it out of sight. Then she turned quietly, went into the den, closed the door, picked up the phone, and dialed the long distance operator.

When his secretary put the call through, Jerry Lawter's voice was filled with concern and anxiety. "Mrs. Bennett? It's not Claude? I mean, the boss hasn't…"

"No, Mr. Lawter. It's still very much touch and go with him. He should avoid undue excitement and alcohol as killing plagues, but as of this moment Claude is all right. The fact is, he just left here, saying he was on his way to see you."

"Fine," Jerry Lawter said more calmly, "I'll be glad to see him."

"You must give him a message, Mr. Lawter, immediately on arrival. He asked me at the last minute to pack for him. And I—I'm afraid I made a dreadful mistake. In the rush, I took the wrong pills from the medicine cabinet. Mr. Lawter…Claude is carrying useless headache pellets instead of the nitroglycerin pills so vitally necessary if he should have…if an attack… Three days… He'll be away three days…"

"I understand, Mrs. Bennett. I'll tell him the very instant he gets here."

"Thank you," Hester whispered. "Thank you very much."

She wasn't aware of moving, until she felt the hot afternoon sunlight on her face. She looked about the yard. A faint laugh came from her. Strange, she'd never before noticed how small and cramped the yard really was.

She crossed to the nearest flower bed and deliberately began pulling the plants out by the roots, one by one. She dropped each plant on the moist earth for a quick death in the sun.

THE FIVE YEAR CAPER

Originally published in **Alfred Hitchcock's**
Mystery Magazine, *August 1965.*

The day was uneventful, except for the incident that occurred as Henry Overby was preparing to close his teller's cage at the end of the working day.

As he was totaling the cash in his drawer, Henry had the sensation of being watched. He glanced up, and there was Mr. Joshua Tipton, the bank president himself, standing in the doorway of his impressive, walnut-paneled office, studying Henry.

Mr. Tipton, a gray-maned old lion, a banker's banker in the ancient tradition, rarely showed concern for anything so low on the evolutionary ladder as mere tellers. Awareness of Mr. Tipton's drawn-out and minute appraisal of Henry Overby seeped through the bank, until just about all of his fellow workers were stealing glances in Henry's direction.

Despite the accelerating nature of his pulse rate, Henry gave no outward sign of dismay. With a properly respectful inclination of his head in Mr. Tipton's direction, Henry continued working with his normal quiet, deft efficiency.

Work in neighboring cages came almost to a halt as Mr. Tipton took it upon himself to stroll all the way across the bank to Henry's window and stood there.

"How are you, Overby?" The austere, craggy countenance nodded cordially.

"I'm fine, Mr. Tipton. And you, sir?"

The president glanced through the wicket. "Have a good day?"

"Very good, I'm glad to report."

"A number of our customers seem to prefer you, Overby. They like to have you wait on them."

"I try to serve with dispatch, Mr. Tipton."

"A commendable attitude." He glanced sharply away from Henry, and work behind the other wickets resumed with vigor. Less severely, Mr. Tipton's eyes returned to Henry. "You've been with us for some time now, haven't you, Overby?"

"Five years, sir."

"A mere breaking-in period in the business of banking," Mr. Tipton said.

"But time alone," Henry ventured bravely, "is only one yardstick. There remains the diligence with which an employee applies himself."

Mr. Tipton's bushy brows quirked to attention. "Quite true. Taken much sick leave, Overby?"

"Never missed a day, sir."

The president studied Henry a moment longer, then cleared his throat. "Yes, well... Nice chatting with you, Overby."

"The pleasure was mine, Mr. Tipton."

* * * *

Henry was able to contain himself until he was alone in his neat, almost barren bachelor apartment. On his record player he put some very cool Brubeck and very torrid Rusty Warren and then, from the tenth which he'd purchased on the way home, poured himself a precise ounce of Scotch to celebrate the occasion. Unlike the slightly built, commonplace Overby of banking endeavors, Henry brazenly cracked back at Rusty, guffawing as he realized he'd topped the gag emitted by the tinny record player.

He danced his way to the kitchenette to stash the Scotch for future special occasions, a birthday ounce, a Christmas ounce, perhaps even two ounces at New Year's.

The usual covey of strutting and cooing pigeons were gathering on the window sill. Henry fed them generously with graham crackers, bran flakes, and bread crumbs.

"Eat hearty, pals," he told the fluttering flock, "toward the nearing day when it will be cake!"

Ah, yes, he thought as he began frying a thin hamburger for his dinner, Mr. Tipton's conversation today has but one meaning.

Mr. Darcy Featherstone, who was now cashier, was going to be made a vice-president of the bank. Everyone knew that. But until today there had been no indication of who might be elevated to the cashier's post.

As cashier, Henry thought, I'll enjoy complete trust, unquestioned access to that beautiful vault.

The culmination of five years of planning, working, and waiting was almost at hand. It made all Henry's past years seem remote and unreal. He could hardly remember the scrawny myopic little boy who, pushed from one unwilling relative to another after his parents had died, had long ago learned to keep his hungers, fears, and hopes to himself.

The day after he got his high school diploma, Henry had risen before dawn and crept from the house of the final relative, an uncle named Hiram. Henry had never turned back.

For the next couple of years, Henry had sampled the world, drifting and working odd jobs. A neat, polite, unobtrusive young man, he had been employed as a hardware clerk when he'd heard of the opening at the bank.

Applying for the job, he'd known he had impressed Mr. Joshua Tipton, then a vice president, as a fellow whose wants and needs were simple and few.

Little did he know, Henry chuckled as he flipped his dinner patty of ground beef.

After his loveless and vitamin-deficient childhood, Henry had a secret yearning for prestige so powerful that it occasionally boiled out of his subconscious in the form of dreams. Slumber might transform him briefly into a renowned statesman, or a famous philanthropist planning an Alice-in-wonderland community for orphaned children, or an eminent explorer pushing far up the Amazon.

But the fiber of Henry's agile mind was far too strong to be satisfied by mere dreams. Prestige, he analyzed, was possible to him only through material things, since he had little prospect of becoming a statesman, philanthropist, or explorer.

He lined his secret sights on four specific prestige symbols: an imposing home; membership in an exclusive country club; a big expensive automobile, and an expensive and somewhat snobbish wife with a family tree, even if she should turn out to be a bit plain.

It was not through choice that he placed the wife at the bottom of the list. He was simply realistic, accepting the natural order of things.

The prerequisite to Henry's needs was, of course, commonplace. Money, money, money: enough to take him far away, to a new name, to a beginning of life.

He'd had no hope of ever coming into so much money, even when he had gone to work at the bank. The position, at the outset, had attracted him for two reasons. A bank teller enjoyed more prestige than a hardware clerk. And he liked the feel of money, the thought of being surrounded daily by so much of it.

Then one day, he'd watched Mr. Darcy Featherstone go into the bank vault where fortunes, plural, were stacked. And the thought had come quite naturally to Henry's mind: If I were in Mr. Featherstone's position, I'd disappear one day, and when they started checking up they'd find I'd become a very rich man. In Mr. Featherstone's position, I could easily alter the record of the serial numbers of the large bills. With free run of the vault I could secrete the bills in my clothing, if I prepared the garments beforehand with hidden pockets and pouches, slip into my topcoat, bid everyone the usual goodbye for the day, and walk out of the bank as a veritable animated gold mine. I could break down the bills later in one part of the country, take the hoard to some nice little town in, say, Vermont. Who would think ever of looking for the boldest of bank robbers around a snooty Vermont country club?

Henry had been jarred out of his trance, a few beads of sweat on his forehead, by the impatient clearing of a customer's throat. The idea hadn't frightened Henry for very long. It became a part of him, another facet in that unknown portion of his personality. The bank vault, only a few yards from where he worked each day, became something more to Henry than mere case-hardened steel and flame-resistant alloys. With the passage of time, the vault assumed the aspects of a hiding place for Henry's own secret treasure trove; a personal depository just waiting the day when he could claim his fortune.

He was young. He had plenty of time. Eventually, efficient worker that he was, he had to be taken into the inner circle, from which he would have intimate and unsuspected association with the treasure. It was his one hope. It was surely worth waiting for.

Meanwhile, he had more than his salary to sustain him. Each day, he would be near his treasure. In a way, he would be watching over it. With a start, Henry came out of his money-spangled fog. Greasy black smoke was rising from the hard lump of scorched hamburger. Not only that, someone was knocking on the door of his apartment. He grabbed the frying pan, blistered his fingers, yelped, reached for a pot holder, and removed the pan to the sink. Then, sucking his burned fingers, he dashed for the door.

With a vacuous smile on her large, damp mouth, Miss Mavis Birdsong was standing in the corridor. She had moved into the building a few weeks previously. Ripened to the point of generosity in face and figure, she was a blonde with large, round blue eyes. There was just a little too much of her for Henry's taste, although he had accepted her friendship from the day she had moved in and crossed the hall to borrow a cup of sugar.

"Hi, Henry."

"Hello, Miss Birdsong."

She gave him a little pinch on the cheek. "Come on over. I made spaghetti like even the Italians wish they could make, more than I can handle by myself."

Henry thought of the charred mess in his frying pan. "Well, I... Fine."

She linked her arm with his, precluding any further hesitation on his part. "I even have wine to go with it."

"If you're sure it won't inconvenience you, if none of your other gentlemen callers...."

"Just a couple guys I know, Henry. But you're the only real gentleman in my life!"

In her apartment Mavis hummed in a throaty voice as she prepared his plate. "How goes it at the bank, Henry?"

"Okay. Well, excellent really."

"That's great. You get a promotion or something?"

"I think I'm going to. I—I'm sure they're going to make me cashier. It's been a long time coming, five years, but I'm certain I'll be more than amply rewarded." He gave a beatific sigh.

"Wonderful!"

Henry gave her a glance. For some reason or other, Miss Birdsong seemed slightly strained this evening.

"I'm afraid," Henry said, "I've bored you with nothing but talk of the bank."

"Not a bit I've enjoyed every minute."

* * * *

Henry woke bushy-tailed the next morning. He bounced out of bed, did his knee bends and twenty-five daily pushups with no more effort than bending a finger.

In the preparation of his breakfast, he grasped the skillet handle and flipped the eggs in a manner that would have brought the envy of a first-rate short order cook.

Even the date didn't bother him today: first day of the month, the day for cashing those endless payroll checks from textile and food processing plants in the area.

Henry made his customary prompt arrival at the bank. The blinds were still drawn on the double front doors, but he knew that Mr. Darcy Featherstone would have already arrived, met the guard, and unlocked.

Henry stepped inside. He promptly ceased all motion as a small, round object was jammed against his back.

"It's a gun, pal." A gritty voice behind Henry imparted the information.

Henry's gaze made a wild sweep of the bank. Judkins, the guard, with a lump on his head and no gun in his holster, was bending over a leather couch where Mr. Darcy Featherstone was recovering from a faint. Against the far wall, the bank's small complement of employees were lined up under the gun of a squat man who wore coveralls and a rubber monkey mask that covered his entire head.

In a similar overall-mask disguise, the man behind Henry herded him forward. "You can fill the sacks, chum."

"We're vegetarians," the second monkey face said. "We like lettuce. All that lettuce you got on hand to meet the payroll checks."

"Save it," the man behind Henry said. "Just be sure to watch them jerks so nothing goes wrong until we get the lettuce into her car." Her?

Henry had a queerly detached feeling. *Her*! Driving the getaway car. Waiting behind the wheel right now, engine at the ready, for her male partners to emerge from the bank loaded with loot Mavis Birdsong. Yes. It had to be. The men in coveralls and masks were the exact size and shape of the pair who had visited her. Her choice of apartments had been by design, as well as her friendship for Henry. She wanted him to tell her about the bank so that she and these two hoodlums could plan a despicable act. "Come on, come on," one of the robbers was snarling at Judkins, the guard. "Get the cashier on his feet and about the business of opening the vault!"

"Right with you." Mr. Darcy Featherstone's voice was that of a whimpering child caught in a sepulchre.

Pressed forward by the man behind him, Henry watched the teller's cages swimming toward him. From the corner of his vision, he saw Mr. Featherstone cravenly rushing toward the vault. Mr. Featherstone was going to open the vault. And these unspeakable usurpers, the greedy pigs in monkey faces, were going to take, in a matter of minutes, the treasure to which he, Henry Overby, had been willing to devote years of his very life.

A wild shriek came from Henry's throat. He felt the hard pressure of the alarm button behind the teller's cages under his toe.

A bell began to clang. A gun blasted. A female employee screamed. Mr. Darcy Featherstone made a dull noise as he fainted and keeled over again.

Henry was vaguely aware of being in motion, the shrill yells still coming from his lips. He had a strange object in his hand which he'd scooped up from the shelf below and inside a teller's cage. He curled his forefinger, pointing the object, and the bank resounded with the blast of gunfire.

Then half the building seemed to fall on Henry's right shoulder. The process was instant. He blacked out.

* * * *

Henry returned to the realm of consciousness with a wince, a groan, a slow opening of his eyes. A doctor, a nurse, and Mr. Joshua Tipton, bank president, were hovering beside his hospital bed.

"Welcome back, Henry," Mr. Tipton said as if speaking to a son. "Did they...."

"They didn't, Henry," Mr. Tipton said. "When their deal soured, they broke and ran. Both got caught. Unfortunately for them, they were stranded on foot. When she heard the commotion, the blonde woman bolted in the get-away car. In her panic, she ran into a bridge abutment. But she was the only fatality."

"Better let him rest now," the doctor said.

"I'll give him something to rest on," Mr. Tipton said. "When you come back, Henry, you're through as a teller."

"I am?"

"The most miserable showing of Darcy Featherstone in a crisis has convinced me that he's not quite the man for the v-p post. Your experience and length of service, along with proof that still waters do run deep, qualify you for the job, I think."

"They do?"

"Welcome to our ranks, fellow executive. Mr. Vice-President!"

"Hmmm," said Henry. He squinted one eye in deep thought. In five years, he realized, he had come to like the bank. Except for that shrimp Darcy, the other employees were pretty nice. And Mr. Tipton…why, the old man had unsuspected emotions behind that leonine exterior!

"You have the personal interest we all must share in the great responsibility entrusted to us," Mr. Tipton was saying. "Even I, Overby, must take a lesson from your courage and intense personal devotion to our fine bank."

"You must?" Henry inquired. His thoughts skittered briefly on a tangent. After all, bank vice-presidents do belong to country clubs. They do buy imposing homes, being in a position to ferret out a bargain. A v-p can invest, handle his money wisely, even purchase a fine car, and court a slightly snobbish fruit off a fine old family tree, although she may be a bit plain.

Henry's ambition began to leap and dance. The mere thought of filching from the vault seemed puerile. Certainly it was unworthy of Henry Overby, vice-president, who in a few more years would very likely occupy the very office in which now Mr. Tipton reigned.

"Yes, Overby," Mr. Tipton's tone was an oratorical flourish. "We are proud to have a man with your sense of duty, your very personal regard for our noble institution. You expressed it fervently, Judkins reported, even if somewhat abstrusely."

"I did?" Henry said cautiously.

"Certainly, man! Don't you remember? As you went down under the gunman's bullet, you were yelling it at the top of your lungs. Overby, the heroic words you uttered were, precisely, 'You can't have the treasure out of my vault…my vault…my vault…'"

LONE WITNESS

Originally published in **Alfred Hitchcock's**
Mystery Magazine, *January 1966.*

Marco tingled with excitement and pure delight when Timothy Watkins came to him in a moment of extreme trouble. Marco didn't reveal these feelings. Instead, he ushered a disheveled Timothy into his apartment on a drizzly midnight with a show of concern and sympathy that appeared genuine.

After all, he and Timothy were supposed to be friends. Timothy's money, purchasing a chunk of Marco's foundering business, had bailed Marco out of deep financial difficulty. And like a true friend and honest man, Timothy had come straight to Marco when it appeared Miss Sharon Randall, a lovely brunette, preferred him over Marco.

When he opened his door on the man whom he secretly hated, Marco took in Timothy's appearance at a glance. Timothy was wet and muddy. His face had lost all color. His eyes were glazed, stricken, not quite in complete touch with reality.

Timothy, Marco knew, had had a dinner invitation from Miss Randall. Marco had spent the evening seething at the thought of the two of them alone in the intimate seclusion of her lakeside cottage.

A big, expansive sham of a man, Marco helped Timothy to the couch.

Timothy began mumbling a garbled apology. "No one else I could think of—had to tell someone; better leave…"

Timothy started to rise, but Marco pushed him back. "No nonsense, now," Marco said. He was so eager to know the nature of Timothy's trouble he would have locked the door to keep him here. "You did exactly right. Just relax and tell me what it's all about."

Timothy was incapable of relaxing. Marco crossed the room to the buffet, poured a stiff drink, and brought it to Timothy, who gulped gratefully, shuddered the liquor down straight, and a bit of color came to his face.

"Marco," he said in a whisper of suffering, "I've killed a man."

"What!"

"A stranger. A man I never saw before. Never knew he was there, hardly, until the car hit him."

All the bitterness went out of the evening, as far as Marco was concerned. He put on a front of gravity and trouble. He dropped beside Timothy and put his hand on the wiry, sandy man's shoulder. "Better tell me about it from the beginning, Timothy."

Timothy was miserably reluctant. "I don't want to involve..."

"More nonsense," Marco said, giving him a slight shake. "What are friends for, anyway?"

Timothy's need was so great and Marco so kind and understanding that Timothy's slate-gray eyes misted. "Miss Randall and I... We had cocktails before dinner and a couple drinks afterward. I left there pleasantly mild. Not drunk, but not completely sober either. Not knowing that a man's life would be in my hands..." He closed his eyes and shivered briefly.

"You were returning home from Miss Randall's, Timothy?"

"Yes, driving along, thinking of her, of our evening. I saw the truck stop at the intersection far ahead. It pulled away, and I know now that the driver had let a hitchhiker out. The truck was going no closer to town than the intersection. The hitchhiker was headed on this way.

"I—I didn't see him until I was through the intersection. He was just there, all of a sudden. On the edge of the road, flagging me for a ride.

"I slammed on the brakes and the car skidded slightly. Felt like it was going to flip over. I hadn't realized how fast I'd been driving.

"I jerked the steering wheel. The car slewed off the edge of the pavement, and I heard a bump, exactly like cold metal slapping meat and bone.

"When I managed to get the car stopped, I got out but I didn't see the hitchhiker. It was as if he'd been a mirage in the rainy night, an impression of a thin, slightly stooped guy in jeans and out-at-the-elbows jacket.

"Remembering the sound of that bump, I began to shake all over, I tell you! I grabbed the flashlight from the glove compartment, ran up the road..."

"And found him?"

"Yes," Timothy mourned, his head in his hands. "In a thicket down the embankment beside the road, his head all bloody—I knew he must be dead."

"How did you know? Did you go down and examine him?"

Timothy lifted his head slowly. "No, I—come to think of it the sight of so much blood—I panicked, I guess. Don't remember anything else clearly until I got here. But he couldn't have been alive with his head battered so badly."

"Did you leave any traces of yourself out there, anything that might link you to him?"

"I—I don't know," Timothy said.

"Then we'll have a look."

"Marco, I don't want to drag you in…"

"Forget it," Marco said, keeping his face averted so Timothy wouldn't see the glint in his eyes. "We're business partners, aren't we?"

Timothy stood up slowly. "You know, I always had the feeling you really didn't like me. Deep down, I mean. Well, after all, you might have felt I stole your girl."

"Come now, Timothy, give me credit for being a bigger person than that."

The highway was a dark, deserted ribbon of slippery black. Timothy slowly stopped his car. "Right over there, Marco," he whispered, although there was no reason for keeping his voice so low. "Across the road. I was heading in the other direction, you know, toward town."

Marco's' raincoat rustled as he shifted his bulk out of the car. He had the flashlight in his hand. "Leave the parking lights on, and if you see another car coming, get out and open the hood like you have car trouble."

"Marco…"

"I know. You can thank me later."

Marco went quickly across the highway and started down the slope. He moved below highway level, the flashlight probing a rough, sparsely-grown landscape. His excitement grew higher. Surely, this was the opportunity of a lifetime. He'd get his business and his girl back. Once he went through the motions of friendship, he'd have to go, finally, to the cops, wouldn't he, before Timothy had a chance to move the body? He had conscience, didn't he? He was a law-abiding citizen, wasn't he?

The topping on the cake was the knowledge that if Timothy had played it cool he might have got away with it. Now, he never would.

Irritation began to crowd the elation in Marco. The finger of light became more hurried in its movements. Where in blazes was the guy, the dead man who would return to Marco everything Timothy had taken? The light swung across the heaviest of the thickets. Stopped. Returned.

Marco moved forward, holding the light steady. He cursed under his breath. Clearly, this was the place where the hitchhiker had landed, where Timothy had seen him. There were freshly broken twigs, an impression where a man's body had lain. The wet leaves had been disturbed where the hitchhiker had dragged himself away.

With a growing sense of having been cheated, Marco moved the light slowly. He could see exactly how the man had pulled himself around, groaned his way to his feet A few feet beyond the thicket was a tattered, soiled handkerchief with a smear of blood on it. The guy had paused there to touch his wounds, steadying, feeling the return of strength.

Marco plunged forward, hoping the hitchhiker had collapsed. Marco's eyes and brain were hungry for the sight of the dead body.

But the hitchhiker had recovered and gone. Marco had to admit the fact. He finally stopped his search and stood overcome by the death of hope. Wouldn't you know it? Those stringy, bewhiskered bums and winos, you couldn't kill them with a meat-axe. A passing motorist had probably picked up the guy. Right now, the bum was no doubt dry and comfortable in a hospital charity bed. The cops would give cursory attention to his accident and invite him to get out of town.

"Marco?"

Marco raised his head. Timothy's shadow was visible up on the highway.

"Marco, what is it? Where are you?"

The sound of the hated voice at this moment put Marco's teeth on edge. He hadn't until tonight known how much he really wanted to remove Timothy, when for a little while it had seemed possible.

And then a thought came to Marco. Timothy had no way of knowing he was down here alone. Without turning on the flashlight, which he'd extinguished when he'd quit searching, Marco called softly, "Get back in the car, Timothy! Trying to attract the attention of anybody who happens to pass? You crazy or something? I'm coming right up."

Chastened, Timothy was under the wheel of the car when Marco returned.

"Let's get out of here, Timothy."

"What took you so long?"

"For pete's sake, I wasn't so long. It only seemed that way to you. I had to find the guy. And then I tried to figure something to do. Thought about moving him. Looked around for a place maybe to hide him."

"Then he's—"

"Deader'n a burned out match, Timothy."

A sob came from Timothy as he hunched over the wheel.

"Look," Marco said, "I'm sorry."

"I'm a murderer, Marco."

"I wouldn't feel…"

"Murderer," Timothy said. He suddenly beat on the steering wheel with the heel of his palm. "I'm a murderer—and the fact can never be changed."

"Hey, now get hold of yourself. We've got to think."

"One second," Timothy sobbed wildly, "I was a decent, law-abiding guy with a business interest and a girl. The next tick of the clock and I'm a killer, and nothing will ever make things exactly the same again."

Marco gripped him by the shoulders. "That's right Timothy. You have to get used to the idea."

"Marco, I'm scared to face the police."

"No need for you to. Crazy if you do, pal. You were drinking when you hit that guy. They'll really throw the book at you!"

Timothy shuddered and dropped his forehead on the rim of the steering wheel.

"But cheer up, pal," Marco slapped him on the shoulder. "There's a way out."

"There is?"

"Sure. I'm going to help you, Timothy."

"How?"

"We'll go back to my apartment I'll give you all the ready cash I've got. You'll have a long head start before that guy is found. They'll never find you."

"You mean—run away?"

"Any better ideas, Timothy?"

"But I'd lose my share of the business, my girl."

"There are other businesses, other girls. But you just have the next twenty years one time, Timothy. Of course, if you want to throw them away, along with the business and girl…" Marco shrugged. "I'm trying to help you salvage what you can, that's all. I see no other way but for you to get going quick, go far, and never look back. And try not to take it so hard, Timothy. You're not the first guy to have a thing like this happen."

Timothy became quieter. He pulled himself erect, reached to the ignition key, and started the car. Marco was glad he had the cover of darkness to hide his elation.

They rode the self-service elevator up five flights to Marco's apartment. Marco let them in and turned on a light in the living room.

He gripped Timothy's bicep briefly. "Cheer up, Timothy You'll start a new life under another name a thousand miles away, and all this will seem a bad dream. Now, I'll see how much cash I can rustle." Timothy moved dully to the window and opened it. He drew in a deep breath of air. The rain had stopped. The night outside was clean tasting and very silent.

Marco returned. "Here's about five hundred bucks, Timothy. Not much, maybe, but used sparingly, it'll take you a long way." Timothy took the money, looked at it as if he didn't quite realize what it was, and slipped it into his pocket. The lower portion of his face parted in a gray smile. "Murderer…" he mused. "You know, Marco, once you get over the first shock of knowing you're a murderer, it changes your whole outlook."

"Just don't think about it, Timothy," Marco admonished him then.

"Why not? Once you've killed, then human life assumes a completely new value. Or should I say lack of value?"

Marco began to feel uneasy. "Timothy, you ought to use every possible minute to put as much distance…"

"I hate to think of losing the business and my girl, Marco. Really I do, especially since there is only one thing that can definitely link me to the hitchhiker. The rain must have washed the tire tread marks from the shoulder of the road, and I can burn my shoes, in case I left footprints. That leaves just one thing, Marco. You, the lone witness." Before Marco could speak, Timothy clipped him on the jaw. As he crumpled, Timothy took Marco's shoulders and directed his fall out the open window. Then he kicked back the throw rug from under the window, which made everything reasonably obvious. Timothy would agree with everyone that it had been most unfortunate for the rug to slip.

PROXY

Originally published in **Alfred Hitchcock's**
Mystery Magazine, *June 1966.*

When I left her apartment, I skedaddled straight to Mr. Friedland's estate. I left the car standing in the driveway and went in the big stone mansion like a coon with a pack on his trail.

I asked the butler where Mr. Friedland was, and the butler said our boss was in the study. So I busted in the study and closed the heavy walnut door behind me quick.

Mr. Friedland was at his desk. He looked up, bugged for a second by me coming in this way. But he didn't bless me out. He got up quick and said, "What's the matter, William?"

I knuckled some sweat off my forehead, walked to the desk, and laid the envelope down. The envelope had a thousand smackers, cash, in it.

Mr. Friedland picked up the money. He looked a little addle pated.

"You did go to Marla Scanlon's apartment, William?"

"Yes, sir."

"She was there?"

"Yes, sir."

"But she didn't accept the money? William, I simply can't believe it."

I couldn't think of an easy way to explain it to him. "She's dead, Mr. Friedland."

He cut his keen eyes from the money to me. He was a lean, handsome man who looked about thirty-five years old in the face. It was just the pure white hair that hinted at his real age.

"Dead?" he said. "How, William?"

"Looked to me like somebody strangled her to death. I didn't hang around to make sure. There's bruises on her neck, and her tongue is stuck out and all swelled up like a hunk of bleached liver. She was a mighty fetching hunk of female," I added with a sigh.

"Yes," Mr. Friedland said, "she was."

"But she don't look so good now."

"Was she alone in the apartment?"

"I reckon. I didn't feel the urge to poke around. Just had a look at her there on her living-room floor and hightailed it here."

Mr. Friedland absently put the thousand bucks in his inside coat pocket. "She was alive three hours ago. She phoned me, just before I went out. I returned, gave you the envelope, and you went to her place and found her dead. Three hours. She was killed between two and five this afternoon."

"Could have been a lot of traffic in that much time, Mr. Friedland."

"I doubt it. Not today. Today she was expecting a caller with a white envelope. William, you didn't see anyone on your way out of the building?"

"No, sir."

"Phone anyone? Speak to anyone?"

"Not a soul, Mr. Friedland, until I got here and asked the butler where you was."

"Good. You're always a good man, William."

"Yes, sir," I said. "I try to be." Which was no lie. I'm a hillbilly from near Comfort, North Carolina, which is back up in the mountains. It's a mighty poorly place, believe me. Mr. Friedland came up there one summer for a week of fishing. I worked for him that week, and when the week was over he said as how would I like to keep working for him. He said I was intelligent and clean-cut and had respect for other people. He said he needed a chauffeur and a man to do errands and personal chores. He said I would have quarters on a nice estate and steady pay. So naturally I jumped at the chance. That was near five years ago, and I'm glad to say that Mr. Friedland has come to depend on me as few folks can depend on a personal worker. He trusts me and knows I can keep my mouth shut. And that means a lot to a big shot newspaper publisher and television station owner like Mr. Friedland.

While I was simmering down and losing the shakes from my experience in Miss Marla Scanlon's apartment, Mr. Friedland was busy on the phone. He called Judge Harrison Corday and Mr. Robert Grenick, who is the prosecuting attorney. They were both close friends of Mr. Friedland. He told them to drop everything, he had to see them right away. He said a thing of utmost importance had happened which couldn't be talked about on the phone. He asked them to come to his study pronto, which they did.

Judge Corday got there first. He was one of the youngest superior court judges in the state. He liked parties and booze, and it was beginning to show around the softening edges of his face. He was a big, reddish man. He'd been a famous football star in college.

He said to Mr. Friedland, "What's up, Arch? I've got a dinner engagement and…"

"You may not want any dinner when you hear what I have to say," Mr. Friedland said. "To save a lot of repetitions, we'll wait until Bob Grenick arrives."

Judge Corday didn't press Mr. Friedland, knowing it would do no good. He sat down and lighted a dollar cigar and tried to read Mr. Friedland's lean, tight face.

Mr. Grenick showed up almost before Judge Corday got his cigar going good. Bald, chubby, and middle-aged, Mr. Grenick had thick, heavy lips and thick, heavy eyes. Both his lips and eyes always looked slightly damp, like a lizard's back that lives in a spring branch.

As soon as Mr. Grenick was in the study and the door safely closed, Mr. Friedland said, "Tell them, William, what you just told me."

"Miss Marla Scanlon is dead," I said.

The judge took it without blinking an eye. The state's attorney, Mr. Grenick, choked, put a hand to his neck, fumbled for a chair, and sat down.

"How?" Judge Corday said, cool.

"Murdered, I reckon," I said.

Mr. Grenick made noises like he was having a hard time getting air.

"By what means?" the judge asked.

"Choked to death, it looked like," I said.

"When?"

"Sometime between two and five," Mr. Friedland put in.

"What makes you think I have any interest until the murderer is caught and I act in official capacity?" Mr. Grenick said raggedly. "I hardly knew Marla Scanlon."

"Oh, come off it, Bob," Mr. Friedland said. "Marla Scanlon worked artfully and most skillfully. One by one she compromised the three of us. She didn't stretch her luck. We three were enough. She had her gold mine. She was content. She didn't intend to incur further risk by developing, in a manner of speaking, a source of silver."

Mr. Grenick got half out of his chair, gripping its arms. "I deny any..."

"Please shut up," Mr. Friedland said quietly. "None of us is on trial, not yet. But we're the three who might have killed her. It's reasonably certain that one of us did. She's milked you the longest, Harrison. I was next. Bob, you're her third and final golden goose. Between us, we've contributed, over a period of time, something like a total of sixty-thousand dollars."

"Too bad we never reported all that stashed cash to the income tax people," Judge Corday said. "They might have taken her off our backs."

"And the hides from our backs right along with her," Mr. Friedland said.

"How'd you find out all this?" Mr. Grenick asked. "About me, I mean?"

"That's a rather silly question, Bob," Mr. Friedland said. "I'm still a top reporter when it comes to digging out the facts. And I have the resources of a metropolitan newspaper at my disposal, don't forget."

"All right," Judge Corday said, like he was on the bench considering a motion by a lawyer. "It's laid out between us. We three were her patsies. Each had the same reason to dispose of her. We re cruising, in a word, in the same leaky boat. Now it remains to determine whether or not we have a paddle. Unfortunately, I have no alibi for the three hours between two and five this afternoon. Have you, Bob?"

"What?" Mr. Grenick was looking sort of gray, like a prospect for a dose of calomel.

"Where were you between two and five this afternoon?"

"I was…"

"Yes, Bob?" Mr. Friedland prompted.

Mr. Grenick lifted his eyes and looked at his friends. "I didn't go in, understand. A block away, I turned the car. I didn't go all the way to her apartment."

"You were going to see Marla?" the judge asked.

"Yes. I was going to appeal to her, to prove to her that I couldn't afford the blackmail tariff any longer. I was going to convince her that she'd have to be satisfied with less—or nothing more at all. I simply couldn't rake up the money. I'm not as well heeled as you two."

"But you got cold feet," Mr. Friedland said. "You didn't actually see her?"

"That's right, Arch, and you've got to believe me."

"Whether or not we believe you," the judge said, "cuts little ice. The important thing is that you have no alibi. How about you, Arch?"

Mr. Friedland shook his head. "I got a call from her at two o'clock. She reminded me that William was due at five with a thousand dollars. I drove out for a quiet, private look at some acreage I may purchase. I came back in time to send William on his errand."

"So any one of us might have killed her," the judge said.

"Listen," Mr. Grenick said in a tight voice, "I didn't do it. But if a scandal of this sort brushes off on me, I'm ruined. The three of us," his eyes looked wetter than usual, "are ruined. There are too many people in city hall and police headquarters who'd like to collect our scalps. We can't hush up a thing as big as murder, not even if Arch does control the press and TV."

"Precisely," Mr. Friedland said. "Sometimes, Bob, you almost convince me you have a mind, in addition to the cunning you've shown in the political jungles. We cannot cover this thing."

"So what do you propose?" Judge Corday asked.

"An unbreakable gentleman's agreement," Mr. Friedland said. "Whichever of the three of us is nailed, he must bear the entire thing alone. He must not turn to his friends for help or implicate them in the slightest. He must stand firm on the statement that he, and only he, was involved with Marla

Scanlon. Whichever of us is doomed will at least have the satisfaction of knowing that he shielded his friends."

"It might be rough," the judge said. "When a man's slapped in the face with murder, the natural reaction is to name others, to confuse the issue, to point suspicion elsewhere."

"I know," Mr. Friedland nodded, "and that's my reason for calling you here. We must decide in advance. We must agree that the two who escape will, throughout the future, stand by the loser's loved ones in any crisis, any trouble, as if the loser himself were still there."

"Mr. Friedland," I said.

He turned his head in my direction. "Yes, William?"

"All the time you been talking," I said, "I been thinking. I got an idear."

"William," Mr. Grenick said in a sore tone, "we've far more important things to consider than any ideas you…"

Mr. Friedland shut him up with a motion of his hand. "I don't think we have anything to lose by listening to you," Mr. Friedland said. "Go ahead, William."

"Thank you, sir. You see, Mr. Friedland, you've been real nice to me, giving me a chance to live like I never knowed people live, when I was a hillbilly back up beyond Comfort, North Carolina."

Mr. Grenick groaned. "This is no time for asinine, emotional speeches."

"Yes, sir," I said. "Anyhow, I'm all through speechifying. I just wanted Mr. Friedland to know one of the reasons I'd be willing to do you-all the favor of standing trial for Miss Marla Scanlon's murder."

I had their attention now, believe me. Right then, you could have heard a mouse crossing the attic, only of course there wasn't none in Mr. Friedland's attic.

"William," Mr. Friedland said finally, "I'm touched. But I suspect that you haven't quite finished."

"No sir, Mr. Friedland. Not quite. All three of you have society wives and fine kids and fancy homes and just everything to make life good. You stand to lose a real passel. But me, I got nobody but myself. And I never before had a chance to get me a stake together."

"How much?" Judge Corday asked.

"Well, you been paying Miss Marla Scanlon plenty. One final payment—to me—will finish it for good. Just chip in five thousand dollars apiece, and I'll protect you all from the aftermath of this terrible thing."

"I won't do it," Mr. Grenick said, "not five thou—"

"Yes, Bob, I think you will," Mr. Friedland said. He eased his backside to the edge of his desk and brought his eyes back to me. "How do you propose to do it, William?"

"It ought to be simple as picking corn when the sun ain't hot," I said, "With your newspapers and TV on my side, and Judge Corday on the bench, and Mr. Grenick handling the case for the state, I ought to come off all right. I'll say that I had been hanky-pank with Marla Scanlon. I'll say she was giving me the boot. I'll say we got in a big fight and I lost my head and killed her without really meaning to. Nobody in this town really cares that she's gone, nobody to question or suspect what you do. I figure the judge should give me about three years for manslaughter. I'll behave good and be on parole inside of a year."

"And then?" Judge Corday said.

"I'll just take my fifteen thousand and go back to Comfort," I said. "None of us has got to worry about any of the others going back on the contract, account of we're all in this together and we sink or swim together."

"William," Mr. Friedland said, "I think you've got a deal. How about it, friends?"

Both the judge and Mr. Grenick were quick to nod.

"I suggest," the judge said, "that you and William contrive to rehearse a bit in private, Bob."

"A good idea," the prosecutor said.

"And you've fine material to work with here," Mr. Friedland said. "You won't have to worry about William botching his part."

"Well, gentlemen," I said, "let's get finished up here with the practice questions and all, soon's we can. I reckon I ought to get to police headquarters in a reasonable time. It'll look better if I surrender myself and show them how sorry I am for what I done to that girl."

"Excellent, William, excellent," Mr. Friedland said.

I got to admit it looked pretty excellent to me too. I'd go back to Comfort a little over a year from now with over fifty thousand dollars, counting the fifteen thousand these men would cough up.

Miss Marla Scanlon, in life, had had an eye on the future. When I'd made her open the wall safe in her apartment before I strangled her I'd picked up a little over forty thousand.

Folks around Comfort, North Carolina, are all eligible for this poverty program the government is running. It'll sure be nice, going back and being the richest man in the whole durn town. The air is clean, the scenery eye-popping, the likker mellow, and the girls all corn-fed beauties. I might even hire myself a chauffeur and personal errand boy—only I'll make sure his name ain't William.

THE CONFIDENT KILLER

Originally published in **Alfred Hitchcock's**
Mystery Magazine, *October 1967.*

Nom Roddenberry took the news of her daughter's death like a durable hill woman. Her sallow, bony face went as gray as fog. Her slate-gray eyes went out of whack as she tried to keep on seeing me. Her gnarled hands lifted and grabbed her wrinkled cheeks, as if she could make a physical pain that would lessen the hellfire scorching her inside. A wail like a cat caught in a steel trap split her thin lips.

Then she steadied, pulled her shoulders together, stood gasping behind the counter in her cafe. "Gaither...Jerl Brownlee murdered my girl?"

"That's what I'm trying to say, ma'am."

She took off the clean white smock that she wore over her simple gray dress as her cafe uniform and came around the counter, a small, spry woman that the Smoky Mountain winters and endless toil had whittled down to a collection of hickory sticks and leather.

"Is Pretty at Doc Weatherly's undertaking parlor now, Gaither?"

"Yes, ma'am."

"Will you walk over with me?"

"You know I will!"

"And tell me the whole of it." Her fingers were like wires on my wrist "Every last detail. You hear me, Gaither?"

She turned over the cardboard sign that hung inside the glass part of the cafe door. The sign said "Closed." We stepped onto the sidewalk. The old lady closed and locked the door, then stood a minute looking up and down the dusty street like she was a stranger, although she'd lived in the town of Comfort all her life.

"Not much here to satisfy a gal young'un who dreamed of fancy clothes and big city excitement, Gaither."

"She wasn't a bad girl, ma'am."

"That she wasn't, Gaither. Just too innocent and ignorant of the ways of the world and too—attractive to men."

With me at her side, Mom Roddenberry thought of the short eighteen years of Pretty's life, I reckon, as she set off with dogged hill-woman's stride. "I'm listening, Gaither," she prodded.

So I told her how Pretty Roddenberry had come to her end, as we tramped toward the old gingerbread house where Doc Weatherly lives upstairs and undertakes on the ground floor.

Pretty had met her death in cruelly simply manner. She'd sneaked up to the Brownlee lodge to keep a date with Jerl. He was the last of the Brownlees, had inherited a timber and tobacco fortune, and figured he was cock of any walk he cared to set foot on.

Jerl didn't show up in Comfort often, preferring to spend his time and squander his money in resorts where fancy women were plentiful. With a bunch of friends, he had boozed it up at the UT-Clemson game last week, which took place in Knoxville. The swanky Brownlee lodge being on a thousand-acre estate across the line in North Carolina, the gang had trekked over and kept the party roaring.

They caroused over land, lake, and mountainside for three days before they fizzled out. Finally Jerl was left alone, surly and restless. He got to thinking of that cute little trick he'd made a few passes at previous when he happened to be in Comfort, so he called her on the phone, and she was dumb enough to sneak up there.

Who knows what went through Pretty's excited mind as she dolled up in her best dress and perfume? Did she think she could tease her way into that rustic mansion and let it go at that? Did she think Jerl would actually take her away from the drabness and boredom of an isolated little mountain town such as Comfort? Did she kid herself into thinking she might even have a chance of marrying into the Brownlee millions?

Ever how her noggin worked, when the showdown came she just couldn't snatch off her clothes and jump into young Jerl's bed. But she'd called her shots all wrong. She hadn't figured on the size of Jerl's spoiled selfishness. His boozing had sharpened all the meanness in him. Even sober, he reckoned that anything he wanted should be his for the taking.

Pretty fought him. It must have been an unholy sight, Pretty struggling and begging for mercy, of which there was none in the inflamed face before her. She barked his shins and scratched his face; then he knocked her down and busted the back of her head. Maybe she struck the big fireplace or a piece of the heavy furniture.

Jerl thought he'd killed her then and there. He dragged her out put her in his car, got in and drove a ways across the mountain until he was off the estate, then shoved her out. He must have thought he was reasonably safe. Days, even weeks, might pass before anybody found Pretty's body. By then, Jerl figured, it wouldn't matter what folks suspected. Suspecting and proving are two different matters. He'd just deny that she ever had come to the lodge. Nobody, he reckoned, could prove that some hill renegade hadn't seen her walking up the road and got passionate ideas.

Only thing, Jerl hadn't figured on a situation which the Brownlees themselves had set up. For years the Brownlee estate had been posted and the old man, before his death, had kept a mean caretaker up there to enforce the rule. As a result, the thousand acres teemed with game, and a mountain farmer with a taste for fresh meat had set out that morning to do a little poaching, thinking Jerl's drinking party had adjourned to the lowlands and wouldn't bother him.

The farmer heard Jerl's car booming around the curves on the gravel backroad, ducked into the timber, and his popping eyes witnessed Jerl's final act. The minute Jerl got back in his car and rounded a curve, the farmer went sliding and tumbling into the thicketed ravine where Pretty's body had come to rest.

A final flicker of life twitched through Pretty's china blue eyes. Her silken mane of yellow hair was a bloody tangle about her face as she tried to speak. The farmer dropped his ear close to her lips and caught her final words. She told him what had happened, as if there was any doubt in his mind.

The farmer ran a shortcut to the lodge, broke a window to let himself in, and phoned the sheriffs office in Comfort. Sheriff Collie Loudermilk had flashed the word to the sheriffs of neighboring counties. Roadblocks were set up in minutes.

With Jerl Brownlee in the net, Collie had sent me, his deputy, to fetch down the body. I'd brought the poor broken thing to Doc Weatherly's, gritted my teeth, and dragged my feet to Comfort's only decent cafe, wishing it was just for a cup of Mom Roddenberry's good coffee.

Mom didn't interrupt my tale once. She had a good grip on herself now. She took my words like the seasoned willow takes the slashing sleet. Her suffering was too deep to show on the surface.

We stopped in the shadow of the porch that rambled across the front of Doc Weatherly's place. Mom Roddenbery lifted a hand and touched my cheek. "You're a good young man, Gaither Jones, and I'm beholden to you for telling me the straight of it."

"She was a sweet, human girl, Mom. She was tempted. And she tried to overcome. You always remember that."

"Yes, Gaither, I will."

"And be sure we'll get Jerl Brownlee, Mom."

She lifted her eyes slow-like, and they were the hoar frost that rimes distant peaks. "Yes, that is all that's left now, Gaither, justice: eye for eye, tooth for tooth. If Pretty is to rest easy in her grave, Jerl Brownlee must reap his due."

I didn't need to answer that one. We were both hill people.

"Again, I'm obliged to you, Gaither. Now, I know you got work to do. I'll just ease inside alone to spend a last minute with my daughter."

I watched her creep up the porch steps. Each one added about ten years to her narrow, bony shoulders. The door of the undertaking parlor opened, swallowed her. I turned, jammed my hands in the pockets of my tan twill, kicked some hollyhocks growing alongside the walk, and cussed my way back up the street to the office.

The short-range walkie-talkie, which the taxpayers begrudged Collie and me out of the mail order catalogue, was crackling when I walked in.

"Gaither, where in dad-blasted thunderation you been?" Collie Loudermilk howled through the static, sounding like a banshee.

"Playing pool and drinking beer," I said sourly, looking across the street at that "Closed" sign on the cafe door. "You bringing in Jerl Brownlee?"

The walkie-talkie like to have spit fire. "He spotted my car blocking Miden Falls road, skidded off the curve, turned over twice, straight down the mountainside."

"He's hurt? Maybe bleeding to death?" I inquired happily.

"He bounced out healthy as a jackrabbit and with the same ideas. I've lost him, Gaither, somewhere in the gorges above Cat Track Holler. If we don't flush him out of this wild country before nightfall, we lose him. He's got the whole compass to aim at, a good chance of making it out of these mountains. If he does that well heeled as he is, next thing we know he may be playing with them French girls in that Riviera place."

"I reckon you need me and Red Runner and Old Bailey," I said.

"Naw," Collie growled, "I'm just fiddling with this gadget in hopes of communing with a braying jackass! *Will* you stop wasting time?"

"You're doing all the talking," I said, and cut him off.

I grabbed the two dog leashes off the wall peg, and skedaddled out of the office, around the old brick building to the dog lot behind the jail. Old Bailey and Red Runner heard me rattling the gate open. They snuffled out of their kennels, long ears nearly dragging in the dust. Their baggy, forlorn eyes spotted the leashes, and a quiver went through both dogs. They perked up quick. I swear those bloodhounds can even smell out the prospect of smelling out a man.

A setting sun threw streamers of golden fire across the peaks in the west and twilight was settling in the valleys when me and the two dogs homed in on Collie Loudermilk's location.

Collie is a skinny, sandy man who looks like he couldn't last out a mountain winter in front of the fireplace, but he's the kind of gristle that can dull a knife. He's been sheriffing in Comfort for twenty years, and knowing him firsthand, it wouldn't surprise me if it's twenty more before I inherit his job.

While the hounds and I got our breath in the shadows of the gorges. Collie shook out a sports jacket that would have cost me a month's pay.

"Lying loose in the back seat of Jerl Brownlee's wrecked car," Collie said. "Let's hope it's his and that he's worn it recent before he pitched it back there."

Collie squatted before the excited dogs, held out the jacket, and they took a good long whiff. I stayed with them, keeping the leashes slack, as they snuffled around for a few seconds. Then with a howl fair to curdle the blood, both dogs hit the ends of the leashes, almost jerking me off my feet.

We tracked Jerl up a long hollow where the briars were as thick as riled-up bees, and across a long stretch of naked shale, where only a dog's pads had good footing. Collie slipped halfway across. He burned skin off his knees and elbows as he slid and rolled twenty feet down the slope. He got up cussing because I was holding up the dogs, waiting for him to climb back to us.

Beyond the shale. Jerl had jumped a spring-fed creek, which held us up for a good ten minutes, and crossed a soggy meadow. Then he'd stumbled onto the dim remains of an old logging trail and picked that route up through the timber.

I didn't have a dry rag on me by this time. I was sweating so hard from the exertion. The dogs had lather on their flanks and wet tongues hanging from the sides of their mouths. Collie looked as fresh as a new-grown stink-weed, eyes anxious on the purple shadows that closed in about us.

As the dogs tugged me along. I began to lose track of the number of gullies we crossed, the patches of underbrush we slammed through. My legs felt as if they had fallen off, and I looked down in the failing light to make sure they were still there, like a pair of pump handles underneath me.

Then all of a sudden my glazing eyes glimpsed Collie's shadow shooting out ahead of us. I still didn't see the flicker of motion that had caught his attention. He splashed across a seep that would turn into a creek during a heavy rain, and dived into a canebreak. A minor hell erupted in there. Sawgrass and reeds rattled. A covey of birds sprayed out in all directions. Cattail fluff showered into the air.

Collie came out just as the dogs and I cleared the seep. He had Jerl Brownlee by the shirt collar, Jerl draped on the ground behind him.

"Got him, by gum," Collie said, backhanding an ooze of blood off his nose.

"You done all right, Sheriff," I said, nodding, "after me and the dogs cornered him for you."

Jerl was about the most bruised, scratched, begrimed, and generally trail-weary young punk you'd ever want to see. Collie and I and Jerl's rubbery legs finally got him back to the sheriff's car. We put the dogs in front with Collie. I got in back to guard the prisoner, who didn't look much like it was necessary. We'd come back for my car later.

Jerl didn't have a word to say all the way back to town. He was doing plenty of thinking, and by the time I shoved him in a jail cell, he'd about decided he was still Jerl Brownlee, cock of any walk.

He watched me lock the cell door with hooded eyes. Then his battered lips twisted in a sneer. "You yokels don't think for a minute this is going to work out your way, do you?"

"Looks like it might," I said.

"You dumb rube," he said. "With my dough, I'll have the choice of the finest legal brains from New York to Los Angeles. There are jurors to buy, judges for sale. There are a thousand loopholes in the law, and ten thousand technicalities. With my loot, I can fight this thing to the highest courts in the land, no matter how long it takes. So before you wallow in any naive sentiments about the workings of justice or pat yourself on the back, deputy-boy, just answer me one question. Have you ever heard of a millionaire ending up in the electric chair or gas chamber?"

His question was still rattling around in my head a few minutes later as I trudged across the dark street The "Closed" sign was still on the door of Mom Roddenberry's cafe, but there were lights in the flat overhead where she and Pretty had lived. I fumbled for the banister of the outside stairway that led up the side of the building to the flat.

The old lady answered my knock, searched my face for a minute, and invited me into a plain, but comfortable and clean parlor.

I sat down on a studio couch. Mom eased to the edge of a chair across from me. A hard stillness came to the apartment.

"Gaither," she said, "you did catch him. He's locked up. I've already heard."

"Yes, ma'am. But I got a dreadful feeling that rich boy will get out of this."

"Why, lad, we *know* he done it! Cold-blooded and mean. Pretty said he did—and she wouldn't tell a lie with her dying breath."

"I know, but we run up the first stump right there. We got a witness that says that she said it. They call it hearsay evidence. The lawyers he can afford will cut our case to nothing."

The old lady thought about it, hands crimping like talons. Then she raised her slatey gray eyes. "Might be a game two can play, Gaither." I frowned. "What are you talking about?"

"Would a mountain jury convict an old woman if she was temporarily pixilated by the murder of her daughter?"

The hairs stiffened on the back of my neck as I began to get the drift.

She rose slowly. "Mom Roddenberry's cafe always supplies meals for the jail prisoners across the street. Tonight you got a prisoner. I'm going down now, Gaither, and fix his supper. I reckon that's why you came over, to fetch the prisoner his tray?"

I gulped. "Well, ma'am… Come to think of it, yes."

"A real mouth-watering meal for the man…" She patted my shoulder in passing. "But don't you dast get forgetful and throw the scraps to Red Runner and Old Bailey."

"No, ma'am," I promised. "I reckon such a fine pair of dogs deserve better than scraps tonight."